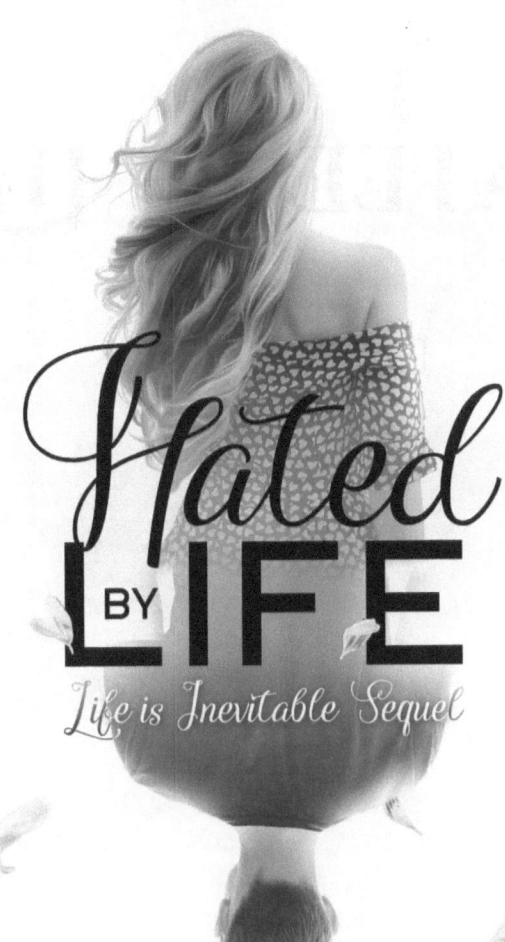

Hated
BY LIFE

Life is Inevitable Sequel

DANIEL SANTOS

HATED BY LIFE

Daniel Santos

CONTENTS

PROLOGUE

J essica stood atop a waterfall in her underwear, wondering how she let herself become someone she hated. Just an hour ago, she had stripped to take a swim in the lake. At the time she'd felt as if her sins were being washed away, but leaving the water brought on the recurring sensation of grime. After pondering her thoughts of inadequacy, she felt even more shame than she did before. To bully Olivia to the point where she'd attempted to take her life indicated she lacked self-control. A thousand regrets rushed through her head, but the most significant one had to be her hostility toward herself. Standing at the edge of the waterfall made her realize just how quickly and easily she could kill herself. And she planned on doing exactly that. At that moment, the world didn't seem real. She felt like she was in a fever dream. With the sun rising in the distance, its warm rays reflected on her blonde hair.

"I'm sorry," she whispered to herself. She didn't believe in the existence of a god, but she found comfort in the fact that her physical beauty might make her look appealing to any deity above. However, in her moment of weakness, she remembered that her beauty on the outside didn't reflect who she was on the inside. Everyone that knew her saw her for what she truly was: a monster. Tears rolled down her face, and she hesitantly put one foot over the edge. Her leg trembled, forcing her to shut her eyes for a moment. *I must do this.* With closed eyelids, she leaned forward and dove headfirst into the rocks below.

ACT I

A LOST TRAIN

Brennan sat on a bench in the train station, towering over some of the passersby as he waited for the woman to answer him. Her sudden appearance didn't distract him from the fact that her voice sounded familiar. He knew without a doubt that she was the one who spoke to him in the fog.

"I know what you're thinking, and the answer is 'maybe'," she said. After she spoke, Brennan sat upright rather than leaning back. Her long black hair hid her eyes, and that white dress of hers made him wonder why she took the time to appear so formal. "Welcome back." The woman spoke as though she knew of his previous endeavors within the train station. Maybe she knew that his soul had traveled here after his first death. In the short moment they had a pause, a train whisked by at lightning-fast speed. The updraft blew her hair up, making it flow magically, like she spawned as an otherworldly being.

"Where is she?" Brennan asked as he stood.

"Where's who?"

"Jessica. Where's Jessica?" Brennan reminisced about the day he died and how the following days had felt like years. He closed his eyes, letting his memories bring him back to the day he hung himself. It was the same day Olivia took her life and met him at this train station. A glimpse of her red hair and her t-shirt flashed through his brain. The image of Seattle's Space Needle covered her entire top. It indicated that she lived in Washington, but Brennan couldn't have guessed he'd live there as well.

He took deep breaths. The desire to find Jessica became his priority, and the woman's lack of insight into his dilemma made him panic. Judging by her sudden appearance, she must've been a spirit, or maybe even an Angel. Surely, if an angel couldn't help him, how would he be able to help himself?

"Are you an angel, just like Haniel?" Brennan asked.

"No, not at all. Angels work under God as his messengers, but I'm here on my own accord." She smiled at him, but Brennan didn't return the gesture. She noticed the frown on his face and asked, "What's wrong?"

He had always had a hard time opening up to people, but seeing as he was desperate to navigate the world of the dead, he sought out the woman's help. "God had given Olivia and me a second chance, so he sent Haniel to give us train tickets that would return us to our bodies, but I messed up. I accidentally switched them, and ever since, I've been living as Olivia, and Olivia has been living as me. I was so desperate to find her and get back to my body, that I used Jessica, and I made her life hell. She's gone because of me."

The woman gave a nod before taking hold of Brennan's hand. The warmth radiating from her skin prompted a feeling of safety within him. It didn't take long until he forgot about the unexpected display of affection. "I understand your sorrow. Losing someone is one of the hardest experiences for all people."

Brennan sniffled and wiped his eye. "I want to find her," he muttered, in a shaky voice.

"And why do you want to find her?" she asked.

"Because in the time we shared together, she's been the only person to stick by my side. My sister left me, my father left me, and my mother never loved me. Jessica was all I had, and now she's gone."

The woman ran her fingers in circles as she cradled his hand in hers. "What will you do if you find her?"

"I'll bring her to this train station, and I'll take her with me back to my world. The world of the living." Brennan stood in a firm stance, staring directly into the woman's eyes. He tried to ignore it, but there was no denying the tear streaming down his face.

"Even though you're not an angel, can you help me?" Brennan's hands trembled and his voice wavered.

"Take it easy," the woman said sweetly. "I sense a lot of desperation in your words. You're worried and I understand, but you must remain calm and let me help you."

Another train flashed by, creating a wind that seemed to slow time down when her hair fluttered. Brennan took in the woman's beauty. He hadn't noticed it before since his sadness over Jessica's death took over his mind, but upon laying his eyes on the woman's delicate lips, rounded cheeks, and blue eyes, they held a hypnotic state of control over him. If she wasn't an angel, then what could she be?

"First off, I think it's important to acknowledge how much you've changed," the woman said, but Brennan wasn't listening. He was too mesmerized by her appearance.

"I'm sorry, what was that?"

"I was just saying that you should feel good about the changes you've made to yourself. It's quite lovely." She let out a giggle and her eyes squinted as she smiled.

"Change..." Brennan hadn't thought about it before, but he had changed, although this woman hadn't been there to experience the shift in his personality. "How do you know I've changed?" he asked. "Have you been watching me?"

"Maybe," she said in a high pitch.

"That doesn't help. Just give me a straight answer. Have you been watching me?" Even though he had changed from a bitter, angry, and childish teenager to a mature young man capable of empathy and compassion, Brennan still retained the flaw of being a slave to his impulses. When she took a moment to respond, he let himself get impatient. "Just tell me already!" He gritted his teeth, but she didn't flinch at his sudden display of madness.

"If you really must know, the answer is 'yes'. Yes, I've been watching you."

"But how can you—" Brennan stopped. Meeting this woman didn't answer all his questions. Instead, she just filled his head with more.

Before he could bow his head in defeat, the woman leaned in to hug him. Normally, he wouldn't accept a hug from a stranger, but this was different. Their skin touching felt so familiar, so safe, Brennan swore rubbing his arms would cause the exact same sensation. His mind wavered and her touch put him in a docile state. "I just realized I haven't asked for your name," Brennan said, forgetting his troubles.

"Don't worry. You were too distraught to be formal." She kept her voice soft and low. "You can call me Lily. Do you like that name?"

"Sounds sweet. Yes, I like your name, but please, can you tell me what you are, if you're not an angel?"

Rather than answering, she walked behind him, and he felt a strong urge to press for an answer, but he froze in place. *Why does she make me feel this way?* Her unique presence put him at a loss for words. She wrapped her arms over his chest and snuggled her face into his left shoulder.

"Let's just say I'm a spirit, and a special one too. But at heart, I'm only a spirit."

Her answer didn't completely satisfy Brennan's curiosity. Knowing she was a spirit wasn't enough. He needed to understand her purpose for meeting him, but seeing that she had an elusive side, this was probably the best he answer he could hope for.

"I can show you what you truly want," Lily said. Unlike other dresses, the one she wore had pockets, in which she kept a small rectangular box.

When she presented it to Brennan he asked, "What is that?" His voice wavered. He looked at the box and wondered about its contents. Was it some otherworldly item from the afterlife? Considering where he was, that seemed very likely. But what would the item be, and what would it do? She brought it to his face and flicked her index finger to open it. A small circular mirror revealed itself.

"If you look into it right now, you'll see something that's true."

Without hesitation, Brennan slightly leaned forward to stare into the glass. Much to his surprise, he saw himself. His own face stared back at him, as though he had never taken over Olivia's body.

"It's me," he muttered. He felt his face while running his fingers around his lips and across the bridge of his nose. He knew that the man in the mirror was definitely him. "How's that possible? We switched bodies. Why am I seeing myself?" His mouth tightened as his confusion began to set in.

"You look so cute when you're flustered!" Lily giggled. "But if you must know, your soul is here, but the body you inhabited is not. In this world, only souls are what linger. There's never been a physical body here before."

Brennan looked at the mirror and his muscles relaxed as he let out a sigh.

"Now, do you know what you truly want?" Lily asked.

"I already told you. I want to find Jessica and take her back to my world."

"Are you sure about that?"

"Yes, of course." Brennan gave a short nod, and Lily pointed at the mirror. When he turned his gaze toward it, he saw him and Jessica holding each other, doing a slow dance while listening to music.

"It appears you're being honest, and I like it. It's important to know the truth, especially when it comes to knowing our deepest desires." Lily whispered in his ear like a snake, and Brennan felt compelled to heed her words.

"Yes, I want to be with Jessica, and I want us to be more than friends," he muttered. "Is she here?" He frantically looked around. "I need to find her."

"I'm afraid she's not in this particular area, but I can help you get to her. I have a special ticket that can take you to places beyond your reach, but you must be sure that it's something you want."

Brennan clasped his hands together, begging Lily to hand over the ticket. She obliged and held out an open palm. A brand-new ticket appeared. Its golden hue shined against the orange lamps posted around the station.

"Just wait here and keep an eye out for a gray train coming your way." She pointed to the tracks behind him as she walked backward and as she did so, she bowed her head, slowly fading out of existence with a sinister smile on her face.

For the next few minutes, the voices from the crowd grew louder. More souls seemed to be entering the afterlife. Then a train came into view, but modern, unlike the old rusty ones. Its white color palette shined brightly despite the dim light. And when it came to a stop, the doors slid open.

"Hello!" a little girl yelled. Her white hair fell down to her shoulders and she gave a wide grin. Her unique appearance and giddy attitude were something Brennan recognized, instantly. The only child he could be talking to right now was Life. The young girl's smile took him back to when he ran into her and her brother at the park that appeared while he was in a state of limbo.

"You've been following me everywhere I go." Before boarding the train, he knelt down and rubbed the top of her head. His touch seemed to make her laugh more, as though it tickled.

"Ticket, please!" She acted seriously. Her hands were placed on her hips and her face was stern. Brennan could only guess that she wanted to play the role of a conductor. He smiled at her attempt to act like an adult before giving her his special ticket. She snatched it quickly, catching him off guard. With her nose stuck high in the air, she proudly stated, "You can come in now."

Brennan stepped through the sliding doors, and found the interior to be just like the subway trains back in his city. The floor, ceilings, and walls were gray, while the seats were made of plastic, showing off their yellow colors. He sat on the chair closest to the door and leaned his head back. Her heard Life plop next to him, but didn't bother to look down. The moment he ran into her, happiness had filled him, but his mind couldn't stop coming up with plans on what to do about Jessica. He didn't know if this train would take him straight to her, or if he would have to travel on foot from another stop. Even then, what would he do once he found her? Just grab her hand and walk out of this world?

And then there was Lily. He imagined himself talking to her. The mirror she'd presented him, showed a glimpse of the life he wanted. *That's what I want. To live my life with Jessica.* He took in what she told him as gospel. He had to know what he truly wanted, and he had to embrace it. Even though he sought to find Olivia as a part of his initial quest, he decided putting that on hold would be for the best. *I'm sorry.* If he could speak to Olivia, that's all he would say. Forcing her to live in his body a little longer seemed selfish, but he justified his actions by telling himself it was all for Jessica's sake.

As the train moved, Life rested her face on his arm.

"What brought you back here?" Life asked.

"I don't know exactly. I just remember running even further away after Jessica died. I was in her truck speeding down a highway when the fog began to roll in. I felt soft arms hugging me from behind, and the voice of a woman whispering in my ear. She said, 'The longer you hold on to me, the heavier I get. What am I?'"

"Is that a riddle? Were you playing a game? I'll play with you! Let me follow you!" Her words put Brennan at ease. Even though she misunderstood him completely, that was to be expected when speaking with a child so young. But that was the charming part of their conversation. Chatting with someone so innocent reminded him of the childhood he could've had, if he wasn't forced to grow up so fast.

Eventually, she nodded off to sleep while Brennan looked out the window. They were a long way from the train station. The scenery had drastically changed. Various pieces of the world outside looked like different countries that had their own unique environment, but the only constant was the lighthouse far in the distance.

It stood tall atop a massive hill, and the sound of water splashing signified that the train left the tracks. It ran over the ocean, skidding from side to side. At first, Brennan didn't mind, but once the bumping and screeching became too much to bear, he realized that they weren't meant to go on water. He gripped the handrail beside him, taking in a deep breath to calm his nerves. He closed his eyes and envisioned himself on solid ground, but the train suddenly jerked to the side. Life woke up as she hit the floor. Brennan hopped off his chair to kneel beside her.

"Are you okay?" he asked. "Did you hit your head?" Life cried and rubbed the top of her scalp. "I guess you did hit your head," Brennan commented. He softly cooed while hugging her. When he rubbed her back, the train jolted to its other side. Brennan used his entire body to shield her from harm, and as they tossed and turned, she gripped onto him even tighter. His torso, smacked into the poles, and his legs hit the chairs. Eventually, the motion flew him into the air before his back smashed through the window. At that moment, he felt the train topple over. The last thing he saw was Life struggling to drag him outside.

MEMORY FRAGMENTS

O livia sat in the kitchen her mind created for her. Ever since that boy beat her into a coma, her body drifted in a world between life and death. It wasn't a pleasant state of being to most, but in this world, everything she dreamed of came to fruition. Places, objects, and people spawned from her desires to bring them to life. Because of this, she was able to live in a cleaner version of her house, rather than the dirt-filled home that came to be after her dad's death. While it's true that this was the same residence, anyone who witnessed it could've been fooled into thinking it was a different house.

Olivia sat at the dining table in the green pajamas her father bought her. Despite the wonderous world she recreated, the knowledge that it didn't truly exist plagued her. As she sat there with her head hung low, Haniel appeared around a corner. He walked toward her, but when he placed his hand on her shoulder, she didn't look up.

"Olivia," he said.

"It's time for me to wake up soon, isn't it?" she muttered and groaned. The air around her moved when Haniel nodded. For the last couple of the days, she could slowly feel herself slipping back into reality. At first, the force of gravity pulling her down became stronger; then the voices of the living haunted her. Her world called for her return. "I wish I could stay here," she whispered. Even though the harsh truth of this world being false lingered in her mind, she'd rather be here, surrounded by memories of her dad. The idea of going back to her stepfather, with his tendency to speak with his fist whenever she did something he didn't like, became too much to bear.

"I know you don't want to leave, but we both know what you have to do."

"Yeah, I have to find Brennan." After switching bodies, she'd experienced everything his life had to offer, and she hated to admit that she was jealous. She raised her head to look at Haniel. Usually, news that went against her best wishes would make her cry, but this time was different. After everything she's been through, she learned to harness her mental and emotional strength. Living in Brennan's life showed her the world from a different perspective.

The sudden change toughened her up since she had to get comfortable being uncomfortable. However, everyone, including her, would undoubtedly have trouble leaving their safe space, but she knew she had to depart immediately. Not just for her sake, but for Brennan's as well. Olivia gritted her teeth and pushed her emotions aside. She told herself that finding Brennan should be her top priority. She leaned back in her chair and placed her hands on her lap.

By now, the sounds emanating from the real world rang in her ears. When she closed her eyes, she took a deep breath. A heart rate monitor accompanied by people reached her senses. They were awaiting her return, but she just wished she could delay their wishes. Haniel put his lips to her ear.

"It's time to go," he said.

From there, Olivia felt herself being sucked out of that plane of existence. Her soul was being shoved back into Brennan's body. The numbing sensation felt like the pain of being thrown against a wall, and once she felt her blood pumping, the feeling of being alive pumped through her. She opened her eyes, only to realize that her vision was blurry. There was an abundance of light, but she couldn't recognize the source. A bright glare bombarded her, but as she focused, the fogginess cleared. She could now see that the bright gleams came from the lightbulbs hanging above her head.

Dozens of bedsheets were piled on top of her. Their weight and density forced out sweat, and when she turned her head to the right, she saw Elly, passed out in a chair. Her short stature seemed to fit in the seat perfectly, and her pale white arms were folded across her stomach. Initially, waking up caused her memories to vanish, but the sight of Elly brought back fragments of the events that transpired. Olivia's suicide became the first piece of the puzzle to come back. The pills she took, her body collapsing, and finding Brennan in the train station flashed through her mind. Everything gradually came back to her. She felt odd remembering that the body she inhabited wasn't her own. Switching into another person's body had caused her so much trouble that she didn't know where to start.

After all the pieces fell back in place, she spoke.

"Ell—" She couldn't finish her sentence. Olivia's throat burned. It seemed that the unbridled strength she felt in Limbo wasn't present in the real world. "Elly," she finally managed to say. Although her voice came out as a mere whisper, the girl opened her eyes.

"Brennan! You're awake! You're finally awake!" Most people would've felt groggy when being woken so suddenly, but joy replaced that sensation within Elly, and Olivia made sure to smile back. "I'll come back. I'll get the nurse!" She made a move to run toward the door.

"Wait," Olivia muttered. Her voice croaked as Elly stood by the doorway. They made eye contact for a moment, but rather than speaking again,

Olivia raised a small handle by the side of her bed. It harbored the shape of a lower case "l" with a shiny red button on top. "I can use this to call the nurse. Just stay here with me."

Elly rushed toward Olivia. She held her hand gently and ran her fingers across hers. This created a sense of comfort that almost washed away Olivia's dread.

"I've missed you so much. Don't leave me like that again," Elly said.

"I promise, I won't." Saying so was nothing more than an act of reassurance that Olivia deemed as necessary. Undoubtedly, their time together would eventually come to an end, and summoning the nurse would be the start of it. After pushing the red button, Olivia continued the conversation. "What happened while I was gone?" she asked.

Elly turned her head away with sullen eyes. "A lot. A lot of bad things." She pursed her lips, and her eyes grew wide.

"It's something *I* have to fix, right?" The people in Brennan's life were always supportive, but they weren't her real friends and family. They only helped her because they believed they were talking with Brennan, but keeping up the act had taken its toll on her mental health. She wished she could be herself in some way without alerting them. She would even take glances at Elly when the lie became too much to bear. But in the end, Olivia would be alone again, or even worse, with her stepfather.

"No, we can fix it. You don't have to take it on alone," Elly said with a sigh. "I'll help you. Nora and I are here to help!" The frown she previously had, turned into a smile. Their abundance of kindness overwhelmed her. *Why should I go back to my body? It's so much better here.* For the first time, Olivia entertained the thought of taking over Brennan's life. After all, when they met, he didn't seem too fond of his second chance at life.

"But what happened to that guy? The one who — who..." She was hesitant to say it. Olivia remembered the boy who beat her into a coma. From what she remembered, he had a feud with Brennan. Neither of them were great people to begin with, but tackling this problem would make Brennan's life easier. *It could also make my life easier.*

"You're talking about the guy who beat you?" Elly asked.

"Yes."

"Well, last I heard the judge put him under house arrest until the rest of the trial is completed. Of course, you'll have to go to court as well."

Olivia frowned and buried her face in her hands. Even now, she didn't seem to be able to live carefree. While living as herself, her stepdad would assault her, and now some random boy who didn't know her assaulted her.

"God dammit," she muttered. Finding Brennan was a goal she put on a pedestal of broken glass. It was important, but came accompanied with a deep-cutting pain. Olivia pushed aside that thought for now. The upcoming trial definitely held importance, but recovering from her decrepit state should be a priority. But what should she do after recovering? Go straight to court or run away and find him like she originally planned? For a moment, Olivia caught herself thinking about the consequences her actions would have. *It'd make it harder for me.* She shook her head as if they would brush away that thought. *It wouldn't be a problem for me! That problem would be Brennan's.* She told herself that she'd leave his body and life behind as soon as possible, so there was no reason to worry about the drama she'd bring him.

"Don't worry. You'll be fine. We're definitely going to win that court case." Elly placed a hand on her leg. Warmth spread throughout Olivia's cheeks. Elly's calm demeanor always put her at ease. If only she could open up to her, it'd make her predicament a whole lot easier to manage.

"That's not what I'm worried about." Olivia looked to the ceiling and mustered the strength to groan. Elly opened her mouth to speak, but stopped when the nurse stepped in. After they got lost in it, their one-minute conversation felt like an hour. The nurse stood there with her hands clasped together over her thighs. At first, she seemed oblivious as to why they summoned her, but when Olivia blinked, she said, "Oh, you're awake! I'll get the doctor."

Elly continued to run her fingers through Olivia's hair as the nurse left.

"Brennan, I have some good news." Olivia's face showed skepticism. After everything that happened, what would constitute as good news? "While you were asleep, I had plenty of time to unlock your phone. I've bypassed the passcode." With Elly's proud proclamation, Olivia's face beamed. That piece of hardware held her back for so long, but now she controlled it. Elly reached into her pocket and pulled out Brennan's phone, but since Olivia had trouble mustering the strength to hold it, the physical labor didn't depend on her. She just laid back while Elly held the screen in front of their faces.

As the phone powered on, Olivia made the decision to snoop through everything. Contacts, photos, social media, and anything that could reveal his lifestyle held importance to her. Having knowledge of who he was would give her the tools she needed to live as him. The original plan was to contact him, but now she just wanted to stay in his body a little longer.

"Go to my contacts list," she requested. Elly did as she instructed and tapped the green phone icon. Unfortunately, no one's personal info made the list. Olivia couldn't fathom why since most people had at least a few friends to talk to, but she guessed Brennan didn't really have anybody. "Tap on my social media apps." There were three of those, but Brennan didn't make a single post. He only followed a few accounts which belonged to various artists and graphic designers. Olivia told Elly to keep looking through his account. Dozens of faces popped up on his feed, but none of them belonged to people at his school. *Damn!* Without any clues to his personal life, what else could she do in the meantime before their meeting?

Feeling disheartened, Olivia formed the urge to recede into herself. She wanted to give up, but she remembered what Brennan told her. *Since we're in each other's bodies, you have to act like me. Be assertive! Stop being a coward!* It seems that even though she had been going above and beyond to be him, her old habits seeped through. In a last-ditched effort to find valuable information, Olivia asked Elly to go through his photos. Then, just like a loyal servant, she obliged. Images appeared onto the screen, and they scrolled through them one by one. Most were pictures of artwork, but as they slowly swiped through the camera roll, photos of different places in the city started to surface.

Elly stopped at a picture of a wooden treehouse. The green roof made it stand out in the forest, and the distance above the ground, the ladder, and the pulley system could satisfy any child's sense of adventure.

"Oh, so you went there," Elly teased. However, Olivia didn't understand why her tone of voice shifted in that direction. A confused expression dawned on her face.

"Why are you looking at me like that?" Elly asked.

"It's nothing. I just don't remember why I have that picture." At this point, Olivia had grown as accustomed as she could to acting as Brennan, so her façade seemed almost natural.

"Well, you probably went there with someone. After all, everyone at school calls it the 'love house'."

Olivia raised her eyebrows in curiosity. "Love House?"

Elly gave a short laugh. "Don't pretend you don't know. Everyone knows what it means."

"I think I'm still really out of it." Olivia let out a deep breath and rubbed her forehead to make the act seem genuine. "That name just isn't popping up in my head." Since the grogginess wore off, and she became filled with energy, enhancing her imitation skill.

"I highly doubt you don't remember," Elly said.

"But I'm serious!"

Elly sighed as though she didn't believe her. "All right, just in case you're being honest, I'll tell you. That treehouse used to belong to some kid who lived in the neighborhood. After he died of a seizure, his parents refused to take it down. Apparently, they believed keeping it would make the other kids happy, but I guess it made them elated in ways they didn't expect, especially since all the high schoolers just went there to smoke pot, make-out, have sex, or all of the above. There were a couple of guys who were notorious for all the drugs they bought, but they go so messed up everyone collectively decided to ban them. Elly's smile slowly faded, the deeper she got into her explanation.

Her gaze also kept switching between Olivia and the phone. Meanwhile, Olivia wondered why Brennan had the photo. He excluded pretty much everyone out of his life. Olivia sunk her head into the pillow as she thought. Elly only came into Brennan's life when she met Olivia after his suicide. If Brennan didn't have anyone else, why would he go to that treehouse? Her brain turned into a mess of possible conclusions, but the boy who beat her into a coma came into the cluster. He assaulted her because Brennan hurt his sister. Olivia's eyes opened wide. *Maybe they were close.* That girl might've been the exception. She could be the only person special to him.

But for a moment she doubted herself. Her memories after waking up were still hazy, but when she closed her eyes to concentrate, she remembered Haniel had the power to show her Brennan's memories while she was stuck in Limbo. And at some point in his past that girl revealed herself to be his girlfriend, but Olivia assumed she became an ex-girlfriend. *I need to find her.* That strong conviction only lasted for a moment, however. It didn't take long until Olivia decided she needed a break. Sorting through this mess since they switched bodies had been taking a toll on her ever since. *I need a break.* The thought seemed selfish to her but she justified it by reminding herself that she always did what others wanted and never what she wanted.

Still, she couldn't help but let her empathy get the better of her. She reluctantly accepted the fact that she'd have to go back to her own life, but she didn't want Brennan to kill himself again when he returned, so seeking out his ex-girlfriend to learn what went wrong, might give her the right lessons she could teach him. Maybe then, he could keep himself from going down a rabbit hole of regret. Then he'd have less reasons to kill himself.

"Elly, I need your help," Olivia said.

"What is it?"

"I think I do remember going to that 'love house'. I went there with a girl, and I need you to help me find her."

"Girl? Who? What girl? Why haven't you mentioned her?"

Olivia racked her brain for more of Brennan's memories, and the fact that the relationship had a big age gap surfaced. "There was just a big age difference," she said. "She was older than me by five years. I had to keep it a secret." Olivia surprised herself at how good she'd become at dissecting his life and expressing it as if she were really him, but her imitation wasn't perfect. She had to rub the creases forming on her forehead to hide her eyes. Their expression always gave away her deceit.

Elly hummed to herself before asking, "Okay, what do you want me to do?"

"I want you to help me find her. Can you do that?"

"Yes, but I need a photo of her." Olivia looked perplexed. "Let me explain first," Elly said. "A lot of phones have their location turned on by default. They're pretty much a tracking device. If she had her picture taken while the phone's location was turned on, I can use that image to track her down." Elly rested her chin in her hand.

"Okay. I don't know how you're going to do that, but as long as it gets the job done, I'm happy with it." They went through the rest of the camera roll to find a picture of the girl, and after a few more swipes, they did. In the photo, Brennan held the camera in front of them while his girlfriend wrapped her arms around his waist and kissed his cheek. Olivia felt relieved when finding it, but Elly's face showed jealousy.

"That's her," Olivia said, ignoring Elly's expression.

"Okay then. If they took that picture at her house, I may be able to find her."

"Thank you. If I could hug you right now, I would." Olivia realized that her words were very different from something Brennan would've said, but it made her happy to see Elly smile again. But her smile reminded her that, unlike Brennan, she had a positive impact on her life. *Maybe I shouldn't return to my body.*

THE LIGHTHOUSE

B y the time Brennan woke up, he found himself lying on top of the ocean with Life sitting next to him. The glow of the moon showed her holding her face in her palms. Her tiny finger caught the tears dripping from her eyes. It took a moment for Brennan to regain complete awareness, but once he did, he quickly took notice of her condition. He figured the crash must've been too much stress for her to handle. After all, if it scared him, it definitely scared her.

"Hey, are you okay?" he asked.

Life turned to him with a short sniffle. "I thought you were…"

Brennan shushed her softly. "Just take your time."

"I was scared!" She cried even harder, and Brennan embraced her in a tight hug. The protection radiating from his actions was reminiscent of what he felt when his older sister held him.

"I'm sorry you had to deal with that. It must've been terrifying." Before proceeding, Brennan let her cry a little more until she regained her composure. Her small body wobbled onto her tiny feet before she wiped her face. That was when Brennan took the chance to ask, "Where are we? The water we're walking on. That lighthouse. It feels odd. I've never seen this place, but I feel so close to it."

Despite his request for an answer, he didn't receive one. Life just kept a steady gaze on him with an unmoving mouth.

"I guess you don't know, huh?" Brennan asked. He gave a disappointed look and placed a hand on his knee to push himself up. He stood tall on the water, despite having half of his feet submerged. "Let's go," he said, taking Life's hand.

As they walked, he couldn't help but ponder why the area felt so familiar. To him, the place resembled one of Florida's beaches. The walks he'd take with his father and sister came to mind, and the image of his dad holding his sister's hand brought on a strange feeling. He hadn't seen the man in years, and his mother's house was a spitting image of hell, but his sister had always stuck by his side throughout their childhood. His body shivered at the thought. Nora, his sister had a place in his heart as the person he hated and loved the most. Yet, despite these unpleasant emotions, the lighthouse made it impossible to think of anything else.

The entire building acted as a beacon for his memories to follow. Over time, Brennan began to realize why the place seemed so familiar. As a child, he and his family would go to a sailor-themed restaurant, and the watchtower proudly stood as the diner's main attraction. His mind begged him to delve deeper into his memories, but did his best not to give into the temptation. Brennan didn't want his burdens to live rent-free in his head anymore. He had to get to that lighthouse without falling apart. So, on he went, with Life holding onto his hand.

The closer they got to the building, the brighter its light shined, but when that beacon became bright enough, it revealed a figure standing in the sea. He squinted, trying to focus his vision. That was when he realized the figure belonged to a woman.

"Hey!" Brennan called out to her. But as soon as he yelled, Life drifted behind him. She tightly gripped his shirt and hid her entire body.

"Brennan," she whispered. "She's a stranger! I haven't seen her before."

He considered her words and decided to keep his guard up. He couldn't see the lady's face yet, so he couldn't tell who she was. He stepped an inch forward, shot his arm out horizontally in front of Life.

"Can you see her face?" he asked.

"No." Life trembled, and Brennan felt like an idiot. With the sky being as dark as it was, the moon became their only light source. Of course, she couldn't see the woman's face. With nowhere else to go, they could only wait. As the figure grew nearer, the taller it seemed to be, but Brennan's fear washed away when he realized it was just Lily. Her black hair was now tied into a bun. This time without a breeze; neither her hair nor her dress flowed. They were completely still.

"I hope I'm not interrupting, but I saw the train crash and I became extremely worried. I just thought it'd be best to check up on you." When she brought her face in front of Brennan's, Life popped her tiny head out from behind his back. "Oh my! Who are you?" Lily asked Life with a chuckle. She made a move to rub the top of her head, but the young girl ducked back to her hiding spot.

"It's okay," Brennan told her. "This is Lily. I met her at the station." He gave Life a smile, but she didn't return it. The only thing she gave back was a hint of fear in her eyes. The action made him confused. Life loved welcomed everyone, but if she didn't accept this woman, what was the reason?

"By the way, I forgot to give you this," Lily said. In her hand lay a polaroid camera. "I hope you like this gift. It's ancient, but I've changed its appearance over the centuries. I figured this look would better suit your generation."

Even though Brennan came into the world in the year 2001, past the time of Polaroid cameras, he decided not to complain.

"What's it for?" he asked. He already knew that it must've been some otherworldly item, but everything here seemed to be used for purposes he never expected. Brennan glanced at Life for an answer, but the little girl shook her head, as if she were telling him not to take gifts from strangers. *What's going on in that little girl's head?* If he had learned anything on his journey, it was that Life was the most trustworthy person he had ever met. She may have been a child, but her intuition never failed to be spot on. However, his need to find Jessica hadn't wavered since he boarded the train. But if working with Lily meant saving her, the means justified the end.

"Well, I'm glad you asked!" Lily smiled at him and clapped her hands together. "Just take a picture of someone or something and you'll see what it or they really are! Try that lighthouse." Lily turned her head and pointed to the building. Brennan quickly put the camera to his face and snapped a photo of it. The film gradually came out, developed, and showed that the lighthouse wasn't a lighthouse anymore. Instead, a regular house replaced it in the photo, but before he could examine it further, Life snatched the camera out his hand to take a photo of Lily. However, once she aimed the lens at her, the woman slapped it out of her hands. "No!" she screamed. "Never do that again!"

Brennan ushered Life to stand behind him. Her sudden hostility put him on edge.

"Relax, she's a kid," he told Lily. "She's probably just curious, as children tend to be." He made sure his words came out as calm as possible, for the sake of all of them. Then, turning his eyes down from Lily to focus on Life, he said, "Isn't that right?" But rather than giving him reassurance, she receded into her hiding spot.

"Very well," Lily said with a sigh. "Maybe your friend will be in that house. After all, there's nowhere else to go." She waved her hand and the camera floated out of the water. The device gently levitated into Brennan's palms. After which she faded away with a frown.

"Why'd you think something was off about her?" Brennan asked Life once Lily vanished. He lowered his voice as if someone was listening to their conversation. Finding Jessica was a top priority, so he wanted to be able to trust Lily despite his doubts.

"Don't talk to her!" Life shouted. "Lily is bad. Bad! Bad!" She stomped her feet as a temper tantrum erupted.

Brennan's annoyance starting to take control, but after spending so much time living as Olivia, he had learned to put up with a lot. He took in deep breaths, but his older version still lay dormant somewhere within himself.

"Shut up!" he shouted suddenly. Life stopped and stared at him. Just like what his mother would do to him, he raised his hand to strike, but when he noticed her eyes begging him to have mercy, he lowered his fist.

"I'm sorry." A feeling of defeat washed over him. *I can't be like her.* He'd always promised himself that he would never become as abusive as his mother, yet the actions he took in his past said otherwise. He wanted to ignore the situation, so he continued their hike toward the lighthouse.

"Brennan," Life muttered.

"Yes?" He took a deep breath, as though his guilt was smothering him.

"I'm sorry for making you mad."

He exhaled. "No, I should be the one apologizing. I never should've raised my hand. But why do you have a problem with Lily?"

"I don't know. She just scares me. You're scary, too, but she's a scarier version of you." Just like most children, Life spoke her mind openly, but her words made Brennan feel self-conscious.

I'm scary?

The lighthouse proved too be much further away that Brennan initially thought. He didn't expect to take a twenty-minute walk across the surface of the water. To make matters worse, Life became too tired to continue just before they got halfway there, forcing him to let her ride on his back. At first, he didn't want to, but seeing her tired face, it made him realize he was pushing her too hard. But when he let her ride him, he began to wonder if the situation resembled an interaction between an older and younger sibling. He had always been the youngest child, so he had a hard time looking at things from Nora's perspective, but carrying Life along the water made him feel like a protector. Especially after she fell asleep on his back. Images of Nora protecting him from his mother's beatings came to him, making each step he took heavier, and pretty soon each memory became a whip striking his heart. The thoughts bombarded him until they came to an end once he reached the shoreline.

"Hey, wake up!" Brennan gently rocked Life until she opened her eyes. He kneeled, and she groggily crawled off his back. She sat down for a moment while he stepped forward, so he'd be able to survey the area. Brennan noticed a faint outline in the air. With his interest piquing, he stepped closer until he found himself facing a transparent box that surrounded the lighthouse. Feeling curious, he reached out to touch it, and when his finger made contact with its surface, a ripple flowed across the cube. He applied more pressure until his limb eventually started to push through. "Life," he said to her. "Let's go inside."

Her eyes drifted open and shut, but when she turned her head to the lighthouse, she popped them open.

"Hey! That place looks fun!" Her hyperactivity suddenly came back, catching Brennan off guard. The young girl jumped to her feet and sprinted inside the box without hesitation.

"H-hey wait!" Brennan tried to run after her, but ended up tripping through into the box and faceplanting into the dirt. The strike to his head caused his vision to blur, but when he finally returned to normal, he realized why she was so excited.

The photo he took earlier showed someone's home. From where he stood earlier, he couldn't catch sight of it, but now that he came closer, it presented itself to him in replacement of the lighthouse. While the outside remained hidden in the night sky, the interior of the box became overwhelmed with the warm glow of the sun. The light slowly spread across the ground, bringing not only brightness, but also a trail of grass and flowers in its wake. Life blossomed around him. For a moment he breathed in the sweet scent, but he fell to his knees when his head stung with an abrupt stabbing sensation that accompanied the intrusive memories.

However, they weren't memories of his family. Instead, his mind became bogged down with replays of his ex-girlfriend. He took another look at the house. An array of warm colors glazed over his eyes, causing him to see in orange and yellow. The colors grew stronger with his headache and only subsided when he fully recollected the memories associated with this house.

It wasn't a regular residence; it was the "love house". A near-perfect replica, with the only missing piece being the tree it stood on. The green roof and pulley system remained present.

Brennan figured Life must've been enthralled by its family-friendly appearance, but he knew deep down that this place was not meant for a child. Brennan rushed through the meadow and burst through the front door. Dust particles floated around the interior, but despite the dirty air, the windows, walls, and floor were polished to perfection. Brennan couldn't do anything as he became enamored by what he saw. Blankets and mattresses slowly faded into existence, all of which were cleaner than the ones he remembered couples using. He scanned the room, expecting to see more furniture, but his expectations were squandered by the sight of a young woman. She sat on a mattress with her back toward him. At first, her figure was completely foreign to him, but upon closer inspection, her gray hoodie revealed who she was.

"Nora?" he asked.

The woman turned around, proving his hypothesis to be correct. Nora, his sister, sat before him. Her presence filled him with hate. In the real world, she was alive and well without him, so why did she haunt him here?

"So, you're old enough to come here?" she asked.

Brennan took a step back. "Yeah, so what? Why do you care anyway? We're not kids anymore!" The word "kid" hurt to say. Ever since their childhood came to an end, their bond with each other had ceased as well. The moment she had the resources to leave their broken home, she did.

"You were always a hound dog around girls," she said. "I knew I'd find you here. I just wanted to see my little brother again. Is that so wrong?"

Brennan knew what he saw had to have been a trick, but he clenched his fist to suppress the urge to knock her down. "No, there's nothing wrong with that. But there is something wrong with leaving your little brother on his own!" Brennan gritted his teeth and stepped forward. "In fact, I'd commend you for coming back, but you never did!" His voice turned from anger to bitterness. His breath turned shallow as every little thing he wanted to say to her spilled out of his mouth. "I'll fucking kill you—"

Nora took him by surprise when she jumped to her feet to embrace him. The familiar warmth of her body and fruity scent disarmed him. Brennan wanted to push her away, but at the same time, he missed her.

"I'm sorry for leaving," she said. "I just had to get out of that house. I had to get away from Mom. I'm sorry." Her voice and tight hug almost put him at ease, but Brennan reminded himself of all the empty promises she made. Her whispers might as well have been the whispering of a snake. He gripped her shoulders and pushed her.

"I guess I was wrong when I said you left," he muttered. "I see now that you were always with me. Whether it was the whispers in the dark or the hairs standing on the back of my neck, you never left. You were always there. Torturing me. Taunting me. You became my nightmares." Brennan tightly shut his eyes so that he wouldn't have to look at her, but he couldn't ignore her ever-consuming presence. She ran her hand around his back and frazzled his hair, and once she let go of him, he opened his eyes. A tear of blood streamed down his face.

"Siblings are bound by blood," she whispered. "So can you forgive me?"

"How would I be able to?" Brennan asked, his voice shaking with anger. "How can I let go of what you did? You abandoned me!" He wanted to smack the sides of his face and scream, but his mind told him to fight. To do her wrong as an act of revenge.

"I'm sorry," she muttered.

"No, you're not." Brennan told himself to scream, to throw her on the ground and pummel her face, but he held back. His lips quivered and his voice became weak.

"You don't have to worry."

"I'm not worried." Brennan gritted his teeth and tried to stand tall, but facing his sister made him weak.

"I know when my little brother is sad." Nora cooed at him and held out her hand.

This pain. This torment. It has to end!

"Stop!" Brennan yelled. His sister fell silent, and he heard his heart pounding. He breathed heavily as if his blood was pumping hard enough to burst through his veins.

"Stop what?" Nora asked calmly.

"Stop bothering me." Even though he wanted to sound strong, his emotions took a toll on him. A quiet voice was all he could manage.

"I'm bothering you?" she asked.

"Yes, and I can't let that happen. I missed you so much, I couldn't stop thinking about you. I'm not letting your memory control me, just like Mom's. I'm done with you."

"That's all you have to say?"

Rather than opening his mouth, Brennan shook his head. The silent gesture solidified his decision to leave. He knew he could hold his feelings back for now, but they would inevitably resurface.

"Good job," she whispered. Nora took a few steps back before her finger turned to stone. With a shocked expression, Brennan watched the rest of her body morph into cobblestone. Eventually she turned into a statue, leaving him to wonder what just happened. If this event could take place, what else would the afterlife have in store for him? He went toward his sister and reach out to touch her stone face, but before he could do so, the house began to rumble. Pieces of the ceiling hit the floor, and Brennan decided to seek refuge outside, but he quickly remembered that he didn't come here alone.

"Life! Life, where are you?"

"I'm outside! Please, help me!" He sprinted out the door in pursuit of her voice, and once he found her crying in fear, his arms scooped her little body up and pushed through the meadow. Exiting the box came seamlessly, as though it wasn't there in the first place, which made their escape feel even more of a relief.

"Are you all right?" She nodded. "Okay, the—" he stopped short. Not only had he just seen his sister transform into stone, now he noticed that Life looked a little older. She stood taller, wearing a longer dress and retaining less baby-fat. What the hell was going on?

THE DIGITAL SEARCH

Tracking down Brennan's ex-girlfriend could've been a curse or a blessing. Finding her meant that Olivia had a chance to ensure his self-preservation, but only if she decided to pursue the idea of going back to her own life. Everyone in Brennan's close circle has been treating her with so much respect and love that just the thought of living with her parents again terrified her. On the surface she told herself giving his life back would be the right thing to do, but she also believed she had a right to be selfish. After everything she's been through, surely she deserved happiness of her own.

Earlier that day, Olivia found herself living in her head surrounded by a cage of self-doubt. The only escape from that hell was Elly's voice, and even then, it still wasn't enough to consistently keep her in reality. After numerous attempts to keep Olivia's attention, Elly decided to go home mid-day. The jealously that crept on her face when they found a photo of Brennan's girlfriend etched itself in Olivia's mind. Seeing Elly so upset made it unbearable to witness her departure. All of this formed a feeling of guilt gnawing at her chest. None of the other girls at school took the time to befriend her, so she felt despair when Elly left, and even worse, to realize that she was the person she trusted the most...

If I live my life as him, she'll be by my side, but she won't see me as me. While it was true that she could keep up the façade of being Brennan, she'd have to go on with the pain that they only loved her as Brennan Claufield. All of these factors became a tornado, wreaking havoc on her mind. Olivia heaved a great sigh and sunk her body into the bed. *Why can't anything be simple?*

Fortunately, Elly's willingness to let Olivia transfer the photos of Brennan's old partner to her phone gave Olivia some peace of mind. Originally, she thought Elly just wanted to make a dart board out of a few prints, but she promised that the coding within the pictures would be able to move between devices. Olivia didn't know what that meant, or if what they were doing was legal, but as long as they could track down the girl, she didn't mind. In the meantime, she retrieved Brennan's phone from under her pillow and began swiping through it. She browsed the internet until a news headline caught her eye.

A High School student was found dead at a lake.

Olivia wanted to ignore the morbidity of the world, but she couldn't help feeling curious, so she read the article.

Two students, Jessica Fermin, and Olivia Benning, from Island Bay High School, ran away last Friday. According to Mr. Jefferson, a teacher at Island Bay High School, they ran away early that morning after assaulting him. As of right now, Jessica Fermin was found deceased, and Olivia Benning is still missing.

Olivia's eyes grew wide when she read their names. *Jessica? Brennan?* Even though Jessica only brought on torturous memories, Olivia would never wish death upon her, and if Brennan ran away, that meant he must be heading to Florida. But was Jessica dead? And why wasn't the cause of her death stated? Olivia's brain started to ask so many questions and make so many assumptions. *If Jessica's dead, Brennan's probably dead! Did Brennan kill himself? If he killed himself while in my body, do I have anywhere to go back to?* Olivia couldn't sit around and wait any longer. She got out of bed but hit the floor when she tried to stand.

Being in a coma put a lot of limitations on Brennan's body, especially his ability to walk. She knew that physical therapy would be needed, but at the same time, she had the common sense to know her time was limited. *But if my life is so hectic, I could just stay here.*

Olivia shook her head at the thought. She didn't want to think that way, but if Brennan did die, then she really wouldn't have a reason to go back. Olivia tried to entertain the thought of living the rest of her life as Brennan, but that only worsened her feelings of guilt. *I can't be thinking like this!* Out of frustration, she began slapping the ground, but stopped when Nora stepped into the room.

"Brennan!" she shrieked. She ran toward Olivia and used all her strength to hoist her body up. "I can get a nurse and—"

"There's no need," Olivia said with a shaky voice. "I was just trying to walk. I can't stand lying in bed all day."

Nora sighed, as though she just witnessed her brother narrowly escape death.

"Well, there's no need to be so hard on yourself. Take some time to relax." She placed Olivia back on the bed and stared at her disapprovingly.

"I need to get out of here," Olivia said.

"No! You have to stop pushing yourself so hard! Just stay here until you get better!" Nora's concern only made it harder on Olivia. She never had anyone be so protective of her except for her biological father. Nora's voice provided the structure she wanted in her life so, she began to tell herself that maybe it would be better to stay as Brennan.

"Please, let me leave," she begged. "I just want to see someone important to me."

Nora's facial expression softened at Olivia's request.

"And who are you referring to?"

"There's this-this-this girl, I've been talking to. We've been talking a lot, and I'd like to see her." Olivia's heart felt as if it was being torn apart. First she wanted to steal Brennan's place in the world, now she was lying to his sister. *I'm a terrible person.*

"Are you talking about that brainiac girl? Elly was her name, right?" Nora took a seat beside her and finally began relaxing her posture. She wasn't so stiff anymore, and her arms weren't folded across her chest.

"No," Olivia said, gripping the phone beneath her bedsheet. She only wanted someone to protect her from herself. If only Elly was here to do that, she'd feel a sense of peace. It hadn't even been a full day yet, and Olivia had already become her own worst enemy.

"Then who are you talking about?"

"Her name is Olivia." Olivia started grinding her teeth together. Speaking about herself in the third person never came easy, and it only added to the lie that she was Brennan. "The last time I spoke to her, she... she..." Olivia had trouble keeping herself together, so Nora patted her back. "I saw a news article headline about a student from her school being found dead near a Lake, and—"

"Hold on," Nora interrupted. "You said her name is 'Olivia'?"

"Yes."

"Did you read the full article?" Nora asked nervously.

It took Olivia a minute of brainstorming to figure out what she was getting at.

"No. I know the article had the name 'Olivia' in it, but that's just some girl who shares the same name." Olivia felt a shard stinging sensation in the back of her head. It felt as if God was maiming her for telling another lie.

"Are you telling me the truth?" Nora asked.

"Yes." Another sting stabbed her brain.

Nora stood and began pacing the room. "How'd you meet your friend?" The tone in her voice indicated a hint of hesitation, alerting Olivia that she didn't fully believe her story.

"I met her online in a forum. She's an online friend, but she's just as real to me as you and Elly."

"Well, I don't know much about online relationships, but a person is a person, and a relationship is still a relationship. I guess it doesn't matter how you meet. As long as you get along." Nora returned to the spot beside Olivia, but still had the face of a detective ready to break a case. "A lot has been happening since you tried to... you know..." Nora couldn't finish the sentence, so she just made a horizontal slicing motion across her neck.

"Yeah, I know," Olivia muttered. "I'm sorry."

"There's no need to be sorry. I just need you to be honest with me."

An awkward silence filled the room, and Olivia wanted to create some distance, but it felt as if a rope was keeping her attached to Nora.

"I..." Olivia covered her face and started crying. While their conversation didn't take any strenuous physical effort, the mental violence she'd created for herself took its toll, and when Nora noticed, she pulled her in for a hug.

"Save your strength. We're going to need to beat that kid in court."

"Court?" Olivia asked, forgetting all about her assault.

"Yeah, that boy who beat you into a coma. We'll show him not to mess with you." Nora made a thumbs-down gesture while sticking her tongue out. It was a nice change to their heavy conversation, but not enough to make Olivia laugh. Talking about the boy might've been morbid, but at least it got her mind off Brennan.

The stress Olivia's mind had to endure in such a short amount of time put her to sleep for most of the day. She'd occasionally slip into consciousness, only to see Nora holding her hand while sitting in the chair next to the bed. Even though Elly promised to come back, she never appeared in any of Olivia's moments of being awake. Maybe she'd busied herself working on tracking down Brennan's girlfriend, but then again, she'd never broken a promise before. So, in those moments of being alert, Olivia felt nothing but emotional turmoil. Eventually, the sun stopped shining through the window, and she just barely felt Nora pat her shoulder before creating a breeze, indicating her departure.

Being all alone, Olivia wondered where Haniel was, and how soon she'd be able to get in touch with him. As strange as he was, Haniel always found the words to lead her in the right direction. But the fact that he hadn't shown up again stirred the fear that she might have to go at this alone, so she reluctantly took the time to come up with a plan. The only thing she could think of was running away, though she didn't know how she'd do that. She couldn't move her legs, and she had no idea if Brennan was even alive. But still, if he was alive, finding someone or some way to get to her hometown in Washington would be her best bet to get to him.

Anger and uncertainty boiled inside her, so she picked up her pillow and smothered herself. Her scream made the fabric vibrate while her throat began to hurt as she aggressively pushed the pillow closer to her mouth. Once she finished, sweat poured from her forehead and she returned to lying still, but the moment she closed her eyes, she heard the door open. She only wanted to fall asleep again, so the commotion caused her sit up and let out a groan. At first, she didn't see anyone, but when she looked down, she saw Death walking over to her.

"Oh, it's just you," Olivia said, relieved. *If he's here, then maybe Haniel is too.* The little boy tried to climb onto the bed despite his short stature, but could only accomplish his mission when Olivia stepped in to help.

"My sister's with Brennan," he said bluntly.

His words scared her, but she figured that if Death watched over her in the world of the living, then surely Life would do the same.

"Is she with him in the afterlife or my world?"

"They're in the afterlife."

Surprisingly, the news didn't make Olivia as sad she expected to be. After reading the full article, it became abundantly clear that Brennan might not have died. A body was never found, so maybe there was a chance he'd still be alive. However, him being dead would mean that he didn't have a place in this world anymore, so she might have the option to stay in his body, but then again, she felt reluctant to say that someone's death made her happy.

"So, he's dead?" Olivia asked. She wanted to ask more questions, but her lung capacity limited the number of words she could speak.

"No, he's not dead. He just went back to the train station." Death stared at her with his hollow eyes, as if expecting a response.

Train station? How could he be back there without dying? And if he's gotten that far, does that mean it's almost time for me to join him?

"Are you sure he's not dead?" Olivia narrowed her eyes on him.

"I'm sure. Someone brought him there. That's why he's gone."

Olivia's brain ran through the possible people that could've brought him there. Death seemed oblivious to what happened, so it couldn't have been him, but she couldn't say for sure if Life did it, since she'd never met her.

"Did Haniel do that? Can he bring us back there whenever he wants?"

"No," Death said with a look of disappointment.

"So, is it Life? Did your sister bring him there?"

Death shook his head.

"Even Haniel doesn't know. We just know that the one who did this is really strong. They're bad and strong."

Olivia sighed. Her situation just became even more complicated. Originally, all she had to do was switch places with Brennan after they were wrongly resurrected in each other's bodies, but now she was letting her feelings get in the way, and with the introduction of this new character, they would probably get themselves into an even bigger mess. The stress made Olivia want to shrink in her body again like she always did, or at the very least she wanted to run away and forget about everyone.

To her, it didn't seem worth the trouble to help Brennan out. His burdens were just pulling her down, and she needed a way to make herself happy.

"Is Haniel around?" she asked. When Death didn't say anything, Olivia became frustrated. "Why can't anything come easy for me?" She looked at the young boy with resentment. She never felt hatred toward him, but right now she needed to put her anger on someone else. "Can you leave me alone?" Olivia asked.

Death gave a sad look. "Did I do something wrong?" His wide eyes showed that he held some admiration for her, making Olivia feel weak. She just couldn't get over the fact that the people she surrounded herself with loved her. It was a stark contrast to the people in her life as Olivia Benning.

"No, you didn't do anything wrong. In fact, you can stay here with me." Olivia said.

The young boy gave a smile, which was a rare occurrence for him. He proceeded to lay on his side with his head in her lap. Olivia allowed him to do so, but the nervous look on his face caught her attention. "There's something more you want to tell me, isn't there?"

Death stared at her as he reached into his pocket. When he pulled his hand back out, he opened it to reveal a mint.

"What's that?" Olivia asked.

"Angels can use their powers to make gifts. Haniel wants you to have this. He said it will help you find Brennan, but you should only use it when you really need it."

"What does it do?" Olivia took the mint from his hand and held it between her thumb and index finger. She examined it closely.

"Haniel said eating it will show you what you're not supposed to see."

Olivia took the vague piece of information in. If Brennan found himself stuck in the afterlife, maybe she needed to see things out of the ordinary to find him. But then again, what would count as "out-of-the-ordinary" at this point? She knew about the world of the dead, their sounds, sights, and people. What more could this mint show her? This mint was pretty much useless in her hands.

Olivia took an empty capsule on the metal tray next to her bed and dropped the mint inside. Surely everyone would assume it was just pain meds and not some mythical gift given by an angel. Still, her confusion and doubts added more fuel to her despair. She shoved the capsule into her pocket and closed her eyes. With the pressure of everyone expecting her to switch bodies, she caved in. Even though her life as Brennan brought so much happiness, she still yielded to everyone else's wishes. For now, her she could only feel comfort in the idea of sleep providing temporary relief, so she never opened her eyes again for the rest of the night, letting the drowsiness slowly consume her.

DENIAL

B rennan kneeled on the ground with a heavy breath. While Life was shaking and trying to comprehend what happened, he turned his head toward her as his brain tried to process a million things at once. Why would Nora be in the house? Was it really her? Why did the whole place collapse, and why did Life look a little older?

"I supposed you don't know what happened back there?" Brennan asked.

"No, I just felt an earthquake, and everything started to fall." As she spoke, Brennan noticed that her voice sounded more, mature, and her vocabulary more refined.

"Why do you look so different?" Life stared at him with wide eyes. She dawned a look of shock without offering an answer. "You look a little older. Maybe, about two years or three."

"I don't know what you mean." She played with her hair, as Brennan's question did nothing to diffuse any confusion. He wanted to push the topic further, but the thought of Jessica loomed over him. He knew he couldn't waste any more time, but being left in the dark didn't help at all. Every part of his body tightened in rage, and his bulging veins showed it.

"This is fucking bullshit!" Brennan slammed his fist on the rocky ground, and despite the scrapes and cuts turning them into a bloody mess, he didn't flinch. "Why? Why? Why? All I want is to find Jessica, but all I find is my sister ready to torture me! And look at you!" Brennan pointed a finger at Life, and she jumped. She tried to stand still, but couldn't. Her body trembled and her eyes watered. It seemed that despite growing older, two or three years didn't offer a drastic change in her capacity to manage stress. Her mind was still dominated by her usual fears of what Brennan might do when he lashed out. Upon noticing her reaction, Brennan stood and dusted himself off. Her horrified face reminded him of his childhood.

"I'm sorry," he said.

"Are you okay?"

"No, not really, but I guess there's not much we can do for now." Life let a frown creep upon her face, but Brennan could tell it wasn't only sadness in her heart. She still feared him, and she had a right to. After all, Brennan had proven himself to be notorious for sudden bursts of anger.

"What do we do now?" Her voice still wavered as she looked at him, but he couldn't bring himself to make eye contact. Brennan turned his head away in shame. The belief that he had mastered control over his emotions had fallen part, and he was forced to acknowledge they were still capable of getting the best of him. He wondered if listening to Lily only made them even more lost. But he knew that the gift she gave him was the only thing he could use for now. So, he thought back to how the camera was meant to be used. *To show things for what they truly are.* Maybe, just like the tree house, this ocean was only an illusion. What if something laid beneath the surface? Something to give Brennan an idea of where to go.

"I'll figure something out." Even though he tried his best to sound confident, he couldn't keep the act going forever. Being levelheaded was always easier said than done, but luckily for him, making up a plan on a whim came easy. That said, he feared his ways of doing things would meet a roadblock. This world was too unfamiliar, and he wasn't ready for it.

Brennan stared into the distance, as if it would change the fact that the ocean stretched endlessly. He wanted to know if an exit existed within the sea, but he realized pondering the question would only waste time. The camera in his pocket offered an opportunity that he had to take, despite the horrific house it led him to. He felt his pocket for the device Lily had given him... In an act of desperation, he snapped photos of the ocean, hoping they would reveal something new.

Maybe one of the areas in the water wasn't a body of liquid at all. Maybe he was right to guess that something hidden laid beneath the surface. Like a door, or a portal, or just anything that could get them out of there. For the next few minutes, the clicking sound of his finger and the film sliding out were the only things to be heard. The first three polaroids showed only water, but his heart rose when he found that the fourth one depicted a massive, pitch-black hole located in front of Life. He turned to her with a grin while she drew in the sand with a stick. She began to walk around the edge of the shore, to look for rocks.

"Don't move!" Brennan yelled.

She paused and turned her head.

"Why?"

"It's the water. Well, actually, there's no water. There's a massive hole in front of you, and I don't want you to fall."

She stood still and wiped the sand off her hands using her dress. Meanwhile, Brennan stumbled his way toward her until they were side by side. "Down there." He pointed at the area in front of them. Life still didn't seem convinced, so he pulled out the photo and presented it to her.

"Oh, it's a hole!"

"That's right." Brennan nodded. He knew that hole offered an exit, but he didn't know if it was safe to jump in. He hesitated, wanting to avoid it, but then he thought to himself, *this house only showed me my sister.* He knew that the place was nothing more than a dead end. *Jessica. I need to find Jessica.* Since there was nothing left for him here, his impulses jumped into action, and usually, when they showed up, he'd always brush away the idea of safety, and this time was no different. He closed his eyes and asked, "Life, how does a prayer work?"

"You want to pray?" she asked, surprised.

"Yes. I might not be a big fan of God, but right now I need his help." He wondered if the big man above would protect him. He didn't know if there were a request that was too much to ask for. Plus, he'd always proclaimed his hatred toward the deity. He just hoped that his love and mercy shined upon everyone in the world.

"Just be honest and say what's in your heart," Life said.

"Got it." Brennan closed his eyes and let the words come from his chest. *Whatever it may cost, please let me find Jessica. I don't care about the danger. I just need to see her, and please don't let me die falling down a hole.*

After that, Brennan whispered, "Amen" under his breath. He opened his eyes wide, bent his knees, and sprung into the air. Life tried to grab him, but her fingers only grazed his shirt, since he was already diving headfirst down the hole. The moonlight drifted past him as gravity lost its pull, making his body lighter farther down. Air bubbles floated past him. Surprisingly, his ears lacked any pressure, and his lungs were always filled with air. He saw sunlight behind a liquid barrier at the very bottom. His body went down faster, like a cannonball being shot.

Eventually, he burst through the border, making his body hit a ray of sunshine. He left the ocean far behind him, as he was now pummeling through the sky. The blue ocean water turned into shards of stained glass falling behind him. The wind tore at his eyes, forcing him to shed tears. He began thrashing his limbs violently, looking for something to grab, but he was stuck in a free fall. The realization of his situation hit him, and he tucked his limbs inside to make a protective shell. Once he was ten feet from the ground, he noticed the world being filled with the brightest green grass and reddest roses. His arms and legs braced for impact, but the moment he slammed into the ground, he rolled forward until the momentum died and he came to a halt. For a moment he just lay on his back, not doing anything. He took in the sun, trying to calm his body as more flowers began to spring from the dirt. The roses were being accompanied by sunflowers, daffodils, and lilies. Despite the intense ordeal, Brennan couldn't help but laugh when he saw the beauty around him.

"Having fun yet?" he heard a voice ask. Brennan stopped laughing and stood. His eyes surveyed the area, but didn't catch anyone.

"Up here," the voice said. Brennan turned his attention to the sky to be greeted by the sight of Haniel, the short and inappropriate angel, and Life floating down, with the help of an umbrella. The young girl had her small arms wrapped around his chest. Unlike Brennan, they managed to land softly, but while Haniel held a firm smile, Life covered her hand with her mouth, ready to throw up. She sprinted far into the meadow and out of sight. The sound of her gagging on bile reached Brennan's ears.

"Give her some time," Haniel said.

'Where am I?" Brennan asked.

"I don't know. I've spent enough time in the afterlife to know that each train has a specific destination. But the strange thing is that train didn't. It seems like whoever put you there wanted you to get lost. But since the train derailed, I guess you got lucky. I've also been trying to track you down. It was pretty difficult because you and Life got lost." As usual, he said the most horrible news with a cheery attitude and a big smile that showed off his shiny white teeth. However, he stopped smiling when he noticed the Polaroid camera in Brennan's hand. "Where'd you get that?" he asked in a serious tone.

"I got it from this woman I met. Her name is Lily."

Haniel put a hand to his chin and hummed quietly.

"There's something about that name that sounded familiar. I'm pretty sure if I thumbed through the handbook God gave all his angels, I could find something about her."

"Angels have handbooks?" Brennan raised his eyebrows.

"Never mind that. Just tell me what that camera does."

Brennan returned his face to a more neutral tone before continuing the conversation.

"Apparently if I take a picture of something, the photo that develops shows me what that thing really is."

"I don't understand."

Brennan pulled out the photo of the tree house to Haniel as an example. "What do you see here?" he asked.

"I see a house."

"That's right, but if you were to look at the building in person, you'd see a lighthouse. But once I took this picture, I found out that the building was actually the tree house I went to with my girlfriend."

"And what did you see when you went inside this building?" Haniel's attention seemed to turn into interest, so Brennan went on to explain.

"I encountered my sister. The interior looked great, but everything went to shit once I talked to her."

"Throw that camera away immediately," Haniel said quickly.

"What? Why?"

"I've seen items like these." Haniel skipped to Brennan's side and inspected the item. Rather than asking to take it, he looked closely, like a curious child. His eyes were like a copy machine as they took in every bit of information. From the handle to the lens, Brennan could tell that nothing was escaping Haniel's eyes.

Finally, the angel stopped and stood tall. He looked at Brennan and said, "I'm right. I have seen items like these. They're gifts given by supernatural beings created by their own power. I even made one and used Death to deliver it to Olivia."

"Olivia? How is she?"

"Hold that thought. I still need to explain. Items like these are special, which is why I'm confused this 'Lily' person gave you one. She must have a reason, and it must be sinister."

Haniel's words put a halt on Brennan's dreams to find Jessica. Lily still seemed odd to him, but undoubtedly her gift had the potential to help immensely. He pictured himself being lost at sea, which was prevented by the use of the camera, but then again, it led him to the hell he found at the tree house. "Sinister? B-but this thing's helped me so much! Because of this, I was able to get to this meadow. It showed me an exit!"

"I'm sorry. I know you don't want to hear this, but I have a bad feeling about that camera. After all, Life told me her worries as we flew down here. A child's intuition is strong. Children are friendly to almost everyone, so if someone makes them scared, then it must mean something."

"But she doesn't understand how important Jessica is to me and how much I need this camera! She doesn't know, and you don't either!"

"You're so lost..."

At his words, Brennan stumbled back. He stared angrily at him. He never got over the fury he'd feel whenever someone challenged him.

"What's that supposed to mean?" Brennan asked defensively.

"I mean, do you know Lily? Like, actually know her? There are plenty of evil beings lurking in this world, and my guess is that she's one of them. I'm thinking that camera doesn't even show you the truth. It's probably just showing you what you want to see."

"I don't understand." Brennan started to let his agitation show.

"Let me ask you something. What did you see in that lighthouse?"

At first, he was taken aback and wanted to argue, but he knew that describing his experience would mean talking about his sister. She opened so many old wounds that Brennan couldn't mend. He shut his eyes tight, trying to get the images of her out of his head. "Hello? Brennan?" Haniel started snapping his fingers until he gave a big clap next to his ear.

"Ah! What the hell do you want?" Brennan's eyes popped open, and he stared at him. "Would you stop making so much noise? You're acting like a child!"

Haniel suppressed his smile before clearing his throat. It seems that whenever he annoyed Brennan, he'd take it as a small victory. "As I was asking, what happened in that lighthouse?" He deepened his voice making him sound more like an adult.

Brennan sighed. He didn't want to respond, but since he was being pushed into a corner, he felt he had no choice. "I ran into my sister. We talked, and it just reminded me how much I hate her. Then this big earthquake happened, I ran outside, I picked up Life and we got out of there." His voice turned into a whisper. It became obvious Brennan could hardly bring himself to talk about the event.

"I see," Haniel said. "Well, I think we both know that you have conflicting feelings about your sister, and it sounded like the earthquake happened right after you began to feel frustrated. It could only mean one thing." Haniel rubbed his chin and hummed to himself.

"Just say what you need to say," Brennan muttered.

"I believe the events taking place are a reflection of your mental well-being. I've learned from my millions of years of life experience that people lost in this world tend to have their emotions and thoughts projected within the space around them. For example, your sister has always been on your mind." Brennan opened his mouth to deny his troubled relationship with his sister, but Haniel shushed him. "This world is like a separate entity acting on its own, and you're basically invading it. You're essentially being punished for being lost, and at this rate, that camera is only going to lead you further into your own personal hell. I suggest you hand it over." Haniel held out his hand, beckoning for Brennan to hand it over.

"No, I'm keeping this, and you can't stop me."

"Now, now, listen to me."

"I already said 'no'! I'm going to this thing to find Jessica!"

"Listen, I know you miss her, and I know she's a big reason you've changed from an angry bitter boy to a compassionate young man, but you have to understand she's gone. That camera might let you see her, but it's not going to be in the way you intend to. Either it's something that'll test your mental strength or it's just there to mislead you."

"No," Brennan muttered. He gripped the camera tightly and walked backward. Haniel followed, but Brennan yelled at him to stay away. "She's not gone! She can't be." He gritted his teeth as he tried not to let his tears out. "If Olivia and I can be brought back form the dead, then the same can happen to her!"

"That's not my decision to make," Haniel sighed. He loosened his shoulders and spoke in a kinder tone. "No matter what happens to her, neither of us has control over it."

"But that's not true! She's dead because I brought chaos into her life. If I'm the reason she died, then I can be the reason for her to come back. I'll find her and fix everything!"

"I hope you understand that when someone makes a decision like she did, there's nothing you can do to change their mind."

Life came running up to Brennan. Her head barely stood over the grass, so it caught him off guard when she placed her hand on his wrist.

"Please, Brennan," she begged. "Please, listen to us."

He looked down at her and bit his quivering lip. Tears poured out his eyes. The angry face he had still showed, but he let his hair fall in such a way that it covered his eyes. He did everything to hide his crying, but nothing worked. Life squeezed his hand tightly, then hugged his leg.

"I can't stay," Brennan whispered. "I'm sorry."

"But—"

"I said 'no'!" He raised his hand, making her take a step back. She covered her face, but when Brennan realized what he was about to do, he lowered his fist. He put one hand over the other and pushed it downward. *Not like her. Not like my mom.* He had to tell himself multiple times not to resort to hitting others. "I'm sorry. But I'm keeping this camera with me, and if you can't accept that, I'll just continue without you." Brennan motioned for her to let go of him. When she receded from her hug, he walked past her and straight toward Haniel. "You can't understand what I'm going through," Brennan said, poking his chest. He marched away into the field listening to Life's footsteps trailing him.

However, he heard her stop when Haniel said, "Just let him be." After that, he whispered something Brennan couldn't decipher. Despite the burning desire to figure out what he said, Brennan put that thought in the back of his mind and trudged forward.

OLD WOUNDS

B rennan's feet swept through the grass, with the smell of flowers scattering through the meadow. Although pleasant, he still couldn't help but complain. Why did he have to be so confused? According to Haniel, this world reflected his mental state, so if that was the case, why would he be lost in a beautiful field of flowers? After all, his mind was still rioting in internal violence. The fury he felt from his earlier conversation still lingered, and no other emotion filled him. There wasn't even an ounce of serenity or happiness.

After wandering for a mile, Brennan sat down and thought to himself. *Jessica. Jessica, I just want to see you.* He plucked a blade of grass and twirled it between his fingers like a child with nothing better to do. His mind stayed on autopilot until he heard grass crunching beneath quick footsteps. He turned around expecting to see Haniel, but Lily stopped by for a surprise. This time she wore a white blouse with a long blue skirt, and her hair fell off to the side.

She gave him a bright smile that seemed to go along with her friendly appearance.

"Hello, Mr. Claufield." She said his last name with a laugh, which Brennan took as a signal that she was trying to be funny.

"Hi." He stood to greet her, and when he did, she held out her palm. A small hourglass rested on it, and just like the other items, this one floated into the air. Brennan got the idea that it was another gift, but what Haniel said about the camera made him hesitate. Lily gave him an odd look, but he quickly changed his expression, as he reminded himself that Jessica waited for him at the end of his journey. So he held out his hand to take it. The item gently landed on his palm, and he brought it up to his eye. The sand within the glass had a blue pigment, and its strand flowed to the bottom at a snail's pace. "What is this for?" he asked.

"Why, I'm glad you asked!" Lily grinned at him before continuing. "Time in the real world doesn't overlap with time in the afterlife. Use that hourglass to keep track of the day. You'll probably get confused because of how inconsistently sand moves, but just remember, once one side is completely depleted, that means a week has passed in your world." She smiled at him and took another look at the hourglass. "Judging by the amount of sand on one side, I'd say a new week has just begun." Lily clapped her hands together and gave a curt nod.

"Thank you," Brennan said. He looked at her. He viewed her as an enigmatic figure holding an uneasy alliance with him. He just couldn't stop wondering why Life feared her, and he believed that if Haniel had been in his position, he'd change all his negative assumptions. However, the thought of Haniel's complete disapproval of his actions came back, putting a frown on his face.

"You have a troubled look," Lily commented. Even though Brennan felt his mouth turning upside-down, it hadn't registered in his head what he must look like.

"I just thought of something."

"And what would that be?"

Brennan opened his mouth to speak, but then hesitated. "It's not important." He immediately regretted trying to open up to her. With a wave of his hand, he tried to dismiss her, but she persisted in getting an answer.

"It's okay. You can tell me anything." As always, her voice remained soft and sweet, almost like a mother whispering to her child. He wanted to hold back his words, but the fact that he sensed no danger made this conversation even more infuriating.

"It's just that earlier, I was talking to Haniel, and he told me to get rid of this camera." Brennan pulled it out and waved it in front of her.

"Oh, Haniel!" Lily said happily.

"You know him?" Brennan asked confused.

"Why yes, of course, I do! We never get along, but we know each other well."

"How?" Haniel told him that he never met Lily. So one of them had to be lying. Brennan leaned forward, hoping he could hear her give an answer, but to his surprise, she looked disgusted. It was like she had a fiery hatred hidden beneath that friendly smile.

"Let's not worry about that for now. After all, you've got an important journey ahead!"

"But—"

"I said 'no'." Lily abruptly raised her voice, before bringing it down. "I'm sorry," she said with a nervous laugh. "I hope you can forgive me. It's rude of me to be so nosy."

Brennan wanted to push further, but once she started working her magic again, he became distracted. With a wave of her hand, flowers, dandelions, and blades of grass rose from the dirt and spun around in a circle below her opened palm. They rotated endlessly, like gears turning in a clock. At first, they moved at a snail's pace, but as Lily's fingers twirled faster, so would the foliage.

Eventually, they molded together into a multicolored backpack. The grass made up most of the pack while the flowers were mostly for decoration.

"Put the gifts I've given you into this," she said. Lily made the bag levitate in the air before sending it toward him. Brennan reached out and caught it.

When he shoved all his items inside, he said, "Thanks."

"Now, I suggest you find a place with a different scenery. That way you know you're out of the meadow." And just like her previous departure, she waved goodbye, before allowing her body to slowly become transparent until she vanished completely.

Brennan continued to get lost in the meadow, only letting gut instinct tell him where to go, and just when it seemed as if his walk was for nothing, he heard the sound of a stream. He let his ears become his eyes, and tuned in to the water flowing downstream. The stream was in stark contrast to the never-ending grass and flowers that he had been seeing for hours. With a feeling of excitement, he knew he had found an exit. Unless this world truly represented a jumbled mess, then surely following the stream to its end must lead somewhere. His legs eagerly carried him all the way to the river spitting down the hillside, but rather than diving headfirst into new territory, he decided to dunk his lips in the stream first.

He took a moment to quench his thirst. He selfishly gulped down copious amounts of water until his belly became an ocean, and when he finished, he quickly lifted his head. Some of the water splashed onto his clothes, but he didn't care because the taste caught his attention. *This flavor. Is this real water?*

He hastily pulled out his camera and lifted it to his face to snap a photo of the river. The film slid out, and he held it in his hands until it completely developed. That's when he didn't find a photo at all. Instead, a blank piece of film looked back at him. The only resemblance of an image was his reflection. Upon first glance, he only saw his face, but eventually, trees appeared. They towered over him, covering the sun with their leaves. He turned around only to see that his environment showed everything depicted in the film. The meadow had turned into a forest. Mist began devouring everything in sight, including his hands. It was like one large cloak covering the entire area.

He stood and paced around the trees. *What happened to the meadow? Why are the flowers gone?* Feeling that he had found the different scenery Lily mentioned and having nowhere else to turn to, he followed the stream. Brennan hadn't noticed it before, but as the scenery changed, the landscape did too. The flat ground became a massive hill that could kill him if he fell off. While he pushed aside his fear of heights, he began hiking down until he reached low ground. On his way there, sticks fell from branches, crunching beneath his feet when he stepped on them. Massive rocks came into view, with one of them having choc drawings all over it. He took a moment to examine the design, making him sigh. They were just pink outlines of two comic book characters from his childhood, but something about them seemed familiar. He closed his eyes and started digging through his memories. His brain showed him two children playing with each other, accompanied by the sound of their laughter. Their voices rang throughout the valley. *Nora.* Brennan's eyes popped open. He remembered now. He and his sister made this drawing on a hiking trip.

They were wandering around the forest, trying to break the mold by hiding from their parents. And once they were out of sight, they attempted to make an engraving in a tree. Brennan recalled himself picking up the sharpest rock he could find, but its edges were still too dull to even make a scratch. At the time, he angrily threw it away when it became evident that his attempts to cut into the trunk were futile. He welcomed the memory with open arms, but why was he thinking about this? The memory didn't have anything to do with Jessica.

"Hello," Nora said, sneaking up behind him.

Brennan turned to face her. "You're just like Haniel. Always appearing and then disappearing. Why? Are you just here to punish me? Mock me? I haven't seen you in ages, yet here you are talking to me when I'm searching for someone who actually had the intention of staying with me!" Brennan stared at his sister without breaking his gaze.

"I'm sorry. I just... I just wanted to see you. Is that too much to ask for?"

Brennan's eyes turned red from the tears that suddenly found themselves sneaking through his eyes. *I have to see what you really are.* He pulled out his camera and took a shot of Nora. She raised her hand to shield her face but when the film developed, it became clear that she wasn't really there. Brennan only saw himself standing in her place.

"What are you?" he asked.

Nora gave a confused look and said, "Don't be silly! It's me, your sister." Brennan knew that her calming tone came from a place of deceit. He told himself that she wasn't real. That the afterlife had been forcing him to chase fragments of himself.

"That's not true." He bowed his head and gritted his teeth. He clenched his hands until his knuckles turned white. Even though they trembled, he managed to push the picture in front of her face. "You see this?" he yelled, slapping his finger on the photo. "It's not you on here! It's me! You're not in it at all! You're not real! You're just the embodiment of something in my head! Something that I'm using to torture myself."

His voice wavered as he felt a great sadness from within. He shut both of his eyes and tried to drown out the negative feelings impeding his drive to move forward. "I can't keep doing this," he muttered. "I can't keep thinking of you so vividly." *Don't forgive her! She can't be forgiven! But I love her! But she hates me.*

She left me.

When Brennan opened his eyes again, the tears took the opportunity to roll out. Nora smiled at him, but he scoffed at her. "I used to love you," he said. "I loved the way you stayed by my side through all of Mom's abuse. I loved the way you smiled at me whenever we played, and I just loved who you were. But you're not the same person anymore."

Nora stepped forward and spread her arms out, but seeing as how she intended to lull him into a false sense of security with another hug, he pushed her away while simultaneously taking a step back.

"Brennan, please let me talk to you. We can be siblings again."

"That's not true. After you left, I always told myself that you could love me like you used to, but you never came back."

"But I'm here. I'm here right now." Her voice started to show a hint of desperation, which encouraged Brennan to stand more firm. He knew he couldn't let his feelings for her hurt him anymore.

"Things are different now. I've found someone else who's willing to be there for me. I'll be the one leaving this time."

Nora walked toward him, but stopped after a couple of steps. Her fingertips turned into stone, and just like black ink dropping in clear water, the stone quickly spread throughout her whole body. Her form and facial expressed became immortalized as she turned into a statue. A smile remained, as if she was a distant happy memory, and her arms stretched out showing a warm presence that used to be. Throughout his whole life, the thought of his sister had been following him. *Shouldn't I be happy?* He stood there wondering why his heart still ached. He successfully faced her with bravery, but the feeling of grief still lingered.

Regardless of his current mental state, he decided it'd be best to trudge on, but before he could walk past her, she slowly started to fall apart. Pieces of her body crumbled onto the ground until she was just a broken statue.

"Goodbye for now," Brennan muttered. He took a knee and opened his backpack. After shoving the camera inside, he pulled out the hourglass.

About a fifth of the sand had already poured to the other end, but it wasn't a clear enough indication to let him know how much time passed in the real world. *What's Olivia doing?*

He quickly brushed the thought aside. Now that he'd dealt with his sister, he didn't want to think about anyone else besides Jessica. She was the only person who understood him, so he had a strong desire to bring her back. He walked down the hill until he got to a lake. By now, the scenery had completely changed. He got to the place where Lily told him to go, but again, he only found torment. Brennan didn't want to acknowledge it, but for a moment he couldn't push aside his doubts. Maybe Haniel was right. These gifts were just leading him down a rabbit hole. Either way, he was knew he was completely and utterly lost. So, for now, he just had to follow the path Lily told him to go to whenever she showed up. He just hoped Jessica would be at the end of it.

THE CHASE

Three days had passed since Olivia had her encounter with Death, and Haniel still hadn't shown up. At the very least the hospital discharged her, so she could distract herself by talking to Elly while they sat on Nora's couch in her apartment. Other than speaking, they searched through all the photos on Brennan's phone. Of course, Olivia felt elated to have the chance to spend more time with Elly, but she couldn't help feeling bad whenever they came across a picture of Brennan's ex-girlfriend. Every photo stirred an unpleasant reaction on Elly's face, making Olivia have mixed feelings about her. *Never took her for the jealous type.* Each time her face crunched up, she resembled a small dog getting ready to growl. Olivia sighed and leaned her head back.

"What's wrong?" Elly asked.

"I'm just tired." By now Haniel's lack of guidance completely hindered her. Everything around her was starting to close in. The court date and the pressure to find Brennan filled her head. Olivia thought back to all the people she met while living as Brennan. Some of them didn't have the qualities he believed they had. For instance, his sister was always the caring type, but the boy was too caught up on the day he left her, that he couldn't see that. Nora always worried about her little brother. Olivia still heard her voice in her head. *You're staying with me for a while. You're not going back*. Even though she held the status of being Brennan's older sister, she resembled more of a parental figure rather than a sibling.

"Brennan," Elly said, snapping her fingers.

"What?"

"You're staring into space again."

"Oh, I'm sorry." Olivia bowed her head and smothered her face in her palms.

"Anyway, about the photos. I was finally able to find out where they were taken." Since waking up from the coma, Olivia's legs were too weak to walk. They'd both began making use of the wheelchair the hospital gave her, so Elly took the laptop that rested on the chair's cushion and began typing away at the keyboard. "Sorry it took so long, but here's what I've found so far."

Olivia leaned over, stared at the screen, and noticed numbers on the top right corner. "What do those mean?" she asked, pointing at them.

Elly giggled to herself as the excitement spread across her face. "They're coordinates. I found them in the source code from the photos. I just copied and pasted them onto Google Maps. Look here." She pointed to a house with a pool in the backyard.

"Are you sure she's there?" Olivia sounded hesitant.

"Yes, of course! After we looked through the other pictures, I saw a pool behind you, and, in case you haven't noticed, this is the only house in the neighborhood with a pool." Elly zoomed in on the image while Olivia let her continue her detective work. She didn't know exactly what went through her mind, but Elly definitely proved to be someone invaluable to her. Parting ways would be a great loss, especially if she never got the chance to confide in her about her dilemma. She ran her fingers across the screen like she was playing "I spy".

Eventually, Elly found what she was searching for. "324 Rosewood Street," she read out loud.

"What are you looking at?" Feeling curious, Olivia took another peek at the screen.

"The address. I found the street sign and the address on the house. Now, all we have to do is take a trip over there."

"Okay? But I think you forgot that the guy who beat me lives there, under house arrest. In other words, he'll be there, and I doubt he'd welcome us with open arms."

Elly grinned to herself before answering. "My mom drives a mini-van, and her favorite holiday is Halloween. I say we disguise ourselves and wait around the area until we see the girl leave, then we talk to her."

"You sound crazy. This isn't some movie where we can just throw on a costume and nobody would recognize us." Olivia folded her arms across her chest and sighed. "That'll never work." Despite the occasional annoyance, Elly's optimistic attitude and almost comedic sense of self had its charm. Even though they had grown close, the fact that Olivia wouldn't be able to convince her of the afterlife, and all the supernatural things that happened, made Olivia feel alone.

"We don't have to make the same type of costumes they wear in Hollywood. A simple mask will be enough to hide our faces from that guy," Elly said.

"And then what? Do you think that girl will just talk to two strangers wearing a mask? We'll look like a bunch of kidnappers! If I were her, I'd be running away screaming." Elly smiled a bit at the mention of scaring Brennan's old girlfriend.

"Fine, I'll just bring my dad's binoculars and we can watch from a distance. That guy won't see us, and we can get the girl when she leaves the house. We'll wait there all night if we have to."

"That sounds more realistic. Still creepy, but realistic. Let's leave as soon as we can, then." Elly let out a sigh, and Olivia sensed her disappointment.

"What's wrong?" Olivia asked.

"Nothing." Elly leaned her head back and stared at the ceiling. Her short arms lazily lying by her side, which was a clear indicator that her mind was stuck on something.

"That's not true." Olivia kept her words blunt and to the point. It was a quality she didn't have in her own life. It only became reinforced once she switched places with Brennan. "I just... I just want to talk to you. All we've been doing is talking about that girl. Why can't you see that all I want is to spend more time together?"

Olivia saw her eyes watering a bit, making guilt seep into her heart. Since enrolling in high school, she didn't have any friends, except for one underclassman she took the time to help. Other than that, she didn't have anyone. Elly was all she had, and here she was making her just as alone.

"I'm sorry," Olivia whispered. "We can talk about us and anything you want on the way there."

"On the way there," Elly mocked. "Let's just go." She made her resentment clear before helping Olivia stand up. Once she plopped down into her wheelchair, it was time to go. Olivia didn't know how to feel about the fact that Nora had been spending more time at work to help buy Olivia the things she needed, but she had to admit, sometimes the alone time felt relieving. At least now, it gave her and Elly the chance to leave the apartment uninterrupted.

They used the elevator to the get to the bottom floor and, once they turned the corner, giant panels of glass windows greeted them. Each one stood at the front of the building acting as a gateway to peer in. A boy stood outside, examining the inside of the lobby through the window. He wore shorts and had a mark on his ankle, indicating that something used to be strapped to it.

"You see that guy?" Olivia asked, pointing at him.

"Oh, shit!" When Olivia made eye contact with the boy, she realized it was the same guy who beat her senseless.

"That bastard is supposed to be under house arrest!" Elly yelled.

"Hey!" he screamed, kicking open the front door.

"There's an emergency exit behind the service desk!" Olivia said to Elly. In a panicked frenzy, they turned around while the boy picked up the pace. He ran toward them, and Elly quickly sprinted to the desk, ripped off the computer monitor, raised it above her head, and chucked it at him. It struck his face, forcing him to fall backward. While he moaned in pain, Elly pushed Olivia through the exit and into the parking lot behind the apartment complex.

"Where's your damn car?" Olivia asked in a panic.

She wanted them to drive away as soon as possible, but since Elly didn't live there, she had to park at the other end of the street.

"We can make it, don't worry," she said between gasp of air. She pushed Olivia's wheelchair as fast she could. Meanwhile, they heard the boy's yelling getting closer and closer. Once they were three-fourths of the way to Elly's vehicle, he caught up to them. His hand gripped the collar of her shirt and yanked her to the ground. Before striking the concrete, Elly's body flew into the air. A scenario where he continued to batter Elly rushed through Olivia's mind, but much to her relief, he turned his attention away from her.

"I'm going to kill you if I have to!" he screamed at Olivia. But before he could attack, Elly stood and hit him on the back of the head with a massive rock. It took all of her strength to raise the stone, but the adrenaline rush must've been the necessary push to make it happen. He held the back of his skull and looked at Olivia. "You fucking-"

She rammed her wheelchair into him before he could finish his sentence. His body slammed onto the pavement before Elly kicked dirt in his eye. After that, they created enough time to get Olivia in the car and toss her wheelchair into the trunk. Then they sped through the neighborhood without looking back.

"Let's call the cops," Elly said, breathing over the steering wheel.

Even though she knew that would be the most plausible thing to do, Olivia decided against it. Alerting the authorities meant staying in Florida. And though she would've favored the idea yesterday, she couldn't stop thinking about Brennan. Taking over his life would be the same as killing him with her own hands, which she wasn't willing to do anymore, but the urge to do what others asked still made her ashamed of herself. So, she reluctantly accepted her fate as everyone's servant. Choosing to go to Washington would fulfill the requirements for her mission, but who would take her? Her situation already caused enough trouble. Nora would undoubtedly be crying when she found out about her escapade, and bringing Elly into the madness wouldn't help her either.

"Let's not do that," Olivia said. She sighed and stared out the window. *Think. Think. There has to be a way to take on the burden alone.*

But her thoughts were cut short when Elly screamed, "Are you crazy? We need them to keep that lunatic away from us! They'll keep us safe!" She whipped out her phone in a panic, and Olivia immediately snatched it out of her hand. She rolled down the window and tossed it outside.

"What the hell are you doing?"

"Stop! Stop yelling and listen to me! We can't contact the police!"

"You're not making any sense," Elly grumbled.

"I know everything is falling apart, but you have to trust me."

"I do trust you. I've been helping you. I even agreed to go chase this girl just so I can spend as much time with you as possible! But I'm not going to follow you everywhere."

Olivia was at a loss for what to say. Obviously, Elly disagreed with the idea of staying silent, and even if Olivia decided to leave her behind, surely, Elly would call the cops when she had the chance. Not only that, but in the disheveled state Olivia found herself in, she'd be caught.

A moment of silence consumed them until Elly broke it. "Yeah, you got nothing else to say, huh?" she taunted.

"I'm sorry, I—" Olivia stuttered.

"Sorry, about what? Throwing my phone out the window? Or how about being crazy enough that you'd actually suggest keeping to ourselves? What's wrong with you?"

Olivia never saw this side of Elly before. Initially, she seemed like the type of girl who would cling onto her arm, but since she started experiencing jealousy and feeling ignored, her mood had changed. Olivia finally realized how much she wanted to maintain their friendly relationship. For the past few days, it was one of the things she'd frequently worry about. Every moment they were together, she wanted to reach out for a hug, but the overwhelming fear of what would happen after she left her, seeped into her mind causing her to recede back into the shield she put up for herself. *I can't act this way.* Despair grew within her, but her mind shut it out. *I need her! I need her no matter what!*

"I'm sorry things are ending up this way," Olivia muttered. The sudden tear in her voice surprised them both, and Olivia left herself wondering how she could go out of her comfort zone so quickly.

"What?"

"I said 'I'm sorry that things ended up this way'! Look at me! Look at everything that's going to go wrong. I wish I could have you! I wish I didn't have to leave you!" Olivia worked up a sweat just yelling at her, and she knew if she could walk, she would snatch the keys out of the ignition to ensure they'd stay together just a little longer.. Her words continued to bother Elly as they pulled into a gas station, parking at a spot next to the store.

"Please don't talk to me like that. I don't know why you think we'll part ways," Elly muttered. Her voice became weak, and the hurt in her voice brought Olivia back to herself. The damage she'd done in such a short period of time finally hit her.

"I'm sorry," she said, and this time, she meant it.

"You're the last person I'd want to leave me." She sniffled and wiped a tear away with her finger. A moment of silence rolled in while the two of them avoided eye contact. Olivia stared at her feet, listening to Elly cry. "I just can't take this! I want to help you, but you're acting crazy! I honestly don't understand. Why are you doing this? I don't get it why you're being so cryptic. Just tell me what you need so I can help!"

"Elly, I'm sorry." Olivia reached over to pat her back, but she slapped her hand away.

"No! Why don't you just tell me what your intentions are? I've been so lost in you, that I blindly followed everything you were doing. Just tell me what you really want. Why do you need to see this girl? And why are you so hesitant to call the police?"

Olivia frowned and took the time to come up with a response. She nervously twitched her fingers. And one accidentally tapped the side of her pocket. Since Death delivered that mint to her, she'd been carrying it wherever she went. *Whoever takes this will see things they're not supposed to see.* She thought about those words and what she should take from it. *Maybe I'm not the one who's supposed to eat it.* She pulled the capsule out of her pocket and popped the tiny piece of candy into her hand.

"What are you doing now?" Elly asked, annoyed.

What if Elly took this? Would she see the things Olivia saw, and finally give her a chance to open up? Olivia didn't know if that assumption was correct, or what it would do to their friendship, but she needed to let her know the truth somehow.

"Elly, this may sound weird, but I want you to swallow this."

"Now's not the time to freshen my breath."

"No, you're taking this." Olivia closed her hand over the mint and gave a hard stare.

"Stop messing with me." Elly held a stern face with red eyes. She folded her arms across her chest defiantly. *I guess I can't convince her.* Olivia took the initiative, and leaned over to shove the mint down her throat. She fought back by kicking her in the stomach, but Brennan's physique made it hard to retaliate effectively. Olivia slammed her hand against Elly's gaping mouth, and pushed her fingers down her throat to make sure she took the entire mint. When she retreated, Elly went into a coughing fit. Olivia's fingers combined with the mint must've triggered her gag reflex, or just outright felt disgusting. Either way, she believed her actions to be perfectly justified. When Elly's body began to relax she turned to Olivia, but screamed. "Who are you?"

"What?" Olivia stared at her in confusion.

"Where's Brennan? Why are you in my car?" She backed away and tried to unlock the door, but Olivia grabbed her wrist to pull her back.

'Relax," she said.

But rather than heeding her words, Elly screamed, "Get away from me, you red-headed freak!"

Redhead? Brennan had the darkest hair anyone had ever seen, so why was she mentioning red hair? That's when Olivia remembered what Death told her. *Whoever takes this will see things they're not supposed to see.* That was it. She was not meant to see Olivia for who she really was.

After coming to that realization, she quickly spoke. "Just give me some time to explain."

"Let go of me!" Elly started throwing punches at her face, but she held her wrist down into the leather seat.

"You're right, I'm not Brennan! My name is Olivia, and I've been stuck in his body."

"Bullshit! Just let me go!" Rather than releasing her, Olivia focused on maintaining control. She slapped Elly in the face and leaned over to pin her down. She never resorted to violence, so striking her friend brought up terrible feelings.

"Stop! I don't want to be rough with you, so just let me tell you the truth!" For a moment Elly stopped writhing and lay still. Olivia looked her in the eyes and said, "I've been stuck in Brennan's body."

"I don't believe you."

Olivia sighed, but continued. "Remember when we first met? It was at school in our graphic design class. You sat in the same cubicle as me, and asked me for my opinion on your artwork. I told you 'it's okay'." Elly glared at her, and Olivia noticed the hint of doubt just barely visible on her face. "You even told me about your brother's suicide. You told me about it when we were in the woodshop room while skipping our first period class. The teacher was out so we had the entire room to ourselves. If I was just some random red-headed freak who jumped into your car, I wouldn't know all these little details. I was the one you've been talking to this entire time."

Olivia let her go and retreated back to her side of the car. Elly slowly rose, but quickly slapped her face. Olivia rubbed her cheek where she was struck. "I'm sorry I hit you," she said. "But I had to control you somehow."

"I don't care about that. I just don't know what to think of this."

"I understand it's a lot to take in, but—"

"Then give me some time to take it in."

Olivia shut her mouth and watched Elly get lost in her thoughts. What could she be thinking? Destroying their relationship meant severing ties with Elly, the person who showed her the most compassion. Olivia's real life had been a hell hole of never-ending abuse, so to finally have a friend take her side brought on a euphoric feeling. She didn't want that to go away.

"How did this happen?" she finally asked.

"How did what happen?" For the first time since their short fight, Olivia made eye contact.

"I mean, this whole mix-up. Why are you in his body? Is he in yours?"

The first thing Olivia did was recount everything that happened. She explained how she committed suicide by overdosing, and found out that Brennan hung himself. Then from there, they met at the train station in the afterlife. Haniel, a strange short angel, gave them train tickets to go back to their bodies, but Brennan was so impatient that he snatched the wrong ticket, and they ended up going in the wrong body, and finally meeting the little boy known as Death.

"This just doesn't seem real, but then again, I don't understand anything that's happened so far!"

"I know it's a lot to take in," Olivia said comfortingly.

"None of it sounds real! So explain to me why we're on this crazy ride to nowhere!"

"That's because I don't know where Brennan is. Death told me he wasn't alive or dead, so I don't know how to answer that. But I'm trying to find him." Olivia frowned, and Elly turned defiant.

"So, you find him and then what?" she asked.

"I'm hoping we'll be able to switch bodies. But first, we need to find his girlfriend. Last time I talked to him, he wasn't so sure he wanted to continue living. I'm guess we could learn about him from this girl, then we'll know a few things for him to avoid, so he doesn't go down another rabbit hole of regrets. I'm pretty sure she'll tell us a lot of the things that went wrong in his life, whether by accident or on purpose. After all, partners tend to open up to each other." Olivia tightened her fist and gritted her teeth. She tried to sound confident in her last statement, but she just couldn't. The few times she'd talked to Brennan, it became strikingly clear that his strong personality caused him to act on his own.

Elly sank in her seat and heaved a sigh. "Okay, I get it now. This girl is going to help us, but not in the way she expects. I'm not sure about this. Why don't we just find him? I'll make sure to be there for him."

Olivia took a moment to think. Elly might be right. But knowing Brennan, he was a magnet for abuse. His mom abused him, and so did his girlfriend. They'd definitely need to show him why keeping himself out the lives of people like that is necessary. In other words, despite knowing that Brennan had Elly, Olivia didn't believe she'd be enough to help him make the right decisions.

"No, trust me on this. I've met him after he killed himself. He's still a mystery to both of us. Giving him a reason to stay alive should be our number one priority."

Elly faced the windshield and looked out into the town. "Fine, I'll take you to this girl, but I'm coming along for this whole trip."

"Are you sure? You don't have to." Even though Elly would be a powerful friend, the thought of burdening her with more problems arose.

"As long as it involves getting Brennan back and saving his life, I'm in." Olivia stared at her and realized nothing could dissuade her.

"Stop looking at me like that," Elly said with a hint of anger. "I'm only helping you so I can help Brennan. Don't get the idea that I like you, because I don't. You're a liar. You took his spot and pretended to be him."

"Elly, there's no way I could've come out with the truth. I—"

"I don't want to hear you talk about us anymore." With a wave of her hand, she motioned for Olivia to stay silent. "From now on, we'll only be talking about how we can save him." Feeling defeated, Olivia obliged.

MAMA

After everything that happened in short succession, the afterlife's only purpose seemed to be to torture Brennan. If his mind could conjure his sister into existence just to taunt him, who else could it bring back? His mom? His dad? What about Olivia? This world turned out to be more like Hell than a state of Limbo. But then again, he'd rather spend an eternity in Hell with Jessica before living the rest of his life by himself. What was the point of staying alive if she couldn't be with him? Brennan's mind remained stuck on Jessica, and his thoughts became torturous when he reached the end of the stream.

It led him to a familiar lake, the same body of water Jessica died in. *This again. Will I have to relive this moment too?* Brennan sat at the edge of the water, staring into the spot where he found Jessica's body. He closed his eyes, and the memory came flooding back. The fear, the pain, and the frantic search through water engulfed his mind. When he opened his eyes again, the same fog that intruded in his dreams made an appearance. They rolled in, but the sun shined even brighter through the mist. The fog became so thick he couldn't even see a few feet in front of him, and the scariest part was that it seemed to be alive.

He heard whispers coming in all directions. "You're a terrible person. You couldn't save her. Why even bother? You actually think she'd stay with you?" The thicker the fog grew, the more the whispers intensified until eventually, they felt like they were inside his head. At first, one voice came to him, but soon it turned into a chorus of people berating him, with each vocalist being someone he knew.

I left you on purpose!

You ungrateful child!

Why do I have to know you for the rest of my life?

Brennan, can we switch bodies?

You're screwing everything up!

His sister belittled him, his mom screamed at him, and Olivia cried out to him. Brennan tried to snuff them out by slapping his hands against his skull, but that aggravated them even more. Their voices felt like knives stabbing into his brain. They injected the poison of negativity into his mind.

"Shut up!" he yelled. "Shut up! Shut up! Shut up!" He threw his head back and screamed to the sky until his throat became soar. Eventually, he received a moment of respite when they finally stopped talking. But that sensation didn't last long.

"Brennan, please come back to me," a feminine voice said. The outline of a woman appeared in the fog. Her voice brought him goosebumps, but he couldn't discern to whom the voice belonged to. The mist clouded his vision and held a firm grasp on his sight for ages to come. Only when she got closer did Brennan realize it was his mother. She stood on the water, above the jagged rocks laying below the surface. One of her toes touched the tip of the lake causing a ripple effect to flow through it. Brennan felt the little boy he once was starting to make an entrance. He wanted to cry, but forced himself to stand stoically in an attempt to hide his fear. Still, he desperately wanted to tremble. To run away screaming in the opposite direction. He felt like a coward for having to remind himself to stay strong, but he found resolve in the fact that he was brave enough to admit his fears. *If I can face Nora, then I can face her.*

"What's the matter? You look scared," his mother said.

"I'm not scared." Initially, he didn't believe his lie to be obvious, but when his mom gave him a sinister grin, he knew he had revealed his true feelings.

"Oh, is that so?" She walked forward, but came to an abrupt stop in the middle of the lake. Their eyes narrowed in on each other as the tension grew.

"You can't hurt me anymore," Brennan said through gritted teeth, but his mother only laughed at his false display of courage. "I said you can't hurt me anymore!"

His mom stomped her foot at his loud proclamation, sending a force strong enough to shatter the ground at the bottom of the lake. "You little shit!"

She dashed at him, but Brennan rolled out of the way just in time to evade her attack. He accidentally bit down on his lip too hard, causing himself to taste blood. While the red liquid trickled, he examined his surroundings. His mother had gone past him and disappeared into the fog.

"I don't have time for this!" he called out to her.

"What's the matter? You don't want to see your mommy again?" Her voice became soft, but Brennan never forgot the evil behind each word she spoke.

He got into a fighting stance, ready to face her. He knew she'd remain hidden, ready to strike when he least expected it. But as he stood there in anticipation, he remembered the camera in his bag. If it could show him the truth, then maybe it would reveal his mother's position. He took off his pack and dropped it onto the ground. His hands hastily rummaged through it. His mom's laughter in the distance caused sweat to pour down his forehead, but through all the anxiety, he managed to grab the camera before she appeared. He took a photo of the fog in front of him, but the film didn't show anything.

"Are you using that gift you got? Do you want to take a picture with me, just like when you were a child?" She made her voice soft again and started cooing at him for added effect. Brennan turned around and took another photo, and when the film developed, he saw her, grinning at him.

She flew out of the mist and into his face. He threw a punch at her, but she dodged it. She reached out and smacked the camera out of his hands. The device shattered on the rocks next to him, leaving Brennan defenseless. After that, she left into the fog.

"You can't get away from me," she said with a laugh. "I'll always be there. When you're with your friends, I'll be the memory that haunts you. When you're with your sister, I'll be the anxiety that fills your body. I'll be everywhere in your life!"

Brennan wanted to give up, but knew that he couldn't give in to defeat. His mother tortured him throughout his childhood, and her control over him still remained long after he left her. If he couldn't best her now, he'd at least try to control her. *I'll show her!* Brennan finally mustered the strength to stand up for himself.

"Enough!" he yelled.

"You can't stop me! I'll be with you forever!" This time, his mother dashed in from the right and struck his face. After that, she hid in the fog and waited about a minute to swoop back in to strike. She performed this trick time and time again, giving Brennan no chance to take a break. But Brennan got up each time he fell. After a dozen more hits, bruises began to appear on his battered face, but he did his best to stand tall. She may be hurting him, but he'd learned to manage the trauma she inflicted. But even then, he felt scared. His mother's laugh cut through the air, and she flew at him one more time before giving him the hardest hit he ever took to the temple. He fell to the ground, disorientated as his vision became consumed by darkness.

Where am I? Why am I falling? Brennan felt his body descending into an endless hole. At first, only a black void surrounded him, but eventually, he touched grass beneath him. Its mildew soaked through his clothes, but it felt warm rather than cold, and the faint white glow of the moon revealed a vast ocean stretching out for miles. When he sat up, he realized he was on an island the size of Nora's small living room. Other than grass, white flowers with glowing petals dotted the area. Upon glancing at the area, his attention immediately focused on the ocean, but the glimpse of white hair in his peripheral caught his attention. When he turned his head, a young girl in a white dress appeared, sitting on the ground.

"Hi," she said brightly. She looked like a pre-teen at about thirteen years old.

"Um, who are you?" Brennan asked.

"You don't recognize me? It's me, Life."

Brennan raised his eyebrow. "But how? The last time I saw you, you were a little kid." He looked down and shook his head. He remembered seeing her grow taller and older, but this was a massive change. "I don't understand this world. Why is everything so confusing?"

Life smiled before answering. "You were never intended to travel this far, so this space of existence is building itself as we speak, and right now, your mind is the only thing that it can use as a reference. This world is based on your subconscious. It's made up of the things you can't see. That's why you're envisioning things that are familiar, but at the same time, it confuses you."

"Is that so?" Brennan was at a loss. It felt as if his lungs were filled with water, making it hard to speak. "Why am I on this island? My mom was attacking me and now I find myself on some patch of land?"

"Well, you felt scared during that fight, didn't you?"

"That doesn't answer my question." Brennan sighed in defeat.

"Oh, but it's relevant. Let me ask you this. Do you ever stop to admit that what you say you want isn't what you actually want?"

Life stared at him with wide eyes, but Brennan didn't know what to say. "I don't understand."

She crawled toward him a little and said, "Your subconscious mind is a mess. It's breaking apart. Judging by what you've seen, it's based on trauma, and that trauma is being projected into the world around you."

Brennan's eyes scanned the area, and the sigh made him disagree with her statement. If his mind was in chaos, why did this place put him at ease? "If my head is just one big mess, why am I in such a calm place?"

Life tilted her head and gave a smile. "Would you mind if I ask another question first?"

"Go ahead." Brennan nodded.

"What would you do after a stressful event?"

The answer to Brennan seemed obvious. Every time he suffered at the hands of his mother's abuse, he'd survive the rest of her rage by hiding in a quiet place.

"I'd go some place to cool down. Some place that's quiet and safe."

"Well, wouldn't that describe this island perfectly?" Life asked, signaling Brennan to scan the entire area. "And wasn't the fight you just had stressful on your mind and body?"

He took a moment to respond. "Are you saying my mind is isolating itself from everything else because of the intensity of what I just experienced?"

"Yes, that's exactly what I was getting at. Sometimes, when we get bombarded by anxiety or any negative emotions, we tend to retreat to a place we never want to leave. It becomes comforting to stay safe, and to never see the world again, but you can't stay here forever. You must regain your strength to leave and face what's hurting you."

Brennan furrowed his eyebrows. He knew what came next. His mother had always been a plague on his well-being. No matter where he went or how long ago her abuse was, he never stopped thinking about her.

"You mean my mom, right?" he asked. "She's the one hurting me."

"No," Life answered, bluntly. Brennan leaned in and listened intently. If his mother wasn't the only demon haunting him, what else could be hidden deep within his mind? Would it be his sister? "There's something else holding you back. Something that's the root of all this. Can you guess what it is?"

He put a hand to his chin as he thought. Eventually, he could pin point the exact emotions he felt when he ran into his mom. Without a doubt, fear controlled him.

"Fear. Fear is holding me back." Brennan was reluctant to admit it, but he knew acceptance was the best course of action. "I'm scared of my mom, and the feelings that come with facing her."

"That's right, but is there anything else bothering you?"

"No." Brennan made sure to answer quickly, without any hesitation.

"Are you sure?"

He shut his eyes to help him drown out his environment. He wanted to skip past this part of the conversation, but he could feel himself wanting to vent. His mind went back to Jessica and his desire to save her. Her death wasn't something he was ready to accept. He needed her, and he knew it.

"I'm sure," he lied.

"Very well." Life didn't seem convinced, but she didn't push forward, anyway. She stood while Brennan remained sitting. She walked over to him and knelt down. "Just like me, your life is changing." She placed her thumb on his forehead. "You're growing into a different person. Can you tell?"

"I'm not so sure, but I do know what's holding me back. Fear. Fear is killing me right now, and I have to stop it." He wasn't hesitant in acknowledging his fear, but his unhealthy attachment toward Jessica and Nora wasn't something he could easily brush away.

"Will you conquer your fear?" Life asked.

"No, but I can control it." He felt the water calling to him like a siren signing, and he became the unfortunate sailor who came across her. Except he knew walking out to it wouldn't be a malicious act. The ocean meant no harm, so he stood and walked off the island. His feet sunk in and he waded further. He closed his eyes, plunged down feet first.

Despite going down, his body suddenly sensed itself going up. He emerged from the lake and opened his eyes. His feet carried him to land in his soaked clothes, and even though the fog still dominated the forest, he didn't mind.

"Is that my little boy?" his mother mocked.

Brennan let his ears guide him to her voice. "I know you made my childhood hell, but I'm not with you anymore. I—"

His mother jumped out form the mist to kick him down. He fell back into the lake, making a big splash as his body hit the rocks. *Control your fear.* He kept telling himself, but couldn't find the strength he expected to have. Brennan had previously imagined himself overpowering his mom, yet here he stood, still taking a beating. *Control. Control.*

Brennan remembered all the times he had pushed everything away. He told Life he'd learn to control his fear, but his habit of avoiding scary people and places hindered him. He couldn't set aside his fear. No one could. He was just trying to eradicate that emotion, not control it. But he told himself that fear was normal and good in healthy doses. Fear wasn't something he should be ashamed of. It was something he should acknowledge and accept.

"I have to admit, I am scared of you," he said. "But I'm willing to accept that."

"Oh, how pathetic of you," his mom cooed.

"It's not pathetic. Accepting your true feelings is a sign of strength, not weakness." Brennan faced his mom. She got so invested in mocking him, she forgot to vanish in the fog. He bravely took steps forward. "I'm scared, and I'm not afraid to say it!"

He noticed his mother's hands shrink until they became tiny stubs at the end of her arms. Then the rest of her body followed, turning into the size of an ant.

"Goodbye, Mama," Brennan muttered. After his victory, the mist cleared, and he walked away.

OLD WOUNDS

E lly carefully drove her vehicle over a speed bump. The conversations between Elly and Olivia weren't friendly at all, but rather bland. Neither hatred nor friendliness filled the air. It just felt like business.

"Where are we going?" she asked.

"Um, we're going to meet Brennan's girlfriend." To Olivia it felt like an obvious statement, since they had been discussing it for hours.

"No, I mean where are we going to meet Brennan?"

"Oh! He woke up in my body, which means he's in Washington. At least that's what happened originally..." Olivia's voice trailed off. She could tell that Elly still intended to keep her distance, but her compassion for Brennan still showed.

"What do you mean, originally?" she asked.

"This sounds bad, but please listen. Ever since I woke up alive, I've been seeing this little boy named Death. According to him, Brennan is stuck in some sort of Limbo. It's like he's alive but in the afterlife."

"What's that supposed to mean?" Worry grew in Elly's voice. For the first time since, they drove for the last ten minutes, she began to show emotion again.

"I don't know exactly. I just know it means he's not in our world. Either he's in the afterlife, or in some blank empty space like I was during my coma. Either way, he's out there and he needs help."

"So, we're traveling where? Washington? Some other world that we don't know how to get into?" Elly's knuckles turned white as she gripped the steering wheel. Olivia could tell the news about Brennan was causing her a tremendous amount of stress.

"Look, you don't have to jump into this whole mess if you don't want to." Olivia made sure to keep her voice low, like a mother talking to her baby, but she couldn't do anything to calm her down.

"No, I'm driving you there, and we'll get him back. I don't know how, but after that, we'll just leave and hopefully, I'll never have to see you again."

Her voice had a firm tone to it, making Olivia feel threatened and disappointed. Other than Nora, Elly was one of the few people she bonded with, so the fact that Elly began to show resentment put her off.

"Elly, why are you so hell-bent on finding Brennan? I mean, why do you care about him so much?"

"You mentioned the time we talked in the woodshop class. Well, I hope you remember me telling you that my brother killed himself."

"Oh, that's right." Olivia turned her head to stare out the window. How could she forget such an important detail?

"Well, Brennan reminds me of that sense of security I felt when I had my brother. I already told you this before. You should remember what people tell you." Elly scoffed at her, and Olivia shrunk into her chair. "If I knew I was talking to you this whole time, I would never have opened up. These last few weeks, I thought I was getting closer to Brennan just like I wanted, but now I see that it's just you. It's disgusting that things ended up this way."

Olivia didn't know whether she should talk back or hold her tongue. Switching bodies wasn't her fault, yet she was being blamed for the misery it caused. And just like her home life with her stepfather, she too was a victim of circumstance.

"I'm sorry," she managed to say.

"Yeah, you should be."

Olivia tried to empathize with her, telling herself that if she were tricked into confessing her deepest feelings to a stranger, and not someone she loved, she'd probably feel betrayal too. Elly was perfectly justified to be angry, but she had no right to take it out on Olivia.

"I'm sorry."

"Just stop talking already." Elly's face returned a blank stare, in stark contrast to Olivia's grief-stricken expression. So, rather than opening her mouth again, she stayed silent for the rest of the ride.

Once they reached the neighborhood, they drove up the road to the end of the cul-de-sac where the house stood.

"I thought we were going to watch from a distance," Olivia said.

"That was the original plan, but that guy just went after us. I'm guessing he's not here but we don't have much time." Elly stepped out of the vehicle and took Olivia's wheelchair out of the trunk. After that, she helped her get in. With the wind cutting through the trees and dark clouds over head, Olivia sensed a rainstorm coming. She hoped it wouldn't make it too difficult for them to get away should they have to make a last-minute escape. Elly pushed her to the front porch before ringing the doorbell. Ten seconds passed, but they received no response. Her finger pressed the button again, and they waited, but Elly groaned when no one came. She started slamming her fist against the door while yelling, "We know there's someone in here! Open this damn door!"

"Calm down," Olivia suggested. "If someone is in there, you're bound to scare them off."

"Fine, we'll do it the nice way." Elly gently tapped the doorbell again and waited. She folded her arms across her stomach and leaned against the wall. "You better be right when you say we can get information out of this girl to help Brennan."

"To be honest, this is just a guessing game. I'm sure she'll reveal something about the mistakes he's made. Then we'll have some info to keep him on the right track, and maybe he'll be willing to stay alive."

"I still think it's better to just look for Brennan and drag him down here. Anyway, do you really think he's so suicidal that he'd kill himself again after coming back from the dead?

"Last time I spoke to him, it seemed so."

"I'm trusting you on this. Since, I've actually been talking to you instead of him, I guess I don't really know him at all. He might be a completely different person now."

If Olivia could turn away, she would. Elly's frowning face put her at a loss for words. *How do I fix this?* She knew full well that not everything could be mended. Maybe the damage between them was set in stone. "I did enjoy our time together," Olivia said with a sigh.

"I did too, but you ruined it."

"Well, I had to tell the truth eventually. Otherwise, you'd never agree to help me. Then Brennan would be on his own."

Elly gave a distasteful glare before retorting. "Just forget about if for now." She tried to speak her mind, but a blonde girl peeked through the window. "I see her!" Elly jumped up with excitement. "She's hiding behind the curtain!" The door opened slightly, and she looked through the crack.

"Brennan? What are you doing here?" she nervously asked.

"Please, let me in. We need to talk." Olivia made her voice as sweet as possible, but the girl seemed hesitant to undo the swing lock when she noticed Elly standing to the side.

"It's okay. She's just an old friend of mine," Olivia said, pointing to Elly.

"I'm not letting you in." She tried to close the door, but Elly quickly slammed her shoulder against it, making the lock break off. "Leave me alone!" The girl's hand gripped the side of the door as her and Elly were locked in a battle of tug of war. With Elly pulling the door open and Brennan's girlfriend pulling the door shut, Olivia became mesmerized by their determination to beat one another.

"No! We need your help!" Elly yelled. "You're going to let us in whether you want to or not!" Everyone was caught off guard by Elly's loud proclamation. Olivia never saw her like this, and never knew it was possible to show this much aggression.

"Hold on!" Olivia said. She looked at the girl hiding behind the door. She kept her expression calm, so as not to disturb her any further. "We just want to talk to you. I'm sorry about my friend. She's just a little irritated." Olivia tried to perform damage control in a futile attempt, and with the door lock broken off and Elly staring her down, the scene looked like a recipe for physical assault.

After a lengthy amount of staring and intimidation, she finally gave in. "Fine," she said. "Elly was your name, right?" She nodded before brushing past her and walking into the house. "Okay then. My name is Eliza." She got a snicker from Elly as she trailed into the living. From there, only Olivia's awkward stare remained as she and Eliza didn't know what to do.

"Would you mind pushing me inside?" Olivia asked.

"Sure." Once inside, Eliza sat on the couch while Olivia stayed next to the curtain. Elly stood behind the sofa, tapping her wrist like she had an invisible watch. Knowing that the gesture meant their time was limited, Olivia got right to talking.

"It's been a while," she said. Just like most of her situations since switching into Brennan's body, she had to improvise.

"So, what did you want to talk to me about?"

A brief pause enveloped the room before Olivia spoke. "I just wanted to talk about us and everything that went wrong." Elly rolled her eyes at Olivia and grunted. "I'm sorry, but could you give us some privacy?" Olivia asked Elly.

"Fine." She walked out the room and up the stairs, and the moment she was out of eyesight, Eliza felt comfortable again.

"If you want to talk about us, I guess that you're talking about the time I hit you. After all, you wouldn't stop talking about it. You even hit me back and broke my nose." Olivia closed her eyes and rummaged through her memories again. She remembered being in the white void during the coma, and Haniel showing her parts of Brennan's life. The image of his fight with Eliza became crystal clear again. The yelling, the crying, and the sound of fist hitting skin came back to her.

"Yes, that's exactly what I want to talk about. Let's just discuss it so we can learn more from it." Olivia shifted in her seat, as she knew the lies she told during this conversation would make her feel guilty for a while.

"Okay, well, first off, I'm sorry I snapped at you. I shouldn't have. You were having issues with money again and I overreacted. Anger tends to run in my family."

Olivia nodded. She didn't know her at all, but after taking a beating from her brother, and being chased out of Nora's apartment, she completely agreed on their lust for anger.

"But you don't seem angry." Olivia thought back to how dominant Eliza was in Brennan's memory. Her current docile nature came unexpectedly. Being so quiet and fragile, Olivia guessed she must've been afraid. "Are you still scared of me? Is that why you're apologizing?"

Eliza's eyes wandered from Olivia to the staircase. "I... I don't know what to say. It feels as if I'm being pushed into a corner. You two barge into my house and force me to talk, so yeah. I'm scared."

"Well then, let's talk about something else." Olivia leaned back in her chair and rested her hands on her lap. "You can start anywhere." She gave her some time to think, believing that it would ease the tension, but there was no going back. The grandfather clock ticked in the background, reminding Olivia that they didn't have much time left.

"Brennan, I'm sorry, but I just remember our bad memories more than the good ones. Is that normal?"

Before answering, Olivia turned her head to the fireplace. On top of the mantel were various pictures. Some were her with adults Olivia assumed to be her parents, but quite a few depicted her and Brennan. How could they be so close yet so hostile at the same time? If she knew why he was so prone to attracting this type of treatment, she could help him avoid it. Olivia wanted to ask her more, about why she and Brennan got together.

"Do you remember when we first met?" Olivia asked.

"Yeah," Eliza said with a smile. "We met at a party. You went with some of the older guys from my college, and I went with my friends." Olivia took a mental note of what Eliza said. She made sure to remember it, so she could scold Brennan like an overprotective mother, but she knew that information wasn't enough.

"Yeah, that was nice. Remember all the things we said when we opened up to each other?" Again, Olivia did a fantastic job at player her role. Eliza continued to speak without suspecting anything.

"Oh yes, of course I do. You always said you wanted a mom. A woman who would care about you, and I told you that I could be that woman. You were so lost, and I was so happy when you opened up to me."

He was looking for a mother figure? The moment Olivia took the time to think, she realized a big mistake Brennan had been making. His mom abused him, he felt betrayed by Nora, and Eliza used him. The fact that he so desperately wanted a maternal figure is what caused him to get into so much trouble. *So that's why he's so emotional scarred and distant toward women.* Now, she knew what to do. If she could get Brennan to have healthy relationships with Elly, Nora, and other women in his life, then he wouldn't be going in such a downward spiral.

"I'm sorry for the way things ended," Eliza said, interrupting Olivia's thoughts.

"I'm sorry too. We had plenty of good times. It's just a shame we remember the bad ones the most."

Olivia leaned forward to look into her eyes. "I'm sorry, but I think it's time for me to go?" Time became a rare commodity. She got the information she needed, so now the time to leave presented itself.

Eliza smiled and placed a hand on Olivia's knee. "If you're trying to get back together, I'd say you're doing a decent job. But I don't know if we can stay happy. You'll probably start off treating me like the most important person in your life, but then sometimes you'll act like you were disgusted by me."

Olivia uncomfortably slouched in her wheelchair. She recognized Brennan's relationship with Eliza. The emotional abuse that both of them contributed reminded her of her stepfather and mother. She always wondered why they stayed together, and now she found herself asking the same question for Brennan and Eliza.

"You said I treated you like you were the most important person to me. I've done a lot of strange things. How did I show you my feelings?" At this point, Olivia was only buying time for Elly to come back. She thought about yelling out to her, but knew that the act would only stir more irrational actions in Eliza. After all, if she already got what she needed, there was no point in staying any longer. She knew what it took to make sure he wouldn't clock out of the world again.

"I liked just about every piece of art you made," Eliza said, cutting through Olivia's thoughts. "You expressed everything I felt. I remember venting out to you, and in minutes you'd create some digital design that reflected that. It was such a nice sentiment." Eliza smiled at her words, and this time Olivia knew it came from a pure source of happiness.

"And this was your favorite memory of me?" Olivia's eyes darted from the clock and back to Eliza.

"Yes, of course! I always had a hard time showing others how I feel, but even though you weren't that animated, you were still able to show who you really were." Olivia sighed.

'Thank you—"

Before Olivia could finish, Eliza's brother walked through the door.

"What the hell?" he yelled.

"Cameron, it's okay." Eliza tried to control him, but he walked past her.

"Why is this guy here? He attacked you! Yet here you are, talking to him as if you're still together!"

Olivia tried to get away, but he grabbed the handles of her wheelchair and knocked her over. She hit the ground, burning her knees on the carpet.

"To be honest, I don't mind getting arrested for murder." Usually, when someone said that, it was an exaggeration, but Olivia got the impression that he was serious. "As long as it keeps you away from my sister, I guess it's okay." He rolled Olivia onto her back and got on top of her.

"Elly!" Olivia screamed. She wanted to wail some more, but Cameron silenced her by tightly wrapping his wrist around her throat.

"Shut your fucking mouth!" He squeezed tighter, to the point where her face started to change colors. She went from white to red, and after a few more seconds, blue. The veins in her forehead started popping out, and she looked to Eliza for help. However, she just cowered in a corner of the living room.

"What's going on?" Elly asked, running toward Olivia. It didn't take her long to realize the severity of the situation. When she saw him strangling Olivia, she sprinted in his direction and kicked his nose. A cracking sound accompanied the strike as her shin made contact with his nostrils. But that didn't stop him. Meanwhile, Eliza closed her eyes and covered her ears. The only sound she made were loud sobs as she begged them to stop the fight, but that didn't stop Cameron from continuing his assault. Olivia figured the adrenaline rush must've been strong enough to keep him unfazed. Elly kicked him again, but he brought one arm up to punch her stomach. She stumbled backward, and took that moment to breathe, but her break didn't last long. Elly quickly got up and looked around for a weapon. She dashed into the kitchen, searched through the cabinets, and came back with a metal mallet in hand.

She swung it at Cameron's head, making him topple over. Olivia gasped for air and began crawling to her wheelchair after which, Elly struck him in the head a couple of more times when he tried to get up again.

"Let's get the hell out of here," Elly said. She helped Olivia into her wheelchair and pushed her outside. The gray clouds from earlier were pouring down rain, and the hard wind didn't do anything to comfort them. When they got to the vehicle, Elly quickly tossed the chair into the trunk before driving away. Looking into the rearview mirror, Olivia saw Eliza running outside, crying and waving at her to come back.

"Thanks," Olivia said.

"You see? I knew we should've stayed away from them. We wasted so much time and for what? Just to put you in danger? Remember, it's his body you're in! Whatever hurts you now will hurt him in the long run."

"It wasn't exactly a waste of time," Olivia said, with blood dripping from her nose.

"What? How?"

"I just learned why Brennan ends up torturing himself. It's the women in his life. Now we just have to figure out how to get him to realize that."

Despite her vagueness, Elly nodded. So, for now, Olivia tried to figure out the best way she could tell Elly what to do once she was back in her body.

ON THE RUN

After their horrifying encounter with Cameron, Olivia and Elly escaped to one of Florida's many beaches. The long bumpy road plagued their ride there. It all began when they drove a few blocks away from Eliza's neighborhood, and only became more turbulent when they entered the city. Relief finally washed over them, since their time on the road had mainly consisted of random twist and turns, just hoping they'd get somewhere. Eventually they landed at the beach, but they didn't aim to take a short vacation. They intended to start their journey of being runaways, and that beach just happened to be their starting point. It was a nerve-wracking feeling. Even on the way to the beach, they drove past numerous patrol cars, each of which caused a stir of anxiety. They didn't know if those vehicles were hunting them down, but taking the risk of lowering their guard wasn't something they were willing to do.

Right now, Olivia sat in her wheelchair, with her wheels at the edge of the sand. She watched the sun setting in the distance. Families were finally packing up their belongings for the day and retreating back to land. She laid her head back, wishing she could take a moment to rest, but she'd already caused enough chaos. Looking up to the sky, she wondered what the afterlife would hold for her. Even though she already stepped foot in the train station, she knew that, despite being intent on living, she'd definitely be forced to go back. After all, no one could escape death. As soon as that thought crossed her mind, she went back to thinking about Elly.

The girl had gone into the store off to the right of the beach to buy a GPS, since Olivia tossed her phone out the window earlier. A call like that would've been stupid in anybody else's eyes, but Elly forgave Olivia because, according to her knowledge, a cell phone was just a giant beacon indicating their position.

Olivia pondered on what she knew about Elly. She had an inkling on intuition that told her she cared for Brennan, but now she believed that the girl was also completely in love with him. While Olivia wondered more about her new companion, she heard footsteps tapping behind her, and when she turned her head, she found Elly staring at her.

"Hi," she said. "I got the GPS."

"Finally." Olivia sighed and moved closer.

"I've got some bad news and some good news." Olivia raised her eyebrow to show curiosity. "I saw us on the T.V. Eliza reported the whole incident. So, the good thing is that Cameron had some handcuffs slapped on his wrist, but the bad news is that they're still looking for us. In fact, our faces and my car were shown to the entire country. I saw Nora crying to the reporter, begging anyone to bring you back. I even saw my dad." Elly's voice trailed off when she mentioned her father, and Olivia felt terrible imagining the sorrow on Nora's face. "Anyway, we can't go home yet. Let's find Brennan." Elly gripped the handles of Olivia's wheelchair and pushed her into their vehicle as fast as possible. Once they were both inside, she turned on the headlights, but Olivia smacked her hand.

"No," she said. "Like you told me, they know what you're driving! It's best we keep our lights off. We won't be completely invisible, but at least it'll be harder to find us."

Elly nodded. "I guess I understand what you mean. But I'll barely be able to see anything."

"Well, at least we'll be concealed. Now, just drive!" As their wheels drove out of the beach's parking lot and over a speed bump, Olivia fidgeted with the GPS until it turned on. A blindingly white screen bombarded her eyes. She didn't know where to find Brennan, so she simply typed in her address. *I hope he's still in Washington.* Olivia reminisced about her previous life with Jessica, her school, and her broken family. If she had to live with her stepfather again, would she have the courage to even stay alive? She cringed at the memory of him, which just gave her another reason to be jealous of Brennan's life.

"Why don't you tell me more about him?" Elly asked, breaking the silence.

"Who?"

"Brennan. Why don't you tell me more about Brennan?"

Olivia leaned her head against the window and ran her fingers through her hair. "Let's see. At first, I didn't think much of him, but after seeing how eager he was to leave, I resented him. While it's true I wanted to leave the afterlife, too, he could have at least been patient enough to get his ticket and not mine. Maybe then we wouldn't be in this mess." Olivia spoke with great conviction, but she couldn't help but feel a little grateful for Brennan's mistake. At least now she got to experience his life.

Elly silently hummed in agreement, being blissfully unaware of Olivia's internal struggle. "Do you miss him?"

"Yes, but only to a certain extent. Despite learning so much about each other's lives, we never got a chance to talk about it."

"So, you wouldn't consider him a friend?"

Olivia hesitated, and a bead of sweat rolled down her forehead. "No, not at all," she admitted. "But I can't just stay in his body forever. That'll take away all the good things he has." *Good.* That word sounded foreign to her. Nothing in her life was ever good, but Olivia perceived most of the things in Brennan's life as "good".

"I'm sorry I got mad at you earlier," Elly said. "I hope you understand." Olivia looked downcast, but let Elly speak anyway. "It's just hard to realize that the person you were getting so close to wasn't the person you knew at all. That's what I felt when I found out you were in Brennan's body."

"I'm sorry. I wish I could've told you. Actually, I wish I could tell everyone. I felt like such a fake person."

"You don't need to worry about that. No one would've believed you anyway."

Olivia leaned her head against the window, longing to have some peace for the emotional turmoil consuming her. "Yeah, you're right about that." She wiped a shallow tear from her eye and flicked it off her finger. "I'm sorry," she said.

"Hey, there's no need to apologize. If I was in your position, I wouldn't know what to do either."

Olivia felt the need to argue, even though she knew it was unnecessary. Elly was right. No one would've believed her proclamation of being Brennan, but at the same time, she was bound to cause pain. Nora already knew she was a runaway, and Elly's father must be distraught. He already lost a son, and now he probably thought the same about his daughter. The image of Elly opening up about her brother's suicide came back to her. Olivia put her palm to her forehead. as if she could push the memory out. But she couldn't stop herself from seeing the tears that came out of Elly's eyes, the quivering of her lip and the croak in her voice. Olivia looked at her and couldn't fathom how she could be so calm. Not a hint of worry spread across her face. To a certain extent, she even seemed a little content.

By the time they reached a motel to spend the night, the time had just struck midnight. They stopped at a broken-down building and went inside to rent a room. The man at the front counter gave Elly the same gaze Olivia's stepfather would give her. Flashbacks of lonely nights with him clouded her thinking, and she found herself shuddering. If Brennan's body was in a strong, healthy state she could have easily intimidated others, but with its decrepit form, scaring the man into submission wasn't possible. After leaving the lobby to go to their room, Olivia still found him staring when she looked back.

They had to go outside to find their next destination, but once they arrived, Elly immediately went through the door and belly-flopped onto the bed.

"Don't worry," she said. "Just give me a few minutes and I'll get up to help you out of your chair."

While she smothered her face into the fabric, Olivia did her best to stand. Even though she would be grateful to receive Elly's help, that didn't change her desire to be independent. She pushed herself to the side of the mattress and gripped the bedframe before pulling herself up. And even though she had to hold it in a death drip, she still felt a strong sense of accomplishment.

Elly looked up at her with her stomach still pressed against the bed. "I guess you don't need my help," she said with relief. "I didn't talk to Brennan that much, but I can tell you're still acting like him. It always seemed like he was trying to bear all his burdens on his own. How many times have you done that?"

"Never." Olivia was quick to shake her head and lie, but when the memories came flooding back to her, she opened up about her stepfather. "I mean, y-yes. I have tried to deal with my problems on my own."

"Oh?" Elly raised an eyebrow at her, and she nodded.

"My childhood was heaven, but my teen years were nothing but hell." Elly hummed, as if it was possible for her to relate, and Olivia took the opportunity to keep talking. "My stepdad did some 'things' to me. Things a grown man shouldn't do to a teenage girl. Do you know what I mean?"

Elly's slowly opened her mouth to speak, like she had to carefully consider what to say. "Yeah, I understand. I'm sorry." Olivia gently sat herself down on the bed, and Elly rolled over to face her. "This might sound a bit insensitive to ask, but why did you let your stepdad get away with treating you like that?"

"I guess I just didn't want to be alone. I stayed in an abusive house because I'd rather be treated like shit than be alone. I'm sorry."

Elly's eyes grew wide, like a puppy trying to comfort their owner. "There's nothing to be sorry about."

Elly hugged her, and Olivia felt as if they had a real bond. It wasn't something based on the lie that she was Brennan. It was a real bond, based on who she truly was.

"Is there anything else you'd like to tell me?" Elly asked.

"Why are you so curious?" Olivia sounded defensive, but she didn't mean to. After opening up to Elly about her personal life, there was no reason to keep her guard up. Olivia simply spoke without thinking, like she normally would.

"I'm sorry. Sometimes I just say things to say things. I'm not used to having someone to talk to."

"Really?"

"Yeah. Really." Elly smiled at her and reached before extending her arm. Olivia knew that she wanted to go in for a hug, but hesitation caught her.

"Is something wrong?" Olivia asked.

"It's nothing. For a moment, I just thought you were actually Brennan."

"Oh, I'm sorry." A frown spread across Olivia's face. She felt sorry for Elly. After everything she put her through, the poor girl must've been having conflicting emotions and opinions.

"Don't worry about it. I'm still getting used to this whole mess." Elly yawned and stretched her arms. She closed her eyes for a moment, but her rest came to an abrupt end when they heard the toilet bowl flush. Both their eyes suddenly darted to the bathroom door.

"Someone's here," Olivia said.

"Shush. Maybe he doesn't know we're in the room." Elly picked up the lamp from the stool beside the bed and tore the cord out of the wall. Both waited silently to see who hid behind the door. Elly kept a brave face, while Olivia didn't even try to hide the fact that fear had a good hold on her.

The door creaked open, and a short man with white hair peeked his head out. Elly chucked the lamp at the door, and he quickly shut it to shield his face. "Stay back!" Elly yelled. Obscenities kept flying out her mouth, but when the man finally stepped out, Olivia realized it was Haniel.

"Elly, stop!" Olivia commanded.

"Why?"

"That's Haniel. He's an angel." Elly looked at her confused.

"Care to explain why she can see me?" he asked Olivia.

"Well I..." Olivia felt nervous and had to force the words out of her throat. "Remember that mint you asked Death to give me? Well, I sort of forced it down Elly's throat." Olivia gave a nervous laugh, but Haniel didn't react at all.

"Eh, that's fine. Did it taste good, though?" he asked Elly. The question made her wince, and Haniel gave a light-hearted chuckle to compliment his nonstop cheery attitude.

"What's wrong with him?" she whispered in Olivia's ear.

'You get used to it." Her voice was short, almost as though she was sighing rather than speaking.

"Anyway," Haniel said, clapping his hands together. "Brennan has also been receiving gifts, and plenty of them too! I'm sorry I could only give you one, but at least mine don't signal that I have an ulterior motive!" Haniel pouted his lips and looked at Olivia with puppy dog eyes.

"It's okay, but what's this thing about an ulterior motive?"

"Um, I'm sorry to interrupt, but why are you here?" Elly asked, pointing at Haniel.

"First off, It's good to meet you! And like Olivia stated earlier, I'm an angel!" He quietly laughed to himself as he told her his heavenly status. He giggled until the excitement got the better of him, and he burst out laughing. Elly looked uncomfortable, and Olivia stepped in.

"Just tell us why you're here," she said.

Haniel straightened his posture and held his chin up high. "I'm sure you already know where Brennan is, but I came to inform you that he's in more trouble than we thought."

Elly turned her head to Olivia for reassurance, but she had none to give. She reminded herself the news Death brought her — that Brennan was stuck in the afterlife. But what trouble could Haniel be talking about? She didn't know exactly what Brennan was going through, but she knew exactly what Elly must've been experiencing. Olivia had first-hand experience in worrying about someone important. Often times in that position, she would jump to the worst possible conclusions, and she could tell Elly was doing the same.

"What's wrong with him?" Elly blurted out.

But rather than speaking directly to her, he faced Olivia. "I've been using Life as my personal little scout, and she says Brennan's lost and he's just going to get trapped in a maze of turmoil. Apparently, he went searching for Jessica after she died."

"Wait, so it was Jessica in that news article. She died," Olivia muttered.

"Who's Jessica?" Elly asked.

Olivia's thoughts raced through her head. It all made sense to her. She remembered Brennan getting closer to her, so who else could it have been in that news article? Two students missing. One of them dead. Olivia started to hyperventilate, and felt a panic attack coming. If she could jump up onto her feet and walk outside to breathe, she would.

"How? How'd she die?" Olivia muttered under her breath.

"Suicide," Haniel said bluntly. He kept his voice and eyes steady.

"You can bring her back, right? Just like how you brought Brennan and me back, right?"

Haniel shook his head. "That's not up to me. I'm just a messenger. God is the one who makes the decisions."

Olivia buried her face in her palms, and Elly ran a hand around her back to comfort her.

"I'm sorry," she said.

"No! No, you're not!" Olivia yelled. "You're just saying that because it's the 'right' thing to do! You have no reason to be sorry! You never knew her!" Olivia plopped her body back in her wheelchair and pushed herself to the front door.

"Olivia, wait." Haniel called out. "I still have to tell you what sort of trouble Brennan is in!"

"I can't talk right now! Just let me be alone. I need some time to think." Olivia stopped at the front door for a moment and looked up to the ceiling. Her chest rose and fell as she took a deep breath. "Jessica may have bullied me, but I never wanted her to die."

She bumped her chair against the door on her way out, and even though the night was in full swing, she still felt a tinge of humidity in the air. She closed her eyes, letting her thoughts sink in. *Jessica? Dead?* She never could've guessed she'd feel compassion toward her. Yet, here she stood, mourning over someone who made her life hell.

No, she did this to me. If it wasn't for her, I'd have one less reason to kill myself. Then maybe I'd have one more reason to live. I'd have stayed alive. Olivia knew her minded was starting a blame game. It put the burden on others for her circumstances, but she'd always found reasons to justify it. She'd tell herself things like that, that she deserved to be selfish. After being treated so poorly by the world, doing things for herself became a necessity. It was a thought that wouldn't have crossed her mind previously, but now her situation forced her more animalistic desires to kick in. The desire to do almost everything for herself remained, but she still held onto some humanity. A small inclination in her told her she had to help Brennan.

As she sat outside biting on her fingernail, she heard the door behind her open. Elly came through and stopped by her side.

Olivia's appearance made her look like the most broken person anyone had ever seen. The way she hunched over, plus the act of chewing on her nail, did nothing but ruin her image.

"You know, I meant it when I said I was sorry," Elly said. "I may not know who Jessica is, but I know what it's like to lose someone to suicide."

Olivia sighed and reminisced about her conversation with Elly in the woodshop class. She made it clear that her brother ended his life, but in Olivia's moment of grief, she still pushed her away. "Don't bother talking to me. I don't care to hear more about your brother."

A hurt expression spread across Elly's face. Her eyes seemed to be on the verge of letting out an ocean of tears, but she regained her composure.

"It's okay." Elly patted Olivia's shoulder. "My parents also tell me that I talk too much. It's just that when I found out he died, I lashed out. No one could calm me down, but in the moments I was calm, all I did was talk about him."

Olivia sniffled and wiped her nose with her forearm. "If only I had a tissue," she said.

Elly smirked at her comment. Even though the situation didn't warrant humor, Olivia felt somewhat comforted by her familiar smile. It didn't help that much, but she'd appreciate anything at this point. "C'mon, let's go inside," Elly said. "That strange angel, Haniel, is waiting for you. We can still help Brennan."

"All right," Olivia said. She sighed when Elly pushed her back in the motel room. She knew their work wasn't done, but having a moment to take a break spoiled her. She told herself there was no point in going back to her own life. Especially not after the gigantic mess Brennan left behind. Haniel sat on the edge of the bed waiting for them.

"We need to be quick about this," he said. "First off, let me find Brennan."

Olivia shook her head as though it would throw away all her confusion. "Wait, I thought I was supposed to do that?" she asked.

"That's what you thought, but remember, I can travel between worlds on a whim, and you can't. Plus, I know someone is misleading him. I believe he has some doubts about this person, but he still thinks she'll be a valuable ally. However, Life and I know that isn't true. From what I can tell, this 'helper's' name is Lily, but considering the deceitfulness she's showing, I doubt that's her real name."

Olivia folded her arms across her chest and gave a perplexed look. "But why would she have an interest in Brennan?"

'Well, throughout time there's been one supernatural being that consistently shows up to lead damaged people astray. It's a woman who's usually a manifestation of someone's negative thoughts and emotions. I'd guess this is what Lily is. Although no one can remember her real name, unless she wants them to."

"So, you're saying Brennan's so damaged that some woman just spawned from his thoughts, and now she's tormenting him?" Elly turned her head to look at Olivia. Olivia could tell by the worried look in her eyes that she sought reassurance but neither her nor Haniel had some to give.

"It sounds crazy, but everything in my world will seem crazy to you. And yes, considering that she's just giving him 'gifts' that send him further down a rabbit hole into his personal hell, I say she's only there to torment him until he breaks. Brennan wasn't even supposed to go to the afterlife. He was brought there, so he's definitely being taken for a reason."

"Wait," Olivia interjected. "If he can be transported there by some mystical being, can't you do the same to me?" Olivia got her face closer to him, thinking she just hit a jackpot of a solution.

"I'm afraid not." At his words, her face fell into despair.

"But why?"

"Us angels can perform miracles and other things that seem like magic, but we don't nearly have enough power to transport people between worlds. It takes a lot to do that, and since Lily is something spawned from Brennan's mind, she's being fueled by his negativity, and knowing him, he holds a lot of it."

"Then how the hell are we supposed to help him?"

Haniel sighed and bowed his head. "Honestly, I don't know yet, but we'll figure something out. Life can help him by biding some time, while I rest long enough to be able to do a miracle that can save him. In the meantime, you should find your body, so you have something to go back to once this is over.

Olivia averted her gaze, and Haniel caught wind of it. "Is there something wrong with the plan?" he asked.

"No-no."

He eyed her suspiciously but eventually let it go. "All right then. Go and look for your body. I'll try to put things together on my end."

Olivia took a deep breath. *If only he could put me in a body that's not my own.* "Where's my body?" she abruptly asked with a false sense of confidence.

"I really don't know. But since Brennan left it, it's been nothing but an empty shell. It's pretty much in a comatose state, so you don't have to worry about it moving anywhere. Brennan disappeared eight hours away from your hometown. I think he was near an inn that had a waterfall. You should look there."

Olivia thought of the news source. There indeed was a waterfall where they were last seen, but it felt horrifying to know she'd be going to the place where Jessica died. She turned to Elly for help. "You're the only one that can get me there. I need you to tag along."

"You don't have to ask for anything else," she said. "I'll be your designated driver and stick by your side until this is over.

Olivia nodded. Elly didn't know it, but Olivia felt grateful to her as an ally, but if Elly were to ditch her, that betrayal would haunt her for the rest of her life.

"Okay, Haniel. Go help Brennan. Elly and I will go to Washington."

THE CHILD IN THE PHOTOGRAPHS

B y now, Brennan realized that losing his camera proved to be even more detrimental than he anticipated. After his conversation with Life, he'd finally accepted the world for what it was, a reflection of his innermost thoughts, emotions, and struggles. Maybe he didn't know himself that well at all, or maybe denial just became the solution to most of his troubles. He wished that he could be a much simpler person, because right now, he was a complex array of emotions.

Right now, he just knew he had to get away from that lake. He didn't know exactly where Jessica was, but she definitely wasn't there. So as he walked deeper into the forest, fewer trees started to appear similar to witnessing the onset of a blank canvas. Initially, the wooded area had an abundance of foliage, but after about an hour of walking in the same direction, the world grew much darker. Trees began to disperse, and an endless patch of dirt stretched for miles across the land.

What should I do? Everything was changing again; his self-doubt began to creep in. *Should I keep going forward? Will I face more torment?* He closed his eyes and inhaled. *No, I need to see this though if I want to get to Jessica.*

Instead of going back, he trudged forward until the world became so dark, he couldn't even see his own hands. He blindly stepped forward, hoping he wouldn't trip or anything, but when he heard the sound of water splashing under his feet, he smiled. While most people would be scared to walk blindly into water, the liquid brought on a sense of comfort for him. Then the moon began to rise in the sky, along with its faint white light gradually casting away the darkness. Brennan took the time to examine his surroundings until it became clear to him that he was standing in the middle of the ocean.

Not this again. However, with nowhere else to go, he followed the moon, and luckily for him, objects started to make themselves known. He knew he went in the right direction when streetlamps, benches, and trees slowly rose from the water. Everything flew up at lightning-fast speed, and he barely had enough time to stop. Brennan almost bumped into a few trees while walking around. He continued to pick up the pace, but a massive tree sprouting from the water appeared.

He came to an abrupt stop to avoid smashing his nose against the trunk. The wood must've been as wide as a minivan, but the oddly enough, a low humming sound emanated from the base of the tree. He got closer to put his ear against the wood, but stepped back when a sliver of light escaped through a tiny cut. It quickly spread in straight lines until it formed a rectangle. A handle appeared within that shape, revealing it to be a door. It only took one step before going through, that he found himself engulfed in an orange glow. The warm rays surrounded him like the sun in the middle of summer. He closed his eyes at the image, and only when the cold started to touch his skin did he open them. Darkness consumed him, but the sound of a match lighting rang through his ears, and a tiny orange flame lived a few paces away from him. With the sound of a child's laughter, it died, and light suddenly sprang out until an entire room was revealed.

Tiled flooring laid beneath him, and he face planted right into it. As soon as he lifted his face, he realized he was lying in the kitchen of his mother's house. *Why am I here? I already confronted her.* He stood, knowing there was something going on his in his subconscious. Something that would prevent him from finding Jessica. He just couldn't pinpoint the problem, but it must've had something to do with his abusive past. The sound of footsteps running through the house made its known. While standing by the stove, Brennan listened intently. The feet sounded like staccato notes, indicating they belonged to a small child.

He followed the sound. It led him away from the tiled floor and onto the carpet. Even though this place held nothing but grief, he still felt the need to find the person running around. He told himself that the act of delving deeper into this broken home signified that he was ready to get over his past, despite the fear that it still held over him. His ears brought him into a hallway that harbored three sets of doors. If he remembered correctly, one led to the bathroom, the other to his mother's bedroom, and the last to the living quarters he shared with his sister.

Brennan stood still and kept his ears open, ready to react at a moment's notice. But instead of hearing feet clambering around, he heard faint sobbing coming from the shared bedroom. He gently opened the door, but upon peeking in, he saw no one. It was only when he felt a hand brush against his ankle that he looked down to see a child version of Nora sitting against the wall.

"Nora?" Brennan asked, confused.

"Are you going to hurt me too?" she asked.

Even though he felt pure hatred toward his older sister, seeing her as a helpless child brought on different feelings. He knew full well how their relationship would end, but seeing her at a time before their fallout, instilled him with nostalgia. Looking at her in this moment made him forget how he saw her as an adult and only showed him how much he loved her as a sister.

"No, I'd never hurt you." He knelt down to her height and looked her in the eyes. Her face had similar features to their mother's, but there was a softness to her cheeks that made her appear friendlier. "Why are you crying? Did your mom hurt you again?"

"No... At least not yet. But she did get mad at my little brother."

Brennan tensed his shoulders after hearing those words. Nora always referred to him as her "little brother", no matter how old he got. Except as a child, she meant it with more love rather than concern. "I'm sorry to hear that," he said. "But I'll make sure you're not on the bad end of her brutal beatings." If he had been the older sibling, he'd have taken the hits for her, and he'd do so without flinching.

"I don't care about that! I'd rather be hurt than see my brother get hurt!"

Brennan averted his gaze to the side. It seems that being protective came natural to both of them. Over time his childhood had turned into a vague memory, but he always remembered the care his sister showed him. Despite the fearfulness that ran through her, she at least did her best to comfort him. Brennan sighed. The time when she'd blindly loved him felt like a precious time long forgotten. He thought back to his encounter with his mother in the forest. Fear was what caused that, and fear was the reason he almost lost that battle.

But what was feeling now? Was it fear, or something else? He had already defeated his mom, so why did he come back to her home?

"Will you help me find my brother?" Nora asked.

"I'm sorry, but I have to go." Brennan got up to walk away in order to avoid another mentally torturous situation; however, he couldn't leave when Nora grabbed his hand.

"Please?" she begged.

He hesitated, but eventually caved in. "Fine, I'll help you."

She hugged him tightly, crushing him with her arms and letting her tears soak his shirt. "T-thank you! Thank you so much!" She buried her cheek deeper in the fabric of his clothes, and he couldn't help but crack a smile.

Brennan gently placed his hands on her shoulders and softly pushed her back. "Do you remember where you last saw him?"

"Um." Nora had a puzzled look before answering. "I think he was in my mom's room."

Brennan's face turned to horror. That room held nothing but abusive nightmares. As a child, time spent in that room meant time spent in hell. He swallowed hard before speaking again.

"Okay, let's go," he finally said. Nora led Brennan to the end of the hallway while his hands shook in anticipation. He desperately hoped he wouldn't see anything he didn't want to see. Once they reached the door, he let Nora continue to take the lead. She gently stepped in, and Brennan shuddered when he followed. Nothing seemed out of the ordinary, but that was what scared him. The sight of the altar and ice bucket placed in the corner of the room brought back so many memories. His mother would pray devoutly each day, but would ironically turn into the devil at night. If bruises appeared on his face, she would dunk his head in the ice bucket to get rid of them.

"Brennan," Nora called out, but not to the present Brennan. "Where are you?" She walked around the bed centered in the middle of the room, but no one was there. She opened the closet door. only to be greeted by nothing. "I hope he's safe." Nora began to cry again, and Brennan went over to wipe her tears. After all, his sister would always comfort him in the past. When they were children, she was there to steady him after a beating, but once she reached adulthood and left the house, their relationship became based on sibling rivalry.

"I lost him," she muttered.

"It's okay, we'll find him." Brennan put on the most confident act he could pull to reassure her, and she fell for it.

"We will?"

"Yes, we will." He rubbed the top of her head, frazzling her hair, and she gave him a wide smile. Seeing her mouth form the shape of a "U" brought him both happiness and sadness. And those feelings pierced his heart, because they reminded him of the innocent bond they had as children. The kind of bond that would be destroyed with age.

Together, they searched the other rooms of the house, making sure to be thorough with each one, and by the time they got to the living room, Nora sat on the couch, exhausted.

"You look sad," she said to Brennan.

He turned his head and asked, "What makes you think that?"

"Well, my teacher showed me flashcards of different faces, and you look like one of the sad ones."

At first, Brennan chuckled. Now that he thought about it, he did have vivid memories of learning about emotions in school, and how stupid he'd believed it to be.

"Are you sad?" she asked.

"A little bit, but you are too, aren't you?"

Nora nodded. "I'm sad that I can't find my brother, but what are you sad about?"

Brennan paused to think. Normally he wouldn't dump his baggage onto someone younger than him, but if everything in this world was just a reflection of his mental state, this version of Nora wasn't real. It was just his mind playing tricks on him.

"I think you're the only person who asked me that. Thank you," he responded with a genuine smile.

"Don't worry! I'll always ask how you feel!" Her words touched his heart just like they did in the past. But the reminder of his childhood also brought on heartache. This type of love from his sister used to be abundant, but now, that entire supply was completely empty.

"Come on, let's go," Brennan said. They finished searching the house, making sure to be thorough, yet they found nothing.

But once they entered the back yard, they found Brennan's child doppelganger. He sat on the new patches of grass at the corner of the fence, digging a hole, completely ignoring the fact that he was ruining the yard. Upon further inspection, he noticed that he had his favorite toy bucket with him. The young adult Brennan stared at the plastic pail, becoming hypnotized with each passing moment. He remembered his toy so fondly. Every time he went to the beach, he always got the urge to dig a massive hole, and the spade would be his lifeline in doing so.

When Brennan walked closer, he witnessed his child self stuffing his hands into the dirt, digging deeper like a feral dog. But that was also when he realized he was burying photos of Nora.

"What are you doing?" he asked his child self. The younger version of him turned around and frowned.

"I'm just digging."

"Okay then. By the way, your sister is here. She's been looking for you."

However, rather than responding, his doppelganger continued to dig. He went deeper into the hole before picking up the pictures, readying himself to toss them in.

"Whoa, hold on," the real Brennan said. He stepped forward in an attempt to pick up the photos, but his hands were met with a bite.

"Stay away!" the young one hissed. "I don't want to see these pictures anymore!"

"Why?" Brennan never thought he'd come face to face with a childish version of himself, let alone feeling so intimidated by him.

"I just don't like Nora!"

"Don't say that," Brennan muttered.

"I just don't like her. I don't like the pictures, and it's her fault I'm throwing them away!"

"But you're the one digging the hole. You're the one throwing those frames into the dirt." He brought his shaking finger up and pointed at the dirt. The patch of grass was a scrambled mess, and worms who were hidden deep within the ground were now reaching the surface.

At first shock set in, but when that started to subside, Brennan felt nothing but anger and shame toward himself. Even though he hated who his sister became, he couldn't deny the fact that he'd once loved her. So, to throw away all his pictures of her was a hard thing for him to do.

"I know, I'm burying them," his child version cried.

He's blaming Nora for his actions. But he's the one doing it.

Brennan racked his brain. *Think.* His mind became an even bigger mess, showing that this world truly projected his inner most thoughts and feelings. Yet, he still wondered why he was watching himself do this. *Is it my fault our relationship came to an end?* He shuddered at the thought and continued to deny it. He'd tell himself to stop thinking negatively, but he couldn't help pondering the question. Was this all his fault? He told himself "no". It was a "no" because, to him, Nora was the one who left.

She vanished without a warning, or at least, it felt as if she didn't leave a warning. He started to belittle himself. Brennan should've seen it coming. She gave him all her attention, but he just dismissed it.

He plopped down on the grass and threw his head down in denial. *She's the one who left! Not me!* Brennan sighed and looked to the sky. The sun still beat down on his face, and when he averted his attention to the boy he once was, he saw himself turn to stone and crumble to the ground.

Then those pieces eroded away, until they were sand being blown by the wind. The world became a blurry mess, with the house, trees, and sky torn apart by the wind. It didn't take long until the whole world disappeared, and nothing but darkness consumed him. Brennan found himself alone. It was a state he assumed he'd be in for the rest of eternity.

"How are you feeling?" a feminine voice asked.

"Nora?"

"No, it's me." A blue moon rose into the dark sky, revealing the grass that appeared beneath him, along with the glowing white petals of flowers that dotted the island. And with the world being a bit brighter, he saw a girl sitting down in front of him. She had white hair and appeared to be about fifteen years old.

"You keep following me here, Life." Her rounded face was thinner, a clear indication that she aged, but not by much. Brennan reached his hand out to touch her face, but stopped midway. While he was definitely curious, he thought it'd be a strange interaction.

"Hello again." She nodded and giggled, sitting up with perfect posture.

"So, you've aged again." Brennan let out a faint smile in an attempt to lighten his mood, but it did the opposite. The shakiness of his voice exposed his vulnerability. "Can I ask you something?"

Life nodded. "Go ahead," she said.

"What exactly is my mind showing me? I know I wanted to find Jessica. In fact, that's the whole reason I'm here. Yet I'm being shown all these terrible things from my life. If this world reflects my mental health, then it obviously doesn't know me at all. I've experienced scenarios I've never thought of, and I'm encountering all these people I have no interest in. What am I doing here?" Brennan looked down at his hands as though he were looking at the tools that made this world.

Life hummed to herself before responding. "First off, I'd like to ask if you really believe what you're saying."

"What? What's that supposed to mean?" Brennan shot a nasty look at her. He was tired of the mind games being played on him.

"This world is my home," Life said. "I know how it works. Therefore, I'm confident that you're just lying to yourself, but which part is the lie? Is it the belief that you only want to find Jessica? Is it the claim that these people and scenarios aren't something that's on your mind? Or is it both?"

Brennan clasped his hands together and avoided eye contact. "That doesn't answer my question." He gritted his teeth and turned his interlaced fingers into a clenched fist. His anger boiled inside him, and he had a strong desire to lash out with a strong desire to yell.

"I don't need to answer your question because you already know the answer yourself." Somehow Life managed to make an accusation without sounding accusatory Her voice remained calm and her tone firm.

"I just don't get it. Why can't you tell me what's on your mind, rather than being so cryptic?"

"My job is to help you, and it doesn't do any good to just command you. After all, a good teacher makes sure their students understand the subject, rather than just memorizing the steps."

Brennan furrowed his brow and brought himself to make eye contact. Out of his peripheral vision, the white flower petals of the daisy beside him grew larger.

"Fine," he said with a sigh. "Let's talk about this."

"I'm glad we're on the same page. First of all, let's look back at everything that's happened so far. You confronted your sister at the tree house, you met your mother at the waterfall, and now you just witnessed yourself burying pictures of Nora. Does that ring any bells?"

Brennan leaned forward and rested his cheek in his palm. "I honestly don't know," he muttered.

"I think you do."

Brennan brought his mind back to what he saw in the backyard and began connecting the dots. He hated Nora and blamed her for the fallout of their relationship, yet it was him who "buried" her. That's when he asked himself, again if their strained relationship was his fault?

He grunted and slapped the sides of his face, shaking his head. "No!" he yelled. "I don't want to think about it!"

"I guess that's because you know why you saw what you just witnessed?"

For a moment Brennan didn't respond to her. He just shut his eyes and tried to drown out his feelings of self-blame. *Guilt! Guilt! Guilt! I'm guilty!*

"You're right. I do know why I was in the backyard digging that hole. Every bad interaction with my sister was my fault, and I'm the one to blame for destroying us. When she moved out of our home, it was to escape our mother's abuse, and I'm a hypocrite for getting mad at her because I'd do the same thing."

"And you think this is the truth?" Life asked.

"No. It's not something that I only think, it's the truth." Brennan held a clenched fist. He only ever used his hands to harm people, but now he knew what it was like to be on the other end of his angry outburst. He exhaled heavily, trying to slowly take in a breath. He didn't want to get lost again. Jessica was always on his mind, but now he couldn't concentrate on her. The afterlife, Life, and himself were showing that Jessica shouldn't have been his first priority. He wanted her to be his priority, but now that conviction was nothing more than a question hanging in the air.

"Well done." Life smiled after their brief exchange. Then the moon began to set behind the horizon and the flower petals slowly lost their glow, making the world completely dark again.

HEAVY BAGGAGE

The darkness faded a while ago, and from it sprouted a world full of grassy plains with a range of mountains. Even though Brennan had begun to learn more about himself, his mind still hovered around Jessica. *She's what I really want. It can't be anything else.*

Despite using those words to reaffirm his false beliefs, he knew. His inner demons were what took hold of him right now, and he wished it didn't take him so long to realize it. *If I want to find Jessica, I have to beat this. I have to get rid of my problems.* Jessica wasn't his top priority anymore, at least for the time being. Figuring out how to fix himself would come first, and that would open the path for him to get her back, but with all of his gifts gone, he wandered aimlessly. His feet took him along the mountain range. The stone beneath him provided just enough friction to keep him from slipping and falling through the air.

It wasn't until he traveled ten yards that he saw a woman standing stoically at the tip of the summit. His eyes squinted as he felt his heart beat faster. Initially, he believed her to be Jessica, but eventually he realized that delirium had taken over. Because when he ran forward to catch her in an embrace, the woman looking at him was Lily. His heart wasn't yearning to see her, so he wondered why she appeared almost everywhere he went.

"Lily," he said. He got closer and noticed that she seemed older. During their first few meetings, she'd resembled a young woman similar in age to his sister, but now she looked a decade older.

"It's good to see you again," she said with a smile. She cocked her head to the side, and Brennan noticed.

"What is it?" he asked.

"It's just that I don't see your gifts anywhere. What happened to them?"

Brennan stuttered as he tried to get his words out. Since the last time they talked, he'd been through his own version of hell, and Lily only gave him cryptic descriptions of places to go to, all of which were torturous.

With a steady gaze but shaky voice, he spoke to her. "Well, I lost the gifts after being attacked by my mom. I lost everything when I ran into her. Then it got even worse when I saw my sister again."

Despite the numbing sensation in his brain that told him Haniel and Life were right to doubt her, Brennan still sought out affection from Lily. It seems that despite having an inkling of knowledge that she led him astray, his bad habit of looking for a maternal figure in some of the women he met kicked in. So, he felt his heart being pulled apart at the thought of turning his back on her. And as of right now, Lily was the only candidate to be his mom... Brennan shuddered at his thoughts. Just thinking about that habit made him feel ugly, and when the most recent events were added on top of that, he just felt even worse.

"It's like I've been traveling from one hardship to another." After speaking, he looked up to Lily for her approval, similar to what he did to all the maternal figures he wanted.

"I'm so sorry." She leaned forward and frazzled his hair with her fingers, making Brennan smile. "Would you like another gift?"

"That would be nice. Yes." Brennan was quick to answer, and Lily held out her hand. A few creases lined her forehead while an item began to display itself on her palm. A black cap came into existence, followed by a marker.

"There you go," she said sweetly.

Brennan picked it up to examine it. "What can I use this for?"

"I'd rather you see for yourself then have me explain. Answer this — what is something you want to find?"

Brennan instinctively took the cap off. "I want to find Jessica," he said. Judging by his past experiences, he knew that he'd be caught in a scenario he didn't expect, but Lily's gifts were the only thing that somewhat helped him traverse this world.

"Very well then. Just write her name."

Brennan was about to open his mouth and ask for a sheet of paper, but Lily just drew imaginary lines in the air with her finger. Then Brennan got the idea to draw in the air with the marker. He raised the black tip above him and wrote Jessica's name. Each letter appeared above his head as though he were writing on a whiteboard, and they stayed there, like lamps hanging from a ceiling.

"Now blow on it," Lily commanded.

Brennan puffed his cheeks, then exhaled copious amounts of air on the words. They contorted and turned into dust just to fly away to his right.

"Follow those scattered pieces and they'll lead you to her." She pointed at the black dust trail they left behind.

Brennan said, "Thank you." He looked at her with a neutral expression. After everything he's been through, he also saw heras an ATM that deposited supernatural gifts, rather than an ally. He figured that the thought of some powerful being just helping him without asking for anything in return was too good to be true. "Why can't you stay with me?" he asked, wanting her to be less enigmatic.

"That I simply cannot do," she said with a frown. "There are people whom you can't travel with forever, and you'll just have to accept that."

After she spoke her last words, Brennan reluctantly nodded and trudged down the slope of the mountain. His feet slid down the rocks, causing gravel to trickle downward. If only Lily stayed by his side, he wouldn't feel so irritated. He had a dream of finding Jessica and bringing her back to the world of the living, but it felt like Lily was hiding something that could crush his dream..

Once he reached the bottom of the mountain, letters flew over the grassy plain. He ran after them, like a child chasing bubbles. He made sure to stay on their trail, not wanting to lose sight of them. He sprinted as fast as he could, but when lighting cracked the sky, he stopped. He gazed up, and surprisingly, there was an actual crack in the sky, as if a piece of glass had been shattered. The world seemed like a giant snow globe, and he found himself in its inner decoration.

A white beam shot down, making the ground rumble, causing him to fall onto his bottom. The intensity of the rumbling grew stronger until it rivaled the most massive of earthquakes. It shuffled him back and forth so much, that he had to dig his fingers into the dirt to keep them in place. The tremor slowly came to a halt after about a minute, and when it did, he stood to see a short man walking in the distance.

"Hey! Who are—" Once he came into full view, Brennan realized it was Haniel, but contrary to his usual persona, he held a serious face. "Haniel? What are you doing here?"

The short angel picked up the pace, and within seconds he turned into a gust of wind. Brennan felt the draft he caused, but couldn't see him since he'd turned in a blur which made it even more surprising when he suddenly stopped in front of him.

"Brennan," he panted, "I've been watching you from a distance. I think I know who that woman is."

"Who?" Brennan became distraught at seeing Haniel's unusually serious face.

"The woman who's been giving you gifts. She's not here to help you. Her name is Lilith, and she's a demon!" Brennan took a step back, sensing that Haniel was about to snatch his marker. "She spawns from the troubled minds of people who are brought here!" He reached his subby arms out. "Give me that marker."

"No," Brennan said firmly. He always had his doubts, but right now, she was just a means to an end. Despite, the uneasiness surrounding her, Brennan needed help finding Jessica, and he knew Haniel wouldn't be too keen on helping him. "Why should I give up everything just so I can turn back? In all my time here, she's helped me find Jessica more than you ever did!"

Brennan didn't want to hear his words, but the worry in Haniel's voice told him that he should cave in. Still, he saw Lilith as someone he could trust to find Jessica, if nothing else, so possibly parting ways with her instilled a feeling of dread.

"Are you serious? After all this time? I can tell you have your doubts about her! Just hand over the marker, and I'll help you get out of here!"

Brennan's eyes held a steady gaze as he gritted his teeth. He didn't want to lose Jessica for good, but his intuition told him that his uncooperating nature would only continue to stir the trouble he already found himself in.

"I already said 'no'!" Haniel stepped forward, but Brennan shoved him to the ground. "Ever since I got here, she's the one who's been guiding me! Not you!"

"Listen to me! She's misleading you. All those gifts have sent you on some random path that led you further down this rabbit hole of lies! Just hand over the marker right now!"

"Never! This thing will help me find Jessica! Every gift I've received helped me get to where I am! If it wasn't for that camera, Life and I would still be lost at sea. And if it wasn't for this marker, I'd still be wasting my time on the mountain!"

"Listen, Brennan, I know you believe you can help Jessica, but she's dead. You can't bring her back."

Brennan took a moment to remain silent. Thoughts of his future plans with Jessica raced through his brain. He imagined himself and her getting out of the afterlife, her accepting who he was, and them keeping in contact for years to come.

"I realize that when you met Olivia and I at the train station, you gave us those tickets and tried to help us navigate our new lives, but this time is different. I'm not here to change my life and get back in my body. I'm here to get my friend back." There was a sharp edge to Brennan's voice. As if he was trying to sound reassuring yet decisive at the same time. He took in a deep breath before Haniel spoke.

"But Brennan, you can't bring her back. She's dead, and that was her choice to make. There's no need to chase her."

Brennan scrunched up his fist, trying to suppress the anger that came from Haniel's statement. "No, that's not true," he said, grinding his teeth. "I can get her back! Just watch!" Even though he was filled with anger, tears welled in his eyes. "I'm not giving this up! This is my chance to fix everything."

Brennan quickly pulled the cap off, and attempted to write Jessica's name, but Haniel slapped it out of his hand. The item toppled to the ground next to him, and Brennan dove for it, giving Haniel a reason to kick him in the side.

"I'm sorry I have to do this to you," he muttered. Brennan saw him stand straight and spread his arms out, like an eagle spreading his wings. His pupils dilated, and his iris turned into gold. After that, white feathered wings sprouted from his back. Brennan assumed he was about to get pummeled, but he couldn't help noticing how beautiful Haniel looked with his wings. Brennan's eyes were glued to the feathers, and he wished he could pluck one for himself.

Haniel floated above him with his wings flapping. "Brennan Claufield." A low commanding voice came from his short body and his vocals had a strong sense of authority. "I'm taking you with me. You don't belong in this world. It's about time you leave."

Haniel put his hands together and closed his eyes. An updraft enveloped him, and his white hair began to float upward. A bright gleam of light sprouted from his chest and, when he opened his eyes, Brennan felt a mixture of fear and happiness. *This must be an angel's miracle.* The light condensed itself into a ball that Haniel held in the palm of his hand. He aimed it at Brennan, but before he could throw it, Lilith flew in from the side and tackled Haniel. Her white dress was torn at the bottom, and in stark contrast to Haniel's white wings, hers were twice the size and made of black feathers.

Her pupils resembled snake eyes, and her hands and feet turned into talons. Her tongue slithered out of her mouth as she hissed at the young angel.

"Stop!" Brennan yelled. But rather than heeding his request, Lilith dug her talons deep into Haniel's shoulders, causing him to scream. The young angel writhed on the ground. "You don't have to fight!" Brennan felt guilt consume him. He finally realized how evil Lilith really was, and the danger he put Haniel in.

Brennan charged forward getting ready to perform a tackle, but she put her hand out in front of her, and Brennan felt a strong force send him backward.

After he witnessed her and Haniel fighting like rabid dogs, she started cutting Haniel's face with her nails, and he bit into her neck as if it were a delicious plate of food. Brennan had been a victim of violence, but seeing them fight exposed him to gore for the first time.

"Don't you want to find Jessica?" she asked Brennan with a quick turn of her head.

"I do, but this isn't the way!"

She grew fangs and hissed at him, yet he didn't lose his courage. He sprinted at her, but the invisible force hit him once again. He grunted and slammed his back on the ground.

"Brennan, I'll be fine. Run!" Haniel managed to say. His wings smashed into Lilith's eyes, cause her to cover them and scream out loud. He took advantage of the moment by flying into the air, but Lilith quickly responded. She dashed into him, and they clawed at each other in the sky.

Meanwhile, Brennan felt completely helpless. He wanted to stop her, but couldn't do anything, so instead he took Haniel's advice to run. He stood on his feet; however, when Lilith tackled Haniel in the distance, their bodies flew to the ground, creating a gigantic tremor that flowed through the land. The ground beneath Brennan knocked him off balance. and he fell face-down. He got back on his feet as quickly as he could.

"Lilith! Leave him alone!" Brennan yelled, but all he heard was her relentlessly mauling Haniel. Fearing the worst, he ran in the direction he last saw them. *I have to help.*

But before he could make any distance, he felt a strong gust of wind swoop in, and in an instant Lilith stood in front of him. She instantly gripped Brennan by the throat and hoisted him into the air.

"Why are you doing this?" Brennan croaked. He struck her wrist with his fist, but the struggling didn't loosen her grip.

"I'm here to kill you! To take over your life and erase any evidence of your existence!" Lilith raised her hand and put her fingers together. Her razor-sharp nails merged together to turn her arm into a spear, and when she pulled her limb back, Brennan looked down. She'd quickly stabbed through his torso, making him cough up blood. *Am I going to die here?* Despite the pain, he still found the strength to grind his teeth.

"I'll kill you!" he gasped. *Why would she do this? And how did she spawn from my subconscious? It doesn't make any sense!* Lilith laughed manically as she repeatedly plunged her arm through his torso. Eventually, his mind started to slip away, and that's when Lilith tossed him aside. Brennan gazed into the clouds as he lay on his back, but once his vision went black, he saw the white flowers again.

Their petals glistened in the moonlight, and he found himself on that little island, hidden in its blue glow. This time, a girl about his age stood over him. She looked down at Brennan while he stared right back at her.

"I guess that's you, Life." She nodded with a concerned look. "Haniel told me Lily is actually a demon named Lilith. She's a demon created from the minds of people like me, but I don't understand how I made her."

Life offered her hand to him, and he took it. "Come, let me show you," she said.

Life led Brennan to the water, and he looked into it. At first, only his reflection revealed itself, but the faces of people he didn't know began to appear.

"What am I looking at?" he asked. The identities of the men and women within the ocean didn't spark any memory, but he felt sorry for each one of them.

"Lilith is made up of malice, and when someone has a strong will, like you, their negative emotions cause her to appear. She becomes the embodiment of their negativity, and she uses that to fuel herself into a stronger being. Her main goal is to act as a parasite and destroy a person from the inside."

"So, she takes over their mind?" Brennan dipped his finger in the water, and the faces frowned along with the ripple effect.

"In a sense, yes, she does."

"But why didn't you tell me this earlier? You felt uneasy around her when we were at the light house. Why didn't you warn me?"

"Haniel tried to get to the bottom of things and so did I, but we just couldn't figure out exactly who she was. It was as if she used a bit of her powers to conceal her identity. And to be honest, you were so blinded by your own desire to find Jessica that you brushed aside every red flag she showed."

Haniel's name sparked a sudden onset of guilt. Brennan knew that the young angel's fight with Lilith was his own fault. If he hadn't been so stubborn, then maybe all of this could've been avoided. "What do you mean, I was so blinded by my own desire?" he asked.

"Don't pretend."

"I'm not pretending." Brennan gazed into her eyes, and she turned away.

"You know deep down that you'll do anything to get Jessica back."

Brennan got ready to protest, but hesitated. Now that Haniel and Lilith had a fight, he finally came to the conclusion that Haniel was right. If he was wrong about the fact that Lilith had been helping him, there would be no reason for her to trick him. taking advantage of his emotions by giving him copious amounts of gifts to fuel the false delusion that Jessica could be "saved".

"Okay, fine. I'll admit it. I was hoping she could help me find Jessica, but I guess I was wrong." The words painfully left his mouth, and he wished they didn't hold any truth, but they did. "I'm weak, and I'm a liar. I need to change."

"You're not weak, but you do need to change. Lilith has gotten too strong, and the only way to take her down is to tackle your inner struggle."

Okay then," Brennan said with a sigh. "But so many things happened that I don't know what I need to face."

"Just take a moment to think about it. You're beginning to lose yourself because Jessica died. How does that make you feel?"

"Well, considering that I've been wrong in the way I've been acting, I guess I'm confused. You say that I have to find inner peace, but I know I'm regressing. And now I have to accept the fact that Jessica's gone for good?" To Brennan, it felt like the world was closing in on him, as if invisible barriers surrounded his body with the intention of crushing him to death.

"I'm sorry," Life said. "I know you'll figure it out."

"How?" Brennan buried his face deep within his hands, but he didn't have any tears left to spend.

"How what?"

"I've been through so much bullshit, and I lack the proper guidance to teach me how to navigate the world. How am I supposed to solve my problems? And not only that, but all you do is ask me questions that force me to think about the past. You can be pretty cruel sometimes." Brennan's mind became a plethora of questions, with each one getting progressively harder to answer. *What do I do? How can I find what I'm really struggling with?*

And as the seconds passed, Brennan started to feel like he was in Hell.

THE BEGINNING OF A NEW ENDING

B rennan spent a good amount of time being cuddled by Life, but eventually, he became numb to her touch. He cried in her arms for so long, he didn't feel them anymore. At the very least he was relieved to learn that Haniel couldn't just be killed. Life informed him that angels never died; they just crumbled after using too much power. It would take them multiple lifetimes, but eventually, they'd return.

"Life?" Brennan asked, looking up to her.

"What is it?" She gave him a warm smile, and he felt a small tinge of hope.

"I'll have to leave this little island again, right?"

"Yes, but only when you're ready."

Brennan gave a weak smile. It felt comforting to have someone to hold on to, but being held by a person he once saw as a little girl put him off. He was supposed to be the adult, the protector, yet here he was using Life as a pillow. Even though she reached his age, he still thought of her as the innocent child he once knew. He used her arms as a protective shell until he finished sulking, and when he finally found the strength to stand, he did so proudly.

"I'm ready," he declared. He exuded fake confidence to make himself seem more capable, but Life saw through his façade.

"You know, you don't have to act tough all the time."

Brennan slumped his shoulders. Usually, people didn't see through his bluff, but this time was an exception. His mind clearly faltered, which was a dead giveaway that his was putting on an act. "I'm sorry," he muttered.

"You don't have to be. It's normal to feel small sometimes." Brennan took her words in and gave a nod of approval. "You should also take into consideration about how the people in your life really feel about you."

Brennan turned his head toward her. He raised an eyebrow as an indication of his own confusion. "What do you mean by that?"

"Remember when you saw yourself burying photos of your sister? You seemed really distraught about that."

Brennan brushed the grass off his clothes and sighed. "I know. I realize now that I've been the one destroying our relationship. I'm the reason my sister and I are so distant. But what am I supposed to do? Just go back to her?"

Life stood and placed a hand on his shoulder. "Yes, I'm sure she'll let you back into her life. After all, she needs you there."

"But why? Why would she need me?" Brennan took hold of her hand and gently put it down. Talking about his sister stirred mixed feelings, but this time, the pleasant ones outweighed the bad ones.

"She wants you to be back in her life, so she can be the happiest she's ever been. And Olivia still needs you to come back to the real world. After all, how else are you supposed to switch bodies?"

Brennan looked to the ground and picked at the grass with his feet. "I suppose you're right. There's still a lot I have to do. But what about

Jessica?" His heart still skipped a beat every time he mentioned her name. He didn't just want her, he needed her.

"I'm sure you'll figure out what to do about her. Follow me," she said, walking out into the water. Feeling curious, Brennan trailed behind her until the liquid reached their waist. Life held out her arm. "Come here," she whispered softly. Brennan held her hand and she pulled him close. "Close your eyes." He obliged and felt her hand touch his chest. After that, she pushed him under the water.

At first, he felt her touch, but the further down he went, that sensation began to fade. Eventually, she completely vanished, along with everything else. He couldn't hear nor see. The world was simply nothing, but after being plunged into the water for about a minute, his wet body dried up instantly.

A warm ray of sun beamed through his eyelids, and once he opened them, he found himself in the same field where Lilith impaled him. He racked his brain to remember where he'd heard Haniel's screams. He breathed in the air, as if the memory was floating somewhere, and once he resurfaced, he let it guide him. He didn't take the time to walk or jog. Instead, he burst into a full sprint until Haniel's body came into view. He lay face-down in the dirt. next to the rocks that fell off the side of the mountain. Brennan knelt down and hovered his hand over Haniel's bloody face and tattered clothes.

"How are you feeling?" he asked. When Brennan spoke, Haniel's ears twitched, and he opened his eyes. Mud and leaves littered his face, but that didn't take away from his childish appearance. "Answer me," Brennan begged.

"I think I'll be fine," he said in a weak voice. "I'll regenerate. I'll be okay, but right now you have to stop Lilith."

"I know, but I just don't know how. Life told me she's a part of my failing mental health, but how can I 'fix' myself? Is that even possible?" Brennan held Haniel's head up with one arm and wrapped his body with the other.

"Brennan, almost a month ago, you died, then were brought back to life. Anything's possible."

As Brennan, watched him suffer, he couldn't help but let a tear drop out of his eye. Haniel may have annoyed him to no end, but seeing him in such a state of decay initiated the empathy he didn't know he had.

"Let me give you something first." Haniel closed his eyes and clasped both hands together. A small ball of light wrapped itself around his palms until they turned completely golden. "I know, you hate living, but please, just give it a shot." After he let out his last breath, his face turned to stone, before that rocky surface spread throughout the rest of his body.

Eventually, he crumbled and eroded, until he became dust blown away by the wind. Brennan watched him float to the sky as a new object appeared on the ground where he once laid. Brennan bent over to pick it up. Upon examining it, he realized he held a harmonica.

I'm sorry, Haniel. The angel must've used his last bit of power to leave something behind in order to help him. Brennan felt bad that he saw the angel as a friend only after he left. But now, he made a promise to himself and Haniel — that he'd defeat Lilith. He didn't know exactly how the harmonica would work; he just knew instruments were meant to be played.

So, he brought it to his lips and blew a hefty amount of air into it. When the notes came out, he heard a woodwind instrument playing in the distance to answer his call. He stood and headed in that direction. He continued this way while blowing more notes every once in a while. However, the trail he followed seemed to go on endlessly. While the grass blades scraped against his ankles, the mountain ranges were always in sight.

Still, despite the long journey, he held faith that the scenery would soon change. He couldn't let Lilith get away. He still didn't want to let go of

Jessica, but Lilith became a greater obstacle, blocking his path to happiness. So, defeating her would make his purpose here a lot easier. His new goal was getting rid of Lilith and reclaiming his life, as well as avenging Haniel. But he'd be lying if he didn't admit that Jessica was his reason to do all this. As he imagined her face, a drop of rain landed on his forehead, then a few more.

It didn't take long until the rain shower completely soaked him in a heavy downpour. Despite being cold and wet, he pressed forward. He wasted no time and blew on the harmonica — and heard notes played back to him once again. This time, they came from his right. He turned his head and finally saw something different. It wasn't just grass blades and trees anymore. A house standing upon a lake made itself known. It stood on tall wooden pillars that went deep into the water. Brennan felt a rush of excitement before dashing toward it. Finally, something different appeared. The mountain rage was far off, and the world was changing once again.

He blew into the harmonica again, and music came from inside the house, so he made his way to the front steps. The boards creaked under his weight, hinting at that they were about to give away, but once he finally got to the top, relief washed over him. Something in his mind told him that this house harbored special sentiments, and if the afterlife had taught him anything, it was that everything had a reason to exist. This place held some importance; Brennan just couldn't come up with a plausible conclusion. When he opened the door, the smell of old wood hit his nose, and dust particles struck his eyes.

Even though furniture encompassed the area, the room still felt empty. Brennan came to the center and stopped at the fireplace, standing in front of the couch. On top of the mantle were pictures of him and his sister.

Why am I seeing her again? Brennan knew that one of the things that created Lilith was the tension he had with Nora. It wasn't just the guilt he felt over losing Jessica. It was a mixture of multiple people and factors.

He picked up one of the photos and looked at it. It showed his sister with a graduation cap. *I remember this day. She finished high school.* Her graduation day may have been pure happiness for her, but for Brennan, it wasn't.

To him, it marked the day she made plans to leave him behind. He looked at her smile, and even though it was genuine, that happiness didn't spread to him. It made him want to punch her. He wanted to break those stupid braces she'd worn at the time. That high school diploma in her hands signified a contract that caused their divide. A contract that would awaken the rage Brennan held deeply within. He wished he could travel back in time to tear it apart. He quickly put the picture back where he found it and picked up another. In this one, he saw his mother holding him as a baby. She had her lips to his cheek while he held a wide grin.

"Do you like it?"

Brennan turned around to see who spoke, and sure enough, it was Lilith.

"You." Brennan gritted his teeth. "You killed Haniel, and now you just show up out of nowhere!"

"Well, first off, I didn't kill him. You can't kill an angel. And secondly, you should know that this isn't an ordinary house."

"You're right about that," Brennan said sarcastically. He pointed his finger at the photos. "This place is just a museum displaying the sickest pieces of art! That's all this place is! Just a museum of all the worst moments of my life! These pictures should be burned!" Brennan reached over to one of the photo frames and threw it on the floor. The glass shattered when it made contact with the wood, and Brennan stomped on the shards. "These pictures are all lies! There's no happiness in them!"

"Oh, but what if you could actually feel that happiness?" Lilith giggled. "I'm sure you already know this world reflects wat happens in your mind, so think about it this way. What is something you truly wanted for your family?"

Brennan hated the constant tone of her voice. It had a recipe of sweetness with deceit sprinkled all over. "Just shut up! You're trying to trick me again." Brennan picked up a broken shard of glass and squeezed it in his hand. Blood trickled out, but that didn't matter to him. His mind cemented the plan of using it to attack Lilith. He walked forward, but bumped into an invisible barrier.

"Just relax." Her smile and cheery voice started to grate on his ears, but his only choice now was to listen. "You can stay here if you like. I mean, the afterlife has its perks." She smiled and walked up to him. He wanted to lunge at her, but couldn't; his body froze in place. Even moving a finger felt like a strenuous act. She chuckled and went behind him, wrapped her arms around his chest, and put her lips to his ear. "I am light and easy, but the longer I live with you, the heavier I become. What am I?" she whispered.

Those words struck a chord with Brennan. He remembered hearing that same question in his head after Jessica died. It happened the moment before he was taken from his world and placed into this one. Brennan realized that Lilith must've had plans for him for longer than he expected. Perhaps his emotions were already reaching the boiling point, and he just needed a catalyst to push him over the edge, and that catalyst was Jessica.

"How long have you been planning on bringing me here?"

"I've always been inside your head. Everyone has negative emotions, even guilt." Lilith leaned into him and nuzzled her face into his shoulder. "Poor boy," she cooed. "You've been through a lot, haven't you? If you stay here, I can let you live happily in this world. Anything you can think of will come true." She waved her fingers in the air, as though she were a witch performing magic. "Your broken family doesn't have to be broken. Look around you. Look at those photos. What if we just made them happier? What if we changed your memory a bit? We both know that's something you want, so stay here and let me show you what I can do."

A photo levitated from the mantle and hovered in front of Brennan's face. The graduation photo changed to an image of him smiling and eating cake with his sister, while in the other, his father stood by his mom as she kissed Brennan's forehead. Lilith made the deal even sweeter by making her voice soft just like a mother.

But that didn't fool Brennan. To him, she still sounded like a snake. He squeezed the glass piece even tighter, drawing more blood.

"I can see you're having some conflicting feelings, but please stay here. Let go of that shard. You don't need it." She gently cradled his hand, and he dropped the glass. "That's it," she whispered. "Now, look ahead." At first, Brennan didn't see anything, but as he stared at the front of the house, his mom and sister began to appear.

"We love you, Brennan!" they said in unison. As the women waved at him, heavy footsteps came thumping up the stairs. A man so tall his face was hidden above the door, stopped next to them, and Brennan couldn't mistake who he was. He knew that it could only be his father. His family froze in front of him. They stood motionless, as if they were only a picture.

"That's just a teaser," Lilith said. "You can be with them if you like. You can live a new life here."

"But it's not real," Brennan muttered and looked down at the broken piece of glass, and just like the shattered frame, his voice was breaking apart. "It's just not real," he whispered one more time.

"But it's real to you. Isn't that what matters?"

"Shut up." Brennan grinded his teeth.

"Oh, but it's true." Lilith ran her fingers through his hair, simulating the love he fantasied his mother giving him as a child.

"No, shut up," he managed to say.

"I know you want it. I know this is the life you desperately want."

Brennan growled, and let his anger fuel his strength. He used every ounce of his willpower to overcome her grip on him and push her away.

He quickly tackled her and grabbed the glass off the floor. He raised it high above his head and looked down at her chest. "Shut up! Shut up! Shut up!"

He yelled this as he stabbed her repeatedly. He did it over and over, and with each thrust, he screamed at her. It wasn't until she lay still, like a corpse, that he finally stopped. But when he dropped the shard to the floor, he didn't see Lilith at all. Instead, he just saw himself, staring back at him. It was his own body lying in Lilith's place, its expressionless eyes devoid of life.

"Is this how it is?" He quietly cried. "Am I just here to fight myself?" He looked at his body once again. Without a doubt it was himself he was killing, but how could that be?

ACT 2

THE GREAT
ESCAPE

T he night seemed to pass by in a matter of seconds. Olivia blinked, and the next thing she knew, she was basking in the warmth of the sun. Its rays peeked through the curtains, revealing the entire bedroom. Elly still slept on her side, snoring loudly while taking up as much space as she could.

Olivia slowly pushed Elly's legs away and gradually stood. She proceeded to practice walking back and forth as sweat rolled down her forehead. The first few paces from the bed became heavier. until her body collapsed. She smacked the ground in exhaustion, making Elly jolt upright at the noise.

"Olivia? What happened?" she asked, looking down.

Olivia pushed herself up with her arms and stared at her. She became spoiled by living Brennan's life. Losing everything and everyone she was given caused genuine heartache and loneliness. But at the same time, she knew she'd lose it all if she continued this trip. *What if I had people to protect me? What if I had a life worth living?* She tried to shut out the thoughts, but they were drowning her. They started an incessant bombardment of cruel words, to the point where Olivia didn't even realize that Elly was helping her get into the wheelchair.

"What happened?" Olivia asked when she finally got a grasp of her surroundings.

"I don't know. I just saw you lying on the floor. You must've rolled off the bed." As Elly said that, she ran over to the curtains and completely pulled them aside. Sunlight assaulted Olivia's eyes.

"You didn't have to do that," she muttered grumpily.

"That doesn't matter. We need to get a plan started."

Olivia watched her shuffle with the curtains, wondering how she could be so calm in their predicament. But then again, she wasn't the one risking her happiness. Olivia believed she was the only one risking anything. She cared about Brennan's well-being, but she also cared about herself.

"Start what? What plan?" Her delirious state left Elly dumbfounded. It took some time, but eventually she remembered their conversation with Haniel the previous night. "Oh, you're talking about getting us to my body." Olivia looked downcast, and Elly snapped her fingers in front of her eyes.

'Hey! Don't zone out on me now. We need to get started." Elly said.

"Fine." Olivia sighed. "Do you have gas in your car?"

"Yes."

"And air in your tires?"

Elly raised an eyebrow before answering. "Yes."

"Do you have—"

That's enough," Elly said, frustrated. "I have everything we need. We just have to come up with a way to get to Washington."

"Let's just drive." By now, it would be easy to mistake Olivia to only be acting as a nuisance, but she didn't care about coming off that way. Anything to delay their journey was enough for her.

Elly's shoulders rose as she sighed. "I know. What I want to know, is exactly where we'll find your body." Olivia remained silent, and Elly gave her a nasty look. "Last night, Haniel said Brennan was taken away when he left the inn. Do you have any idea where that might be?"

"I'm sorry, but no." While Olivia told the truth, she still told it with the intention to sabotage them. She hoped that her lack of knowledge would be enough to put a dent in their plan.

"He said it was at a waterfall, so Brennan was definitely surrounded by nature."

"Elly, unless you're in one of the few big cities of Washington, you're surrounded by nature everywhere you go." She smirked at Elly, as if she was outsmarting a naïve child.

"Fine then," Elly pouted. "Why don't you give me a description of where you lived?"

"I lived in some small town no one knew about."

"Well, wouldn't a small town be a big contrast to a city? Surely it'll stick out."

Olivia shook her head. "You need to leave this state sometime. Washington is filled with small towns no none knows about. My town is even on its own little island. If Brennan traveled to an inn eight hours away, he's nowhere near where I lived."

Elly sighed and leaned forward with her chin in her palm. "Whatever. We just know we'll find your body in Washington. That's the best we have. We might as well just drive there first." She went behind Olivia's wheelchair and gripped the handles. "I'm going to push you to my car. Are you ready?"

"Yeah, let's go." Olivia did her best to sound eager, but her disappointment still seeped through in her voice. When they exited the room, she felt a strong urge to go back inside. *Stay! Stay! Stay!* Eventually those words left her mind as she began to mumble them, and Elly caught wind of it.

"There's something wrong, isn't there?" Elly asked. Olivia acknowledged her with a nod, but refused to speak up. "Tell me what's going on."

Olivia exhaled slowly and turned her head to the side. Yet again, she declined to answer.

"I see. But when you feel more comfortable, tell me about it." Without saying anything else, Elly pushed Olivia faster and quickly placed her in the passenger seat. As always, silence plagued them as they drove. The only voice they encountered was the robotic speech of the GPS, but that lack of human connection made Olivia feel terrible.

"Elly," she finally managed to say. "Maybe there's something else we can do. Maybe we don't have to get to Washington." It was a long shot, but Olivia was starting to get desperate. She just wanted a little more time living as Brennan. Even if that meant saying something out of the blue, with no logical reason. One of the things she liked about his life was the people in it, so if she wanted to stay in his body, at the very least she'd like Elly and Nora to be with her. Convincing Elly to stay by her side seemed like an impossible task, but Olivia felt the need to try.

"Didn't Haniel already make it clear that we have to find your body? We don't have time to do other things, or even think about doing other things."

"I know." Olivia sighed. "But please, just listen to me." She kept her tone weak, hoping that Elly's never-ending sympathy would kick in and force her to listen.

"Well then, you better have something good to say," Elly retorted. Olivia tried to come up with some words, but nothing came to mind. She opened her mouth and then shut it again. She shook her head.

"I guess that's it then." Elly scolded her. "We're going to Washington."

"Yeah, I guess so." Olivia let the car ride continue in silence for the next few minutes, but eventually, she lost her mind. "Just tell me something about him!" she yelled.

"Huh?" Elly glanced at her, confused.

"I know this is sudden, but please tell me something about Brennan." Olivia decided that if she couldn't live the rest of her life as him, she could at least have a vivid daydream about it. She needed to hear Elly's voice more, so the sound of it would stay in her head long after they parted ways. If daydreaming about her time spent with Nora and Elly had to become her whole life, she'd do it as long as it made her happy.

"You already know I didn't talk to him that much."

"I know, but think of it this way. Once he's back, you'll want to get to know him, right?" Olivia forced out a grin despite her desperation. Listening to stories about Brennan's life would calm her down, but she deemed it necessary to put up a confident act, hoping that Elly would take her seriously.

"Yeah, I guess." She took a moment to think before rebounding with an answer. "Well, Brennan always seemed like a normal guy to me. There wasn't really anything special about him, but that's what made him special to me. Everyone else just looked as if they were trying to prove themselves, but Brennan just stayed true to who he was. He didn't care what anyone else thought. He just wanted to be himself. Of course, now I know that there was a lot more going on in his life, but I still liked him."

"I see," Olivia muttered. *Just himself, huh?* She realized that she could learn some good lessons from his attitude if she just tweaked it a little. Maybe just soften up his rougher aspects. "Was there anything else you liked about him?" Olivia asked.

"He's a good graphic designer!" Elly seemed more excited to say that.

"I can tell. Is there anything else?"

"Um, I can't think of anything else."

"That's okay."

Their conversation was enough to let Olivia imagine a better life worth living. When they came to a stop sign, Elly gently pressed the brakes and asked, "Is there anything else you wanted to talk about?" She seemed more invigorated than earlier as if talking about Brennan gave her the strength to go on.

"No, but thank you." Olivia yawned and leaned back in her chair while a smile spread across Elly's face. But during her happy moment, Olivia realized that she wanted his life more than she initially thought, so tried to come up with ways to leave Elly behind just so she could be Brennan. Even if for a short while. *Brennan, I deserve your life. Not you.*

While resting in her chair, Olivia fell asleep, slipping into the white void. Clocks floated all around her. Their ticking made a constant ring in her ears, and not a single one was in unison with another. A dark shadow appeared on the ground and made a move toward Olivia. Fear gripped her, but when a boy around her age emerged from the shadow, she let her guard down. Something about him seemed so familiar she was willing to put aside his terrifying entrance. His hair was dark as midnight, and his face had firm cheekbones with a strong chin.

"Who are you?" Olivia asked.

"It's me, Death."

At first, she didn't believe him, but when she looked into his eyes the image of his child self flashed in her mind. She remembered his timid behavior and the cold stare he gave.

"So, it is you," Olivia stated.

Death nodded. "I'm tied to you, just like how my sister is tied to Brennan. That's why I've grown older."

"Wait, what's that supposed to mean?"

Death stood tall and looked down at her. "With the gravity of the situation, you've mentally matured and I had to keep up with you." Olivia took in what he said. *I've matured?* "I see you're a little lost," Death said. "However, now is not the time to explain. Brennan is in a lot of trouble, and you need to get back to your body right away."

"I know." Olivia slumped her shoulders in disappointment. "Everyone talks about him and how much they care about him, but why doesn't anyone care about me?" Olivia looked exasperated, yet Death didn't offer any support. "Why do I have this burden placed on me? Why can't Haniel just come here and help me out?" Before continuing, Olivia's outrage came to a halt when she noticed Death's frown making an appearance. "Why are you giving me that look? Are you disappointed in me?"

"No, but you should know that Haniel's gone. He won't be here to help you anymore."

"Gone?" The word harbored a strong meaning to her. Her father was gone, but was Haniel's "gone" meant the same as her father's death? "Is he dead? Is that what you mean?"

"Not exactly. Angels can't be killed. He just lost all his power to continue for the rest of this lifetime. He'll come back in a few hundred years."

Olivia felt a shock wave surge through her body. "But that can't be." For a brief moment, a happy thought crossed her mind. *If he's gone, is there anyone to stop me from taking over Brennan's life?* Olivia felt angry at herself almost as soon as she posed the question. "Who's going to help us now?" she asked, brushing aside her selfish desires.

"That responsibility falls onto to me and my sister."

Olivia had a hurt look on her face. Haniel was temporarily dead, and the kids she once knew were forced to grow up so fast. This wasn't something she expected at all.

"All right then. Tell me why you're here."

Death nodded. "I'm sure you see the clocks floating around us."

"Yes," Olivia said abruptly.

"Clocks always represent time no matter what world they're in. Brennan's time is running out, because he's slowly being consumed by his past burdens."

Olivia turned her head away. She didn't want Brennan to suffer, but then again, suffering had been a part of her whole life, and nobody cared. It seemed that the entire plan to solve their dilemma rested on her, yet she wasn't offered any comfort. Everyone just wanted to use her to fix everything. Even Elly admitted to tagging along only for Brennan's sake.

"What happens if I don't fix this in time?" Olivia asked.

Death stood firm and stared up at the clocks. "Most likely he'll fall victim to his trauma, and you'll never switch back to your old bodies."

Olivia let a small grin creep across her face. Leaving Brennan in a never-ending cycle of mental violence would be her biggest act of cruelty, but why shouldn't she do that? Her whole life had been nothing but physical and mental turmoil.

"I'll make sure we get to Washington as fast as possible," she lied. *Take a detour. Detour. Detour.*

"I'm glad we're in agreement," Death proudly stated. He gave a nod of approval, and Olivia went into a dreamless sleep.

When she woke, the sun had already begun to set. The orange sky gave a wonderful sight, that she planned on seeing every day from now on.

"Olivia," Elly said. "We're almost out of Florida. We'll be in Alabama soon. Let's find a motel for the night, then sort out our next move tomorrow."

"Let's do it." Olivia stared straight ahead as she tried to will an escape plan. Nothing came to her mind for now.

SHATTERED DREAMS

B rennan's feet felt as if they were encased in cement blocks. When he turned around, his family stood, frozen in time. He wanted to sprint at his sister and embrace her, but the moment he took one step, everyone turned into stone and crumbled just like Haniel. At the sight of this, sorrow and anger filled his heart. He walked over to the dining table and gripped one side of it. The veins in his hands popped out at the tightness of his grip before he screamed and used every ounce of his strength to flip it over. *Fuck! Fuck! Fuck!* The dishes came crashing down after, which he repeatedly stomped on the already-shattered silverware. He pulled the bottom of his shirt toward his face and held it up with his mouth, exposing his stomach.

He held a jagged piece that was once a plate. *Is it possible for a soul to kill itself?* If this had been the real world, all he would have to do was thrust the piece into his stomach and cut it open, but he didn't know if the desired effect would take place here. Brennan squeezed his hands tighter, which drew more blood. He held his eyelids shut and raised the broken piece of silverware in the air... but rather than stabbing himself, he screamed before dropping everything he held. He fell to his knees and cried. *Lilith. She's a part me.*

Brennan tried to slow his breathing but failed to. He desperately wanted to kill her. He desired nothing more than to wrap his hands tightly around her throat and squeeze until she drew her last breath.

I can't kill her if I'm dead. Brennan was never one to let someone hold dominion over him, let alone let himself lose a battle. He slowly got back on his feet. It seemed that the only satisfying way to end his struggle would be to kill Lilith or, in other words, kill a part of himself. Once he got to the door, he stepped over the stone pile that was once his family.

"Lilith!" he yelled to the sky. "Come here! Face me!" He screamed louder, but no one came. It was just him in a field of grass. Feeling directionless, he brought the harmonica to his lips and blew into it again. As always, he didn't play a rhythm or melody; he just exhaled into it, hoping for the best. The wind carried his notes through the air, and when he heard a response coming from behind, he turned around.

They came from beyond the lake house. However, Brennan didn't know their exact location. Without a doubt, it would take him on a journey spanning a vast distance, but it was a journey he was willing to take. He trudged forward, assuming that something traumatizing waited for him.

The sky darkened with each step until it became night. Stars dotted the sky, and Brennan anticipated seeing another apparition. He didn't know who or what it would be this time. All he knew was that it would involve the people close to him. But would it be someone he had yet to see, or would it be his family again? As he thought, a figure hidden in the dark made itself known. He saw its feminine form in the distance. *Not this again.* He gritted his teeth, getting into a fighting stance.

If this was just another act of mental torture, it would undoubtedly be a fight. The woman walked closer, and Brennan's eyes popped open.

It's you, Jessica. His body told him to run forward and hug her, making it impossible for her to leave him again, but his mind told him to keep his guard up; that was easier said than done. His hand rose in the air and his fingers twitched. His brain told him to steer clear of her. That for her to appear like this was too good to be true. Yet, at the same time, his body couldn't suppress the urge to stay away. He put one foot forward, only to change his mind, coming to a complete halt. Not everything in this world was how it seemed to be. He knew she was just an apparition, that she couldn't be real, but to him, an apparition was better than nothing.

"Hello," she said, nervously. Her voice almost forced a tear out of his eye. All the memories of their short time spent together came flooding back to him. Her soft vocal chords warmed him up just as much as her body did. But considering everything that previously happened, he didn't know if this was another one of Lilith's tricks.

"Please, help me. I don't know how I got here." Jessica had a scared expression as though she were a lost child in an airport. Her face made Brennan want to go in and comfort her, but he still hesitated. *Lilith, this is your doing, isn't it?* "Please help me. I'm so scared."

Jessica fell forward, and Brennan caught her in his arms.

"I was with a friend," she said. "Her name was Olivia. Can you help me find her?"

Brennan thought back to the waterfall. He only got to know Jessica while he was stuck in Olivia's body, so Jessica never knew who he really was. He didn't reveal himself as Brennan Claufield. To her, she was getting to know Olivia, not him. Jessica's fear looked very real, her confusion reminiscent of Brennan's when he woke up in the world of the dead. "Please, I just got close to her and now she's gone."

Brennan's eyes grew wide. *Closer? She remembers all the time we spent together!* "Jessica, I..." Brennan tried to force out words, but his sobbing held him back. He genuinely wanted to believe that she wasn't just an illusion. That the person he was talking to was really Jessica. But after countless encounters with made up versions of his loved ones, this wouldn't be any different. But the touch of her clothes, her skin, and the feeling of her breath on his chin just felt so familiar he didn't want to let go.

"I'm sorry I did this to you!" Brennan said. A tear rolled off his chin and landed on her cheek, but once she felt the droplet, she stood and held her hands out in front of herself.

"I'm sorry, but I don't know you. I think you're just mistaking me for someone else."

"Jessica, it's me, Brennan."

"You're Brennan? Olivia mentioned you."

"Yes, yes, she did!" Brennan made sure to mention himself when he lived his life as Olivia, but despite that, he was glad to know that Jessica remembered his name. A small amount of joy entered his heart, but that was all it took to make him smile. "Jessica, let's go home."

He reached out to her, but she stepped back. "I don't understand what's happening. I don't even remember coming here, and now you're taking me away? Where's Olivia?"

Brennan bowed his head and sighed. "Jessica, there's something I have to tell you, but we can't stay here. This world isn't meant for us! I'll explain everything as we go!"

"Can it wait? Let's just find Olivia first."

"No, listen to—"

"Olivia can't be far from here," she interrupted while scanning the area. "We traveled together. She must be here." Upon speaking her mind, Brennan looked all around him, hoping that Lilith wouldn't show herself.

"She's not here," he said bluntly, with a quick breath.

"What are you talking about?" Her fear seemed to be replaced with the same indifference he noticed when first meeting her.

Brennan gritted his teeth. If she was so hellbent on seeing Olivia first, the chance of them running away immediately would be non-existent. "I know this is hard to hear, but you're not in Washington anymore. In fact, you're not even alive. You're dead."

Jessica folded her arms across her chest, letting the frustration seep into her mind. "Now is not the time to play games! Just tell me where Olivia is!" She stomped forward and pointed a finger at his face, but Brennan stood motionless. He looked at her with his pupils dilating.

"I'm telling you the truth. I don't know how else to say this, but you're dead."

Still not willing to accept the truth, Jessica said, "I've had enough of this. If you won't help me, I'll just find her on my own." She gave an irritated sigh, and turned on her heels, but before she could walk away, Brennan placed a hand on her shoulder.

In a last-ditch effort to get her to realize the truth, he began recounting the events leading up to her death. "I was there at the lake. You drowned yourself."

He saw her tense every muscle in her body before facing him. "How do you know about the lake? Did Olivia tell you?"

"No, she didn't have to. because I was there."

"What do you mean?" Jessica raised an eyebrow and put her hands on her hips.

"I was Olivia. I was in her body. Every time she mentioned Brennan, that was just me talking about myself." Brennan leaned into her hoping that his love for her would shine through in his voice. And when Jessica opened her mouth to speak, Brennan interjected. "Olivia and I switched bodies when we died and were brought back from the dead. Just like you, we took our lives, and I've been trying to fix this."

"Stop lying to me." Jessica gritted her teeth. "Everything you're saying is impossible! It's absurd!"

"But it's the truth!" Brennan yelled. He sounded more aggressive than he meant to, so he quickly lowered his tone before placing both hands on her shoulders. He looked into her eyes. "If I wasn't Olivia, how would I know about the lake? I remember lying in bed with you while you talked about your father. I remember everything. I even remember when you slammed your desk onto the ground during our English class."

Jessica pushed him back. "No!" she yelled. "You're not Olivia, and I'm not dead!" She turned to walk away, but Brennan grabbed her again. "Get away from me, you freak!" She gave him a good slap on the cheek, and he fell backward.

Brennan quickly jumped on his feet, letting his determination drive his actions. "I can't do that! Look around! This world is too fantastical to be real! You're dead! You drowned at the lake, but I'm here to bring you back!"

"Shut up!" She screamed so loud Brennan felt his heart stop. Tears of anger welled up in her eyes. "Why is everyone messing with me? Did Olivia put you up to this? Did she tell you everything we did and just left me here? Did she backstab me like my friends did?"

"No, I would never do that." Brennan got closer to her. "I love you, and nothing's going to change that. I'm getting you out of here."

Jessica couldn't suppress her tears anymore. They came flooding out like a broken dam. "Don't say 'I'. I may not know exactly what's going on, but I do know I was talking to Olivia, not you!"

Brennan raised his hands as if to show he surrendered, and Jessica let out a small sniffle. "Everything will be okay. I'm here to help."

He hugged her, and surprisingly to him, she didn't resist, but she didn't reciprocate either. As he held her in his arms, she gently shook her head.

"No."

Her simple answer was enough to make Brennan's heart melt. The wind started to howl and grass blades whacked his knees. The ground beneath them shook softly, and gradually escalated into a full-blown earthquake.

The rumbling brought him to his knees, but Jessica stood still. She was motionless, and for a moment Brennan saw her face contort into Lilith's, then back to herself. She was Jessica, then the next second, she was Lilith.

"So it is you," Brennan muttered. "It's not Jessica. It's you, Lilith." His teeth made a grinding sound as his face transformed in the physical manifestation of anger. Brennan could feel his heart thumping through his chest. The cold sensation on his skin turned into a fiery feeling. One side of him that harbored the hatred he had for Lilith conflicted with the despair for losing Jessica. He didn't know whether he should be angry, or sad, or both. He just knew he'd lost her again. This encounter was just another test, and obviously, he failed it.

He got up in a wobbly stance. "What's the purpose of this? What are you trying to show me?"

Brennan's mind became a tangled mess again. He told himself that this meant Jessica was gone for good, but at the same time, he denied that revelation. He remembered his last meeting with Life. She and Haniel may have wanted him to find himself, but that wasn't why he was here. Jessica was his only motivation, so if he couldn't save her, then he could at least avenge her. Getting rid of Lilith became his new drive.

A tear rolled down his eye as Jessica whispered, "Forget me." Brennan tried to hold her hand, but the tip of her finger turned to stone, and that stone spread through her whole body like black ink dropping into water. It started with her index finger before consuming her whole hand. He knew this might be the last time he'd see her, so he went in for another embrace. His arms wrapped around her cold, hard body, but his mind willed the feeling of her warm skin into existence.

"I love you," he said into her ear. A tiny tear dripped from her stone eye socket and flowed onto his shoulder.

"Goodbye." He heard her voice in his head, and after that, her arms crumbled, then her legs. And as he held her torso, he felt it slowly breaking apart until she turned into a pile on the dirt.

Brennan's chest slowly rose and fell. The deep breath he took in didn't cause an onset of relaxation. Rather, it was his way of slowly taking in what he just saw. First, she was there, and now she was just a pile of stone in the dirt. Taking it in all at once would be too much to handle, so he took everything as slowly as possible.

But eventually, he realized that he could handle the grief. Even though it was immensely difficult, he knew he could handle it, so that feeling of sadness soon changed into a bitter sense of triumph. He knew that, in time, she wouldn't be a burden he had to carry. She'd simply be a great person in a field of happy memories. However, to him, there was nothing sadder than seeing the person who created those happy memories become nothing more than another happy memory.

He clenched his hand. Forgiving himself and the people around him was something he had to do, and the less self-destructive actions he took, the more he would weaken Lilith. Maybe the pain he endured would take her down. He felt like a fearsome giant being awoken from a long nap. He put the harmonica to his mouth and looked to the sky. He blew through it, making the notes come out, and once he heard the response he expected, he followed it.

The night wore on, and Brennan wondered why he was able to go on without any sleep in this world. He still walked around, fully awake and functioning like a normal person. Time worked in odd ways here, but he figured that he should take a moment to rest. After all, even though not a hint of exhaustion made itself known, the lack of sleep scared him.

He made sure the harmonica was still in his pocket before lying on the ground. The grass acted as a blanket, keeping his entire body warm, and eventually, he zoned out the sound of the strong winds until he fell into a deep slumber.

"Welcome back," Life said. Brennan opened his eyes upon hearing her voice and saw her standing over him. This time she hadn't aged at all.

He quickly sat up and found himself on the island with the white flowers. "If you're worried about not getting any rest, don't worry. Think of this place as a comfort zone. Your mind immediately heals while you're here."

Brennan rubbed his eye with his finger and yawned. "So, this is where I'll be for the next eight hours?"

Life nodded. "You could lie there and relax, or we could talk. However you choose to pass the time is your choice."

A smile crept across Brennan's face. Ever since he entered this world, despair plagued him, but whenever Life came, his negative emotions would subside. "In that case, I'd like to talk to you."

"What shall we talk about?" Life asked.

"The people in my life that I've been seeing over and over again are appearing because of Lilith. How many more times will I see them?"

Life hummed and put a finger to her lips. She folded her arms across her stomach, which wrinkled her white dress. "I'm not sure, but I guess you'll only see them as many times as you need to. Your mind is still rioting in violence." Brennan frowned at her response. "Why the long face?" she asked.

"It's obvious I still need to get over my past, but I have to admit, it's a tough thing to do. I just saw Jessica, or a replica of Jessica. I learned to let her go, and I have, but I can't say it wasn't painful."

"I see." Life stared into his eyes with an innocent look, but it didn't put Brennan at ease. "Facing your inner demons can be tough, but it's something we all must do."

"Life?" Brennan sighed.

"Yes?"

"Do you even know what it's like to be human? I mean, do you know what it's like to feel our emotions and do the things we do? It's hard to believe you've ever held trauma in. That's the type of stuff that'll break you and make you into a different person, or both."

Life shook her head. "Not exactly, but I know someone who has." Her quick answer caught Brennan off guard, and he found himself staring at her, dumbfounded. "You seem surprised." She giggled.

"Yes, of course, I am. This whole time I thought you've just been this perfect magical being. I never thought you'd have experiences like that." She pouted as wrinkles spread across her forehead. Her face turned to disappointment. "I'm sorry," Brennan said. "That was rude of me."

"No, it's okay. I understand that my happy demeanor must make it come at a surprise, but remember, even happy people have hard times."

"Yeah, I guess so." Brennan scratched the back of his head, avoiding any and all eye contact.

"But it's time I tell you a story." Life sat next to him and got ready to talk. "Way back in time there was a man, who had a mix of black and white hair. At first, he was innocent. He mostly kept to himself, but as humans, foliage, and animals sprang upon the earth, it became his job to watch over them. Eventually, all living things were destined to meet him. He would welcome them into the afterlife, and he enjoyed his job, but every creature resented him for it. Not a single soul wanted to depart from their life. To leave their family and friends behind seemed outrageous. Instead, they preferred to stay in your world, the world of the living.

"However, it was humans who made it worse. They constantly shamed him, and made entire cultures despise him. The loneliness plagued his mind. Therefore, he took an ax and split himself in two, so that he would always have a friend. That friend was a little girl with white hair. She harbored his cheery attitude and childlike innocence. Meanwhile, he was reborn as a young boy with dark hair. That boy held the burden of continuing his job of meeting deceased souls. He was shunned by others, but the girl was loved, and anyone would do anything to keep her happy. It didn't take long until he became jealous. He wanted to put himself together. To become one person again, but upon realizing the fondness others had for her, he accepted his fate. He loved all living beings and only desired to see them happy. Much like you, he carried the burden that he believed he had to bear alone. But that girl came to comfort him. She helped him along the way."

At the end of her story, Brennan felt more at peace. "I think I know who you're talking about." He didn't have to mention who the girl with white hair was for he already knew her name.

"And I believe you when you say that," Life said. "I also believe you know that there's no need to torture yourself by living alone."

Brennan hesitantly put a smile on his face. Life was right, and using that story as an example showed him that it could apply to his life as well. He could embrace someone's help. He didn't need to do everything on his own.

Life reached to the side and plucked a dandelion. She held it in front of her mouth and blew the pappuses off. They floated in front of Brennan's face, and he closed his eyes. Once he opened them, a great feeling of strength flowed through him.

"Know that when the time comes, I'll be there for you. We all will." Life smiled at him and, for the rest of the night, she and Brennan watched the stars in the sky.

GOING HER OWN WAY

Olivia and Elly spent the previous night at a motel within a small town in Alabama. She remembered the excitement on Elly's face as they entered the state. Apparently, she'd never left Florida, and despite the situation, she reveled in the unfamiliar sight. Even though she was usually a happy person, the sudden spike in her mood caught Olivia off guard. By now the sun had risen high in the sky, and a little bit of strength returned to her legs. Olivia finally had the ability to slowly move her lower body over the bed and walk to her wheelchair, but striding considerable distances was still too much. She rolled away from the bed, toward the window near the front door. Upon moving the blinds aside, sunlight hit her face, making her eyes squint.

"Good morning," Elly said groggily.

"I'm sorry, did I wake you?" Olivia turned her head with a concerned look. She may have been planning to escape whether or not it caused chaos, but Elly radiated a peaceful atmosphere when she was calm. Olivia was hoping she could experience that peace a little longer.

"Nope, but the sun did." Elly yawned and stretched her arms before going to the bathroom. Running water sounded and the desire to escape returned to Olivia. *If only I could use my legs.* Even though her fantasy consumed her, practicality started to creep in. Sure, she might be lucky enough to run away, but going back to Nora and seeing even an ounce of normalcy was a long shot. When Elly stepped out of the bathroom, Olivia gave her a fake smile.

"What should we do first?" Elly asked.

Olivia thought about how she could take advantage of the situation before responding. "Let's find a market to buy some food. We ate pretty much everything during our drive."

Without hesitation, Elly nodded and screamed, "Yes!" Olivia had never seen her get so excited over food, and she hated to be the one to ruin it. She hoped her ulterior motive to slow them down would turn into an opportunity to slip away. "Let's go," Elly giggled as she pushed Olivia out of the motel room. Once she stuffed the wheelchair into the trunk, they drove off, letting the GPS guide them to the nearest supermarket.

The road trip didn't take that long, and when the store came into view, they were quick to enter. Upon entering, Elly suggested they split up. She took on the role of getting snacks while she tasked Olivia with finding some drinks.

"I'll find some premade food and candy. You get some water and energy drinks." Elly spoke as if she were a pack leader, and Olivia hummed in agreement. By the time Elly left eyesight, Olivia went down one of the aisles, looking for a case of water bottles and a pack of energy drinks, but a homeless man sleeping against the wall caught her eye. He was slumped at the very end of the shelf near the pharmacy. A pair of crutches lay next to him.

The moment she looked, Olivia believed the crutches to be a blessing from God. Surely, being able to walk would provide a chance to leave on her own. She quietly made her way toward the man and stopped to lock her wheels a couple of feet away from him. She slowly got onto her feet and stumbled to the wall. By the time she reached out to grab the crutches, she had to painfully bend over to pick them up. A grin spread across her face... until she accidentally bumped the end of his foot. The man stirred from his sleep. At first, he didn't respond, but once Olivia made haste to leave, she caught his attention.

"What the..." he muttered. It took a moment for him to register what happened, but when his mind became filled with energy, rage filled him. "Hey! What the hell do you think you're doing?" he yelled.

"Shit!" Olivia bit down on her lip and picked up the pace. almost to the point where she toppled over, but the intense amount of focus she had helped her maintain balance. Luckily, the man was dependent on the crutches just as much as she was. The moment he stood, he fell over, knocking down a shelf of greeting cards. It slammed to the floor, creating a large boom that echoed through the building. Both customers and employees rushed to his aid as envelopes from the shelf scattered in the air. The scene demanded enough attention that Olivia managed to leave unnoticed.

The outside air felt like a refreshing breeze on her skin. She breathed heavily while thinking of what to do next. Escape was her only desire, but she didn't know where she'd escape to. All she knew was that getting away from Elly would be her first step. While on her way to their vehicle, she noticed a sharp, jagged rock lying on the cement. She mustered enough strength to bend over and pick it up. From there, she quickly closed the distance between herself and the car. Olivia stabbed the sharp end into one of the tires and watched it deflate.

I deserve to be selfish. Brennan's life is mine to take.

She felt the eyes of a small crowd watching her speed-walking through the streets. Her eyes frantically scanned the area, and when she noticed a patrol car turning the corner, she ducked into a nearby alley. The dark shadow that it cast was enough to keep her concealed in broad daylight. She took a moment to rest, and pushed away the remaining feelings of guilt spinning in her head.

"This is the right thing to do! I have to put myself first!" Her hyperventilating caught the attention of a woman walking by.

"Are you all right, sir?" she asked.

"Get away from me!" Olivia snapped at her, making her jump at the response. She immediately ran away, leaving Olivia surprised by her own actions. *What have I become? Am I okay?*

Her old habit of second-guessing herself returned. Deep down she knew this was wrong, but when she recalled all the times she let others walk all over her, she used that as a justification for her decision. Olivia turned her head away from the sun and continued down the alleyway. She trudged along with the rats while feeling like one of them. The stench of garbage seeped its way into her nose, but she pushed forward, hoping to never see Elly again. When she got out of the other end of the alley, a shadow still loomed over her. No longer did she walk in the light. She fell into complete darkness, following a path that led to her selfish dream.

Absolutely nothing eventful happened while she walked further into town. It was as if the events that transpired never even happened. The only chaotic thing left over was the negative thoughts clouding her brain. She berated herself with harsh words while praising herself with affirmations. *You shouldn't be running away. You should be ashamed of yourself. You deserve this! Go get them!* But as she kept going, those words started to hold more weight, and their negativity became accompanied by the presence of something following her. It felt dark, like a blanket of loneliness consuming her.

Every time she turned her head, she saw the dark silhouette of a man trailing her. He didn't seem to be walking in a straight line. Instead, he teleported wherever her eyes went, and once she finally got a good view of him, he quickly ducked out of sight. If she could travel faster, she would, but her arms were already struggling to maintain their energy to swing the crutches back and forth. Eventually, the imminent exhaustion became too much to bear, and she came to a complete stop. The park she found herself in seemed like a comfortable place to collapse. She didn't plan on taking that thought seriously, but she gave in. However when she fell forward, a strong hand gripped her collar and pulled her to her feet.

"Do you realize what you're doing?" a deep voice said. Olivia shuddered when she felt his touch, but that died a little when she found out she was only being confronted by Death. Still, her messy, fearful expression was in stark contrast to his emotionless face.

"Why are you here?" she asked.

"I'm here to put you back on the right path. I saw you running away earlier. This isn't right."

"A path?" Olivia scoffed. "A path for me?" She stood tall glaring at him. "Why do I have to follow this 'path' that I never wanted to follow in the first place? Why do I have to live the life everyone else set out for me? Can't I get what I want for once?"

Death loosened his grip on her. His presence became more calming, like he was ready to let them depart as equals. "You're thinking about this the wrong way," he said in a soft voice. "You need to listen when I say you have to get back on track."

"No, you listen to me!" Olivia raised her voice rather than maintaining her composure. "Since my dad died, I've been doing things for other people! I let my stepdad abuse me, for his sake and my mom's! I stayed as that 'good girl' just so I wouldn't hurt anyone. I genuinely believed it was better to get hurt than to hurt others, but now I see that's not true. It's time I make my own choices."

"And you can," Death retorted. "Just finish what you and Brennan started. Then once you're back in your body, you can go live the life of your choosing."

"Do you honestly think I can act on the choices I want to make? I'm not going back to that Hell I came from! I'll be living with my mom and stepfather while being surrounded by people who never cared about me!"

Olivia turned around to walk away, but Death held a firm grip on her shoulder. The action was so rough that she was reminded of the squeezing pain her stepfather forced on her with every grip. "Let go of me," Olivia said, gritting her teeth.

"I'm afraid I can't do that."

"Yes, you can, and yes you will!" She stabbed him in the chest with one of her crutches, but that wasn't even to make him stagger.

"Even if you manage to escape, I'll follow you. No matter where you go, I'll be there. No one can hide from me. It's inevitable that we run into each other again."

Olivia let the rage build inside, causing her face to turn red. "Shut up!" She brought a crutch to his face and jammed it into his nose, but still, it wasn't enough to make him move. "Let me go!" she yelled. Olivia repeatedly thrust her crutch into him, but nothing could make him falter. "You're an idiot! I'm not going back to my life as the old me! Never!"

Death grunted and leaped into the air. Her eyes followed him and opened wide when he tackled her to the ground. She struggled to get out of his hold, but to no avail. He had her on her back while she fearfully looked into his eyes. She saw the reflection of a dark world in his pupils.

"You're not doing yourself any good," he said. "This isn't the right way to do things. You can't just steal someone else's life."

"Bullshit! That's what I'm doing right now!" Olivia swung her fist at him, but he grabbed her wrist and held it down. "So this is it? You're going to force me to make a decision that's not my own? Just like everyone else."

"No I'm not." His voice was blunt, but he moved decisively. "I'm not forcing you to do anything. I'm just going to show you something very important." When he said that, Olivia let out a shriek as she tried to regain the strength to move. She fought back valiantly while a pool of black clouds surrounded her body. Initially, they came from behind her back, but they flowed out to swallow her. Fear became an overwhelming feeling as her eyes grew wide.

"Let me go! I'll kill you! I'll—" Before she could finish, the sound of glass cracking reached her ears, but when she looked around, the scenery showed that she was still in the park. But the ticking didn't stop and her body began to feel weightless before the black clouds engulfed her.

When the darkness faded, Olivia found herself in an empty void, much like the one she spent time with Haniel in. The only difference was that this was black instead of white. In this world, the strength in her legs returned, but she still stumbled as she stood. Being stuck to a wheelchair for so long almost made her forget how to walk.

Other than that, the void wasn't completely empty. The last time she was there, clocks were plastered all over the place, but this time, nothing but mirrors hovered above her. One of them gently floated downward and landed in front of her. She stared into it and realized that she was looking at her real self, not Brennan. She started to hyperventilate. Seeing her old self mae bad memories surface. Memories that reminded her that her old life was a hell she didn't want to return to. She ran her nails across her cheek, letting a tear roll down her face.

"How are you feeling?" Death asked, walking out of the glass.

Olivia jumped at his sudden appearance, but quickly turned that fear into resentment. "Where am I? Why am I myself? What did you do to me?" She wanted to grab his throat, but she already felt the physical limitations of who she really was. Brennan stood taller and stronger, while she was a few inches shorter and nowhere near as strong as he was.

"You're in the world of the dead. In the world of the living, you're bound to the body you reside in, but here, it's only your soul that's seen."

Olivia brought her hands to her face to examine them. She patted her entire body and looked down at her legs. Death was right. She was herself. "But why?" Olivia walked forward, while Death towered over her like a massive wall.

"Because in the afterlife, your soul is the only thing that comes here."

"Well, if I'm already here, can't I just find Brennan and leave? After all, he is stuck in this world, isn't he?"

"I know the logistics of this place is hard to comprehend, but all you have to know is that it's not possible to get to him. For now, he's lost, because his mind created a prison for himself. Just like how this endless void is your prison."

Olivia sighed and looked away. "So that's it, then? My life was my own prison, and now I'm stuck in this world in another form of torture. Why can't I just live the life I want to live?" After ending her sentence, she took a glance at Death and noticed a rare frown on his face.

"Because the life you want to live is Brennan's, not yours."

Olivia pushed him, but he didn't budge.

"Fuck you!" she spat. "I can't believe I have to deal with this! I wish Haniel was still here! At least he had some personality to him. You're just about as interesting as a brick."

Physical touch didn't make him falter, but the mention of Haniel forced a shake in his legs. "I know you're frustrated, but please do as you're told."

"But I don't want to! I want to make my own decisions, and if one of them is taking Brennan's place, then so be it!"

Death shook his head in disappointment. "You're being difficult."

Olivia sighed with a form of anger accompanied by tears. "I just want a decent life. That's all I want." The years of torment she endured hit her all at once. She let out an ear-shattering scream and cried. "Everything was taken from me! My childhood! My dad! My happiness! Everything was stolen!"

She jumped up and got ready to assault Death. Her fist flew through the air, but didn't connect with his body. Instead, a hole grew in his chest, which caused her hand to slip through and crash into the mirror. Even in this world, she felt pain, and the blood dripping from her hand proved that. *I guess I'll always be the victim.*

"How long will I be here?" she asked Death. Olivia tried her best to change the subject, but she knew it would ultimately come back to her getting scolded for wanting to be selfish.

"You'll only be here until you start thinking straight."

"And what if that never happens?" She balled her hands into fists and glared at him.

"In that case, I'll make it happen."

His words held an eeriness that put Olivia on edge. Ever since Death grew up and left behind the child he once was, he'd been enigmatic. "What's that supposed to mean?" Olivia said, gritting her teeth.

"It simply means that I'll do my best to change your view of the world."

Olivia let out a sigh. "People's perception of things doesn't just change suddenly. I'd rather spend the rest of eternity in this void than go back to my old life. At least here there's no one to hurt me." Olivia stood tall as if to defy him before walking away. She sat a few feet from Death and slumped forward. "This world is rotten. No one cares about people like me, so they can all leave."

Death's mouth turned into a frown for a moment. "I hope you make the right decision."

"I'm sure my 'right decision' is different from your 'right decision'." A tear slowly rolled down Olivia's cheek while she stared at her reflection in the broken glass.

DEAD WEIGHT

B rennan awoke to the sunlight looming over him. The flowers, island, moon and Life were completely gone. Despite spending hours watching the stars with her, it felt like he'd slept the whole night.

His hands and feet felt rejuvenated enough to give him the strength to stand. He brushed the grass stuck to his clothes and pulled out the harmonica. His lips pressed into it before he exhaled air a puff of air through the instrument. As always, the notes carried themselves, but this time, they flew over the mountain ranges to his right. *Another hike.* Even though he felt a tad disappointed at having to walk for miles again, at the very least he had a sense of direction.

He made his way to the base of the mountain and looked upward. There wasn't a clear trail to follow. He just knew that he had to walk in that direction. Brennan placed one foot on the stone to begin his ascent upward. The vast majority of his steps were carefully calculated, while a few were part of a small lucky streak keeping him from plummeting down. Rocks and dust slipped off to the side, making a small landslide. He made sure to keep staring ahead, but the urge to gaze below held dominion over him. After traveling a few yards from his starting point, he took a deep breath. He'd never suffered a fear of heights before, but scaling a mountain wasn't something he expected to do.

He took one more step, which ended his lucky streak. His foot slid to the side causing his leg to fly over the edge. The action accidentally made him spin when he tried to regain balance. As a last effort to stay on top, he grabbed one of the rocks and held it as tightly as he could. Dangling over the edge, and screaming internally, Brennan rotated his body so that his stomach faced the mountain. From there. he had the ability to get a good grip onto another stone, although holding on with both hands only gave him the strength to stay in place. He still couldn't pull himself up.

He gritted his teeth and tried to muster more power, but it felt as if weights were strapped to his waist. A pair of footsteps tapped against the stone until they came to a stop at the edge. When Brennan looked up, he saw Lilith, standing over him like a giant.

"Having fun there?" she asked.

Brennan's fear suddenly boiled into anger. "When I pull myself back up, I'll kill you!" He clenched his teeth as he tried to lift his body weight, but much to his surprise, he couldn't do a pull-up.

"I don't think it'll be that easy." She pointed to his waist, and his eyes followed her finger. Upon glancing down, he realized why he felt so heavy. He wasn't just lifting his own weight. He saw his mother, sister, and Jessica holding on to him. They must've always been there, and his mind just now manifested them into tangible beings. Their bodies were nothing more than dead weight pulling him down.

"Oh my," Lilith said with an evil laugh. "It appears they're holding you back. Will you be able to let them go?"

Brennan felt his fingers weakening. Even if he had time to knock them down, he probably wouldn't have any grip strength left. His fingers gradually started to slip back, until he let go of the rock. He shut his eyes, and felt himself fall, but that intense feeling was short-lived. Lilith's hand wrapped tightly around his wrist, and when he opened his eyes, he saw Lilith, as the center of his lifeline. She was the only thing keeping him from going in a downward spiral. She wore her signature grin, and Brennan felt horrified to know that he was at her mercy.

"Well then," she said with a smile. "Will you let them go? You know they're only holding you back."

Brennan told himself that they weren't really his loved ones. They were just figments of his mind torturing him, but the thought of letting them go hurt. Seeing their distraught faces stuck in his mind like glue. Even though they weren't real, he still wanted to save them, and the approval of his mother would be a nice touch. She may have beat him, but he never stopped fantasizing about the life could've lived had she loved him. And Nora... now that he'd seen just how wrong he was for lashing out at her, he wanted to mend their relationship. Acknowledging his faults was just as painful as losing Jessica, but he'd already accepted her death.

"I'm sorry," he whispered. With a flick of his ankle, he tossed Jessica aside, and she turned to stone. The air whistled as her statue plummeted, only to stop when she broke into pieces on the ground. After he heard her shatter, he looked at his mom. She smiled at him. The sudden change in her expression froze him. *A smile? She never smiles.* Brennan closed his eyes, but the image of her happy face was already burned into his mind.

Brennan, I love you. He heard her voice whisper in his thoughts.

She's not real. She doesn't love me. He needed to deny her fake sigh of affection, but the desire for her love to be real held a firm grip on his heart. He greatly underestimated the value of receiving a genuine smile. He got ready to move his foot, but stopped. Her happy face never wavered, even as a tear drop slipped out of her eye. Brennan wanted to cry too, but he wouldn't let himself do so. His mom never loved him, and he had to accept that. Despite how easy it was to long for a relationship that could never be, he did the harder thing and accepted her hatred.

"I'm sorry, Mama." He repeated that phrase as he stomped her face until she let go. Her body flew to the ground as it quickly turned to stone. This time, he didn't even wait until he heard her crash. He immediately turned his attention to Nora. She held onto his ankles, so it should've been easy to shake her off, but the mistakes he made in their relationship were heavier than her body.

"I promise I won't leave you," she said.

Brennan finally let his tears out upon hearing her words. "You left me, but you still loved me."

"I'm sorry," she said. Her lips quivered and her pupils dilated.

Brennan found it hard to make eye contact, but he forced himself to do so. "No, you don't have to say that. I'm sorry I blamed you for my faults. I destroyed our relationship. It's my burden to bear."

"But you're my brother. Just let me take you with me."

"I can't do that." Brennan gritted his teeth. He always wanted her to come back, but nothing in this world would follow him into his real life. Even though he feared that he may have ruined their relationship for good, he would rather live feeling guilty in the real world, than staying in a paradise that wasn't real.

Unlike everyone else who held on to him, Nora hoisted herself up, until she was able to climb over him and stand on the ledge with Lilith.

"Well, isn't that unfortunate? It looks like you couldn't stop your sister," Lilith taunted. "Will you help me do something?" she asked Nora. Nora nodded. "On the count of three, I want you to kick him down. I'll let go of my grasp, then you stomp on his face." Lilith laughed, but Nora remained silent. Even though she seemed eager to do her part, she chose not to say anything.

"Ready?" Lilith asked. "One, two, three!" As soon as she finished counting, Brennan used his remaining strength to yank Nora off the edge. He couldn't change the past. Just like how he couldn't change the fact Jessica died, he knew he couldn't change the fallout with his sister.

With a heavy sigh, he pulled Nora off the edge, and the moment she stumbled, he felt euphoric. As if a great weight was lifted from his chest. Lilith waved at Brennan as he and Nora fell. Next to him, his sister turned into stone during their freefall, and in a panic, he flapped his arms as if he could fly. His harmonica flew out of his pocket, but the wind passed through it, creating a few notes which brought on a response. But this time it came from the ground below. *Is that where I'm supposed to go?*

He shielded his face with his arms and braced for impact, but no impact followed. When he moved his arms out of the way, he found himself standing on the island where he would talk to Life.

"Good job on finally letting go of your sister," a figure said in the dark.

"Life?" Brennan asked. "You sound different." But it soon became clear that he wasn't talking to Life. Lilith stepped out of the shadows, and Brennan put his guard up, ready to fight.

"If you hadn't let go of the grudge you had with your sister, I'd have finished you off. It's too bad I have to let your despair consume your mind, just so I can get rid of you."

Brennan narrowed his eyes on her. Now that he finally let his past grievances go, she barely held any power over him, and thus couldn't finish him off when he hit the ground. "Stay away!" he yelled. Brennan got into a fighting stance, and Lilith giggled.

"It's funny how, despite your progress, you still have struggles. Doesn't that make you laugh? Even I was able to invade your safe space because of the feelings you hold inside!" Lilith smirked and held a firm gaze on him. "How do you expect to overcome your struggles when you still find a way to get caught up in them? Do you even know that I exist just because of you? That I'm a manifestation of everything wrong in your life?"

"If you don't keep your distance, you'll regret it," Brennan muttered, but she crept forward. Seeing that there was no way to reason with her, he took the initiative and dashed forward, making the grass flow with the breeze as he went by. He didn't want to listen to her anymore. He knew that now was the time to kill her; otherwise, he'd be stuck in a never-ending cycle of self-hate. He tackled her to the ground and sat tall, in a mounted position. He looked down at her, reading to attack with a flurry of punches, but hesitated when he noticed her face rapidly switching, from Nora, his mom, Jessica, and back to herself.

"No!" he yelled. "You can't control me anymore!"

"If that's the case, then why did you stop? Shouldn't you be killing me now?"

Brennan thought about her words for a moment. After everything he'd seen, he knew that getting rid of his problems was impossible. They would also appear in his life no matter what, and new ones would always emerge. At first he felt despair when realizing he couldn't kill Lilith for good, but then he came up with a new plan. If he couldn't solve his grievances, he could at least control the effect they had. "I can't kill you... but I can control you."

"Do you even know what you're talking about, or are you too much of a coward to fight back?"

Brennan wrapped a hand around her throat and squeezed hard. "I'm not a coward and I know what I'm doing."

Despite the pressure he applied to her throat, Lilith found it easy to grin. "If that's the case, why don't you go ahead and get rid of me?"

"Because it's impossible to destroy every ounce of guilt and trauma that I feel." Brennan took his other hand and choked her. He breathed heavily as the air around him turned cold. His breath became visible, and came out like fog.

"So do you give up?" She raised her hands and gently cradled Brennan's head. Her fingers ran through strands of his hair like a mother holding her infant.

"No, giving up is not an option." After saying those words, he tightened his grip, and Lilith's throat seemed to shrink into the width of a paper. "I just know that it's futile to try and completely erase my past. It will always be there, and nothing I do will ever change that. But I can still take control!"

Lilith let her hand touch his cheek and her voice echoed in his mind. *You're so young, so misguided, and so naïve.* She gently caressed his face and Brennan grinded his teeth.

"No, I know what I'm doing. Your insults won't hurt me anymore." By now, his body shook by a combination of the force he exerted on her, the cold, and her eerie words.

Insult? No, I'm just telling you the truth. You push everyone away, and in the end you'll be alone. Just you and your guilty thoughts. "Her giggle infected his thoughts.

"No! Shut up!" Brennan yelled violently, his spit splattering on her face.

Why can't you see how weak and stupid you are? You only bring harm to those around you. Give up.

Her laugh rang in his brain, but Brennan fought of the urge to flinch. His only objective was to take over her before she took over him. Brennan slammed her neck further into the grass, and put all his weight on her body. This time, the only resistance she had was her negative words. Physically, she couldn't fight anymore.

You're just a boy. A boy who'll never be strong enough. A boy who just wants to act tough when, in reality, you're just running around pretending to be someone you're not.

"I should kill you," Brennan muttered. He stared at her with tears seeping from the corners of his eyes.

But you won't. If he had gotten into this fight earlier, he would've impulsively lashed out at her for saying that phrase, but he just stared at her intently. *It's okay to give up.*

Without saying anything, Brennan squeezed with the last bit of strength left in his hands.

The flowers that dotted the island had their petals turn whiter than Life's hair and, as they began to shine, he remembered her. He brought himself back to when he initially met her at the park. It was after he died for the first time. The image of her child self in a white dress was still clear as day. Back then he'd seen her as an innocent child playing with her brother, but no that but now that she had grown up and became more accustomed to the harsh realities of life, she was mentally and physically more mature. Yet, that childlike happiness still lingered.

Brennan looked at the flowers, and they began to blossom. All he could think about was Life. She taught him to go... Not only in this world, but in his own as well. New flowers grew from the dirt, and stood proudly among the grass.

Will you give up now? Lilith's voice whispered in his head, interrupting his thoughts.

"No," Brennan said in a cold voice. He sat tall and looked down at her.

What are you going to do then?

Brennan looked down at her pale face and kept a stern expression. "I'm going to take control of my life."

You can't do that. Your trauma and grief will swallow you whole.

"No, not anymore." He sniffled when his tears made his nose runny, and Lilith smiled. He didn't know if it was because she was trying to break his conviction, or if she was just laughing at his troubles one last time.

So, you're getting rid of me? Despite her imminent defeat, she held a straight face as the wind blew by.

"No," Brennan said bluntly.

Then what are you going to do?

Lilith cocked her head to the side like a curious child, but that didn't deter Brennan. "I can't get rid of my past. I can't live without guilt, fear, or grief, but I can learn to live with it. I'll control you, not the other way around!" Brennan's eyes bulged out at the sight of her, while his hair turned white.

Prove it. Lilith smiled, but Brennan knew it was an act to play with his negative emotions.

"This is my curse. This is my burden, and I'll accept it for what it is." Brennan knew he had to erase her control over him. He knew she was him, with the only difference being that she represented all his negative emotions, and so, he decided to change her energy into something else.

He wrapped his hands tighter around her throat, causing her to let out a weak breath. The puff of air she exhaled flew into the atmosphere and floated over the grass. From there, it sprouted new life. A variety of flowers grew from the ground. From the reddest roses to the yellowest sunflowers, life flourished. After, feeling a sense of accomplishment, he squeezed tighter, causing her throat to become just as weak as a shriveled up raisin. As she exhaled again, the world was filled with more life. The grass became taller and greener. Her body slowly began to fade, starting with her feet. The transparency started in her toes, and slowly drifted upward until she was completely gone, leaving nothing behind except her dress. And in the wake of the aftermath, a young woman stood a in the dark, barely being illuminated by the moonlight. Her white dress and rounded cheeks showed off innocence. She looked more like a tall child rather than an adult.

"So, you've done it," she said.

"Who are you?" Brennan asked in a commanding tone. He stood up from the ground while another flower grew next to him.

"You beat her. It's over, isn't it?" Once the moonlight finally illuminated her full figure, Brennan realized it was Life who spoke to him.

"Yes, you're right, but I didn't destroy her. I just took control." Brennan's hands shook, but Life skidded across the water to steady them. They trembled for a few more moments, but once her skin touched his, Brennan's hands remained still. "Guilt and grief aren't things that can just be forgotten," he whispered. "I've won, but that doesn't mean I've purged my demons."

"I see," Life said. She let go of him and looked to the moon, like it was a beacon of hope. "What are you going to do now?"

"Since the job is done, I'll find a way back to the train station. Hopefully, things will finally be over by then." Life nodded and patted his shoulder. "But I need to ask you something," Brennan said.

"Go ahead."

"Once I get there, will there be a way for me to get back to the real world, so I can help Olivia?"

"Yes. Actually, I was hoping you'd ask that." She smiled at him, and Brennan quickly returned the gesture.

"All right then," he said with a newfound confidence. "Tell me how I'll do that, and I'll be on my way."

"You can always get a new ticket. The main booths will give you a pass to Heaven or Hell, but there are some special vendors that are willing to sell other tickets. That harmonica Haniel gave you is quite valuable. You could definitely trade it for something good."

Brennan pulled out the harmonica and stared at it. The instrument shined in the moonlight before he tightly wrapped his hand around it. Even though he was glad to finally leave, he couldn't help but reflect on the lessons he learned. "It's settled, then. Just show me the way to the station."

Life placed a hand on his shoulder. "You don't have to walk there. Lilith was the only thing keeping you from coming back, but since your mindset's changed, the station will come to you. Just take this moment to rest."

Brennan obliged and sat crisscrossed on the ground. He closed his eyes and took in a deep breath. His stomach bulged out as air filled him, then emptied once he exhaled. "Now, lie down," Life instructed him, and he followed. Brennan let his back touch the grass, and slowly let sleep overtake him.

When he opened his eyes again, he sat on a bench in the train station. He stood and looked around until his attention was caught by Life, waving at him. She waited next to a man with dark hair, bearing an expressionless face. Brennan briskly walked toward them, and Life gave her usual giggle.

"Who are you?" Brennan asked, addressing the man.

"It's me, Death," he said.

Brennan thought back to the park in the white void. Just like Life, Death was only a child then, yet here he was as a grown man. "So, you're big now too." Brennan said.

"Yes." His answer was short and blunt, and Brennan didn't feel the need to press further, so he followed them the moment they beckoned him over. They walked past booths and wandering souls until they stopped at a vacant machine. It had a tray with a sign above that read "exchange".

"What's this for?" Brennan asked.

"You put something of value on it, then say what you want," Life said, with Death nodding in agreement.

"So, I can ask for my ticket?"

"Yes," Death spoke. "You could even ask for a ticket that brings you back to your body."

"Wait, does this mean I can go back to my life?"

"Yes." Despite the good news, Death's voice was still cold as ice.

Brennan had to think for a moment. He wanted to help Olivia, but the thought of having all his troubles over was just too tempting. He looked up at Death and asked, "Is there anything I can do for her?" Brennan wanted to his question to gauge whether or not it'd be in his best interest to go back to his old life.

"I can't think of a definite answer right now," Death responded. "I feel that it would be in your best interest to return to your body, but I can't deny that Olivia isn't in the best headspace currently. She tried to run away to take over your life."

"My life? Take it over?" The words alone shocked him. He remembered Olivia being a docile and kindhearted girl the first time he met her. He'd even felt bad for pushing her around, so he didn't expect her to take the initiative to run away.

"Yes, she held a great amount of jealousy when living your life. In her eyes, your life was nearly perfect, and she was too burdened by her past to carry on."

Brennan sighed at the word "burden". For so long, he'd only focused on himself while ignoring the pain of others. After seeing the world through Olivia's eyes, and experiencing firsthand the abuse of her stepfather, he understood why she'd be jealous of him. Both of them had things rough, but now Brennan was sure they'd be able to survive in any situation other than their own.

"I guess you never really know a person until you set foot in their skin," Brennan muttered to himself. Initially, he would've felt like she'd backstabbed him for trying to take over his life, but he didn't blame her. After all, there were people and things he found in her life that comforted him, such as Jessica. Brennan brushed aside his desire to put everything behind him and start his life. If he ever wanted to do something for someone else, this was the right moment. "I want to help her, so how can I do that?" he asked.

Death gave a short hum. "I can't think of a good answer. In fact, I'd even recommend you just go home."

"No, I won't do that." Brennan instantly shook his head, and upon his quick proclamation, Life, who had been entirely silent, clapped her hands in agreement.

"If that's the case, I suggest you find a way to make it easier on her, should she choose to live her life." Her childish happiness began to seep through. It was as if Brennan's change in character was worthy of a celebration.

"Okay, so where will I wake up once I get back to the real world?"

"I took Olivia's soul with me, so I can talk to her privately without interruption. She left your body in a park in a small town in Alabama. You'll end up there."

Brennan stood stoically with his chin held high and a firm gaze. "I guess that settles it. I'm ready." With a wave of Death's fingers, Brennan's harmonica floated out of his pocket, and onto the tray that popped out of the machine. It instantly sucked the item in and whipped out a ticket in return. When Brennan read it, he saw his name.

"Don't lose it this time," Death lectured.

"I'll make sure I won't." Brennan's voice was firm, with a great amount of conviction. He took another look at Life, the woman he once saw as a little girl. A smile slowly crept across his face, but eventually, he couldn't hide it. "You helped me when I couldn't even help myself," he said to her.

"I only wanted to see you succeed. After all, I don't like seeing others in pain." She bopped his nose with her finger, causing him to smirk once more.

"Now, I'm the one being spoiled. Thank you." Brennan went in for one last hug before retreating.

"I wish you best the of luck!" Life said, happily. She jumped and clapped her hands together.

"Will I ever see you two again?" Brennan asked both of them.

"Of course, you will!" Life exclaimed. "But hopefully, it'll be when you die of natural causes rather than a premature death!"

"All right then, I guess this is goodbye for now." Brennan turned around and walked away, as Life and Death waved at him. When they were out of view, he waited in front of the tracks until a train came by awaiting his entry. After that, he was off to return to his body.

ACT 3

WHAT COULD HAVE BEEN

O livia sat in the center of the black void, and, despite being left in darkness, her eyes were able to see, like a cat with night vision. The clocks ticked incessantly as she zoned out. *If Death wants to keep me here, then I'll let him.* To Olivia, anything was better than living her life. She never knew she'd start to resent Death, the little boy whom she thought so dearly of. If only she could live in her own fantasy, just like she did in the white void. At least if that were the case, she could fine some solace, but she just had to be trapped with her own thoughts. Her reflection in the mirror stared back at her, and she felt it tormenting her mind. All she saw was a broken girl with nowhere left to turn. A girl who was just a victim of circumstance.

"If I can't live as him, then I don't want to live at all." Olivia whispered those words to herself and let them linger in the air.

"Are you sure about that?" a voice asked behind her. She quickly turned her head to be greeted by the sight of Death standing patiently.

"Yes, I'm sure." Olivia clenched her fist as she finally let the fiery hatred Brennan had for the world infect her. She kept her voice and head low.

"Do you intend to take your life again?" Death asked.

Olivia thought back to her suicide. After she'd died the first time, she felt like it was the biggest mistake of her life, and at the time, all she wanted to do was go home, but now she believed that her all-loving personality brainwashed her. She didn't have that assertiveness Brennan wanted her to have back then. But now she did, and she intended to use it for her own desires.

"I'll just say that the answer isn't a definite 'no'." She tried to read Death's face to see if it showed any altercation to his attitude, but he remained expressionless. "I just can't handle this," Olivia said. "I want to live the life I want. I don't want to shrink into a smaller version of myself anymore."

"That won't happen." Death's steel gaze never wavered as he spoke. Instead, they kept their attention on her without breaking.

Olivia sighed and turned her head. "That can't be true. All you people want me to do is go back to the hell I used to live in. There's no point in trying." She looked into the mirror again and felt despair. She still saw a broken girl reflected in the glass. Olivia had a strong urge to punch her through it. *Do it! Destroy it!* She raised her hand before lowering it. Even doing something as easy as striking was too hard for her.

"I might not be able to get your life together by myself, but I can help, and the choice to capitalize on my aid will ultimately be up to you." Death reached out his hand to hold her, but she scooted back.

"I'd kill myself right now if I had the chance. But like you said, Brennan needs help, and I guess I'm forced to do what everyone else wants." Just that statement alone made Olivia feel pathetic. One side of her wanted to turn on everyone, yet the other side wanted nothing more than to let her empathy kick in to protect those around her.

"Things have changed." Death's sudden shift in tone and subject caught Olivia off guard, but that didn't mean her attention wavered.

"What are you talking about? What's changed?"

"Brennan's escaped the hell his mind put him through. He's stronger than we all thought, and now he's going to return to the real world. He'll be back in his body. There's no need for you to help him anymore."

Olivia put her hand on her hips. She felt betrayed once she got the news of Brennan's success. After having an exhausting conflict within herself, finding out that he no longer needed aid made her feel like she wasted her time. "So now what? Am I going back to my body?"

"If you wish." Had this happened weeks ago, she would've been happy, but now, this just meant she couldn't live Brennan's life anymore.

"What would you do if I just went to my body, only to kill myself?"

Death folded his arms across his chest. "I wouldn't do anything. Once you board the train you're meant to take, I'll never see you again, until the day you die."

"So, you're not going to stop me?" On the outside she kept a straight face, but deep down she wanted him to notice her pain.

"No, but I do encourage you to live the rest of your life." Olivia glared at him.

What game is he playing? She expected Death to be more aggressive in his attempt to stop her. Maybe by physical restraint. She didn't expect him to just give her a choice.

"You're planning something, aren't you?" Olivia asked, balling her hands into a fist.

"You're right," he said after a moment's hesitation. "I was planning on showing you what a world without you would look like. However, it's up to you if you want to see it. Would you care to entertain me?"

Olivia's mind told her to say "no", but her mouth remained shut. She could've been decisive by choosing to end her life quickly, but here she was, letting self-doubt creep in.

"Fine," she said, giving in to curiosity. "But don't expect me to change my mind." She gritted her teeth, and Death held his hand out. By now she'd become familiar with the odd gestures otherworldly beings made. She knew that taking his hand would be necessary for the time being. Death only had to wait for a few seconds before she made her choice, and when she finally placed her hand in his, he squeezed it tightly. His arm pulled them together, and he hugged her. Olivia felt a strong sense of calmness, like an elderly person accepting the life they'd lived. A black fog rolled in and enveloped them. At first, his body felt tangible, but his touch left her senses quickly, and once her vision returned, she found herself in a new place instead.

Olivia felt weightless, like a cloud flying high above. In fact, she even had a bird's eye view of her surroundings, but her sense of sight wasn't the only thing that told her where she was. She could feel the cool breeze of Washington consume her as though she had a real body, and the laughter of children sounded everywhere. She found herself staring at the road in front of her parent's house. She remembered playing here with the other children, and one child in particular took a liking to her. Olivia didn't remember that much about the girl. All she could recall was the fact that she immigrated from Japan to the U.S. She pondered how their relationship came to an end. *Did she move away?*

"Hey! Hina, look at me!" Olivia's child self said. She rode on a tricycle while Hina pushed herself around on her tiny metal scooter. The idea of being inseparable to a childhood friend was a foreign concept to her. Everything that happened right in front of her felt completely new. The present Olivia floated toward the girls, watching them playing. Hina smiled, as she rode around Olivia in circles. They giggled like while being hyper, just like normal children, but something caught Olivia's attention. Both her and the younger version of her, couldn't stop staring at a massive purple bruise hidden under the end of Hina's skirt. "What's that?" the young Olivia asked, pointing at her thigh.

Hina came to an abrupt stop as she dropped her scooter on the con-create. She ruffled her skirt, pushing it down to hide the bruise. "I don't know." Her quiet voice trailed off, but being the curious child that she was, Olivia pressed forward.

"Did you walk into something? Did that weird kid down the street ride his bike into you?" Olivia sat down and put her hand on the purple spot. Hina jumped at her touch. That's when Olivia reacted with fear. She knew that she'd hurt her friend, but didn't know why the bruise caused so much pain. Hina stood with her head low, crying her eyes out. The present Olivia knew exactly what kind of turmoil Hina must be going through, especially after she witnessed Brennan's abusive childhood through her own eyes.

As the children sat staring at each other, their short moment of vulnerability was interrupted when a silver minivan parked beside him. Inside sat an Asian woman with bags under her eyes. She bore an expressionless face, with her small mouth in a short frown.

"Hina, it's time to go home." Upon seeing her, the young Olivia waved, but the woman didn't return the gesture. She may have seen her as an innocent mother, but the present Olivia had a sneaking suspicion that the woman wasn't as innocent as she seemed. She could tell from the fear in Hina's eyes and the young girl gripping onto her friend's jacket sleeve.

"Please let us play a little longer!" she begged her mom. The woman gave an irritated look that she made no effort to hide. With a sigh, she stepped out of the car, and pulled her child up by the wrist. Hina began kicking and screaming. The young Olivia immediately sensed danger. Even though she initially didn't believe the woman to be a danger, she trusted her friend over her own instincts. If Hina cried so much at her mother's touch, then something was wrong.

"Stop!" Olivia's child version ran up to Hina and yanked her out of her mother's grasp. The woman grunted in rage and stomped forward.

"Get back here!" she screamed. Hina's mom raised her hand at them, causing Olivia to pull her friend behind her back. She used her face as a meat shield. The woman's fist struck her in the eye, causing a pang of pain to shoot through her face. Olivia let out a loud cry, as the front door of her house opened.

"What the hell are you doing?" Olivia's mother yelled. She stomped off the front porch and onto the road. The two women stood staring at each other before starting their screaming match.

"Don't you dare hit my daughter!" After loudly proclaiming her demand, Olivia's mom gripped the woman's earing and tore it completely off. She immediately clutched her torn ear before retaliating with a strike to the face. Olivia and Hina huddled together crying, as other parents from the neighborhood came out to investigate their screams. Men and women running across the pavement echoed all around as the other children's fathers stepped in to break up the fight. The present Olivia did her best to zone out the sound, but couldn't do it completely. Only when the world turned into a blur and everything darkened did the chaos around her cease. Only then she found herself in the black void with Death again.

The moment Olivia was able to completely comprehend that she wasn't in the past anymore, she breathed heavily, like a child waking from a terrible nightmare.

"I'm sure you'd rather be here than there," Death said plainly.

"Yeah, you're right, but why would you show me that? Why would you show me some little girl who was being physically abused? Not only that, but I don't even remember her."

Death looked into her eyes without blinking. "I'm trying to show you that you're the reason that little girl was not taken home that day. As scared as you were at the time, your actions, intuition, and empathy prevented that child from receiving a fate that was much worse."

Fate. That word echoed in her mind. Throughout her entire journey, she always believed her fate to be in someone else's hands. After all, everything she did was for the sake of others, such as Brennan. But never entertained the idea that someone else could also be a victim of circumstance.

"So what? I got the entire neighborhood involved, but what happened then?"

Death quickly waved his hand in the air, causing a tear in reality. It acted as a television, showing the aftermath of what happened. Everything went by at lightning-fast speed, but the images all stuck in Olivia's head. From Hina crying to the neighborhood coming together, and finally to Hina moving in with a different family.

"You may have not been able to see it then, but you acted on the fact that someone else was living in fear. Your compassion to help your friend turned her life into something she could enjoy. Although you never saw her again nor remember her, you at least changed her life."

Olivia knew what he was trying to do. She didn't want these past events to change her mind; however, she'd be lying if she said they didn't make her a little more hesitant. "I liked you more when you were a child!" She pouted and folded her arms across her chest.

"Childish innocence will always die. I had to grow up," he told her. "There's no stopping it. It's inevitable." Olivia glared at him before turning her back. "How about I show you another possibility?" he asked.

"The first one wasn't even necessary, so why show me another one?" she muttered.

"You're wrong. What I just showed you was important, and you should learn from it."

Olivia sighed. "No, it's not."

"You were able to touch someone's life, and you've done the same for others. It's best you realize that." Death stood tall and said those words proudly. "That's what I wanted you to learn, because if you bring love and peace to your parents, you can do the same to those around you. You may not know it, but, you've always made people's day due to your kindness."

Even though he gave a slew of pleasant words, Olivia didn't say anything or acknowledged it. Instead, she let her feeling of doubt take over.

"You seem to be at a loss for words."

"I am," she said. "But if you want to prove a point, I need you to make me believe it. Show me something else. Something that's more intense. Something that I played a bigger role in. Then, maybe I'll believe you."

'Very well then. That shouldn't be a problem." With a snap of his fingers, a black swirling portal appeared behind her. "Step through that entrance and see this for yourself."

Death pointed his slender finger at the darkness, and Olivia turned to look.

"Fine, but if there's nothing noteworthy inside, I'm ending myself again." The feeling of the portal instilled fear in her, but she knew that stepping through it would be necessary, so she did. But first, she closed her eyes and with a sigh, found herself in a boy's room. Post-it notes were plastered against the wall next to the bookshelf.

A boy with dark hair sat at his desk. His back was turned toward her, and his pencil ran back and forth across a piece of paper. His messy handwriting dappled all over the page, but abruptly came to a stop when he stood. He made a move to walk back to his post-it notes. Initially, Olivia's eyes were busy taking him in, but once she saw his face, his name immediately surfaced. Thorin, the boy wandering the halls of the school. He and the other freshman were split up into groups, while volunteers like Olivia showed them around.

The people who were meant to guide him had left him behind. She also recalled him to be an avid reader. The words scrawled on the notes were quotes from various books some of which she recognized. She definitely took a liking to him, but never considered him to be a friend. He was simply an acquaintance she met by pure coincidence, but why would that put her here? Why did Olivia get transported into his bedroom to view his past? After he sat on his bed, she noticed his usually calm demeanor change. He sunk his face into his hands before falling back to lie on the bed.

After rolling over onto his side, he curled into a ball and let tears flood his face. The sight of him crying caught Olivia off guard. She'd never seen him weep, let alone show that much emotion. In a sense, he was as calm as Death. Olivia floated around the room to see if she could find more of his belongings. Maybe then, she'd get a better sense of the kind of person he was, but the only thing she had were the quotes stamped against the wall. Each note harbored words that came from darker stories, meant for troubled teens. She recognized the novels they came from. Most were young adult books that made commentary on social issues like suicide and depression. Olivia wanted to read every single note both out of curiosity and concern, but her desire never came to fruition. Thorin got up from his bed and stormed out of the room.

Olivia followed him into the garage, taking into account that the house appeared mostly empty. But then again, it was the beginning of the school year. Maybe he just moved into town as an unknown student. No one would've met him yet, so she assumed that loneliness, or even homesickness, plagued him.

When they arrived in the garage, Thorin moved a few boxes aside. Initially, they blocked the front of a wooden workshop bench, but once he had a clear path, he headed toward it. On top of the bench laid a silver key which he used to open the locking in the corner of the room. Inside were numerous firearms. He stared at the guns for a long time before bringing his shaky hands to a shotgun. He ran his fingers from the barrel to the stock. The massive size of it, almost ran from one arm to the other. He took it, sat down, and spread it across his lap. Feeling horrified, Olivia went closer to him, hoping he was just there to admire it.

She wanted him to put it back into the case and lock it up, but he didn't. Instead, he rotated it so that the barrel faced him.

"I'm sorry," he muttered to himself. After those words left his mouth, he quickly replaced them with the barrel of the shotgun. His finger traced the entire body until it rested on the trigger. He closed his eyes and, in her head Olivia screamed 'no', but when he pulled the trigger, there wasn't a loud bang. Rather, only the clicking noise sounded. He proceeded to pull the trigger repeatedly, but nothing happened, and when he examined the gun, he realized there were no bullets. He dropped it to his side, and frantically searched the locker, but it seemed that the ammunition was hidden elsewhere. Relief washed over Olivia. She wanted to hug him. To whisper into his ear and remind him that everything would be all right, but she couldn't bring herself into the past. For now, he just got a lucky break.

Changing all these events wasn't something in her control. But now, she knew why she was here. She remembered asking Death to show her something intense. Something that she played a part in. *Was all of this happening behind my back?* After witnessing what could've been a grotesque scene, Olivia found out what exactly what Thorin was going through, and hoped that she stopped him at some point. If this was where Death wanted her to start, she prayed that it was just a sad beginning to a happy ending.

Thorin returned the gun to its resting spot, and after he cleaned up the scene, he sat in silence. It seemed like he was thinking of something. Olivia assumed he told himself, that he was a failure. That screwing up a suicide attempt meant he couldn't do anything right. He rested his hands on his lap and looked down. His body slowly started to shake. He let out a whimper, and that was when he began to cry.

"I'm sorry, I never knew." Olivia spoke as though he could hear her, and she genuinely wished he could. If she was able to travel to the past, she'd do it, just to help him. She'd befriend him, so she could say, *'In the end, everything will be all right.'*

THE RETURN

W hen Brennan awoke, he found himself lying on his back. After standing up and looking around, he realized Death was right. Olivia had left his body at a park, but he didn't mention that plenty of bystanders gathered in a crowd watching over his body. Some asked if he was okay, while others didn't have any words to say.

"What happened?" a woman asked.

"Nothing, I just fell." Brennan stood and dusted himself off. He noticed a pair of crutches on the ground beside him, but being brought back to Life gave him the strength he needed to control his body. It was the same rejuvenation he felt when Haniel resurrected him in Olivia's body weeks earlier, except this time, it felt more natural. Olivia's body had physical limitations he wasn't used to, such as less stamina and strength, and now, he felt like an actual person and not an imposter. His fingers moved without himself having to exert copious amounts of concentration. *Where am I?* Clearly, he found himself in a park, but that didn't help in pinpointing his exact location. He just knew he was in Alabama, like Death told him.

"Move! Move!" he heard a girl yell. Brennan turned his attention to the crowd of spectators and saw a short girl shoving past everyone. When she got to the front, he immediately knew who she was. It was Elly. *Why is she here?*

There were so many questions he should've asked Death before going back to his world. First off, Olivia left Florida, and she was traveling with Elly, which already threw Brennan off. He never really talked to her. At most, they exchanged brief sentences when working together in class. Other than that, he barely knew her.

"Olivia!" she said.

Brennan was shocked to hear her say Olivia's name.

"Elly? What are you doing here? How—"

He meant to ask her how she knew about Olivia, but she cut him short. "Let's get out of here first. The only reason I found you was because of how much attention you attracted. Apparently, everyone saw you walk out of the store, and they recognized your face from the television. We need to get out of here, now!"

"But..." Even though his crutches laid in plain sight, Elly didn't notice him standing at all, and Brennan guessed that it must've been the adrenaline rush taking over her. They ran into town, and she yanked him into an alley. He tried to leave, but she grabbed his arm.

"Stop, stay here. We need to hide."

"What's going on?" he asked. His mind became a jumbled mess. *Why is she here? How'd she come to know Olivia? What the hell do I do next?* All these questions and more dominated his mind.

"You go first. Tell me why you left the store, why you can run, and why I see you as Brennan now."

"Elly, how do you know about Olivia? And what do you mean with you want to know why you see me as me?"

Her face became a blank stare. Even though he never interacted with her that much, he still knew that expression as confusion. He saw it numerous times when he tried to teach her about the new tools in their art software. She raised her hand to put it to his face, like she was amazed at seeing him. Brennan stepped back at the odd interaction and looked bemused.

"Elly, tell me why you're here." From how easily she got stressed in class, Brennan remembered her being prone to panic, so he kept his voice as calm as he could.

"Brennan." Her lip quivered as though his arrival suddenly shocked her. "Brennan, it's really you! Olivia told me everything about your situation while she was in your body! Oh God, it is you!" She slammed her body into his chest with a tight hug. Being caught off guard by her reaction, he improvised by gently rubbing her head. It might have been strange, but then again, what wasn't strange about this world?

"Thanks for the hug, but tell me everything that happened so far." He tried to get her to retreat from her grasp, but she wouldn't. Elly held him tightly and let his arms cradle her. Brennan felt uncomfortable, but he knew that he would get an explanation soon.

She began to recount the events that led up to this moment. She started with seeing Olivia at school without knowing who she really was, explaining the lovely feelings she had for him, the betrayal she felt when Olivia revealed the truth about their dilemma, and ending with the recent event at the park.

Brennan sighed. To him, Elly must've gone through hell. Just a couple of weeks ago, when he was in Olivia's body, he'd convinced Jessica to take him from Washington to Florida. He intended to meet up with Olivia so they could plan a way to switch bodies, but instead he just put Jessica through torment. A torment that she lived through, before she decided to end her life. He didn't want Elly to fall into despair. She and Olivia became runaways, just like him and Jessica. He looked down at her and rubbed his hand in circles against her back. He imagined her committing the same actions as Jessica, but he quickly brushed that sick thought away.

He took it upon himself to protect her, no matter what.

"I'm just so happy to see you." Elly beamed. "I just want you to be here with me."

"Don't worry, I'm not leaving."

After he reassured her, she retreated from her hug with a teary face. "We can go home soon."

Brennan shuddered at her suggestion. "Well, don't get too excited yet. We still have to figure out how we're going to get our lives back to normal. Plus, I still want to help Olivia."

When Brennan uttered those words, Elly paused for a moment before a disappointed look spread across her face. "Yeah, I know, but it doesn't hurt to celebrate a little, right?"

"I know. I'm sorry you had to go through this, but I can't leave Olivia behind."

"I understand. In fact, I don't even want to think about leaving her. If it wasn't for her help, I never wouldn't gotten you back!"

Elly held his hand, but Brennan pulled back. Her display of affection still came unwarranted to him. Being thrust into a hug made his stomach a little queasy. "To tell you the truth, I never noticed you before."

"I know. But now you can. And together we can get the job done." She leaned into him for another hug despite his continued shock at her acts of affection. But her touch still brought on memories of the time he spent with Jessica, and how her life went downhill since he convinced her to help him.

"I see. I'm not planning on forcing you to tag along while I help her. In fact, I don't want to trouble you anymore. You can leave, if you like."

"No, I'll come with you. What I said about her was true, and if you're in it, then I'm in it." She puffed her chest out, like a soldier standing in formation. But despite her proud appearance, Brennan was still worried. He didn't want her to feel pressured, or even hurt herself like Jessica did. He put Jessica through so much, and even though he rarely talked to her, he saw Elly as a fragile person he needed to protect.

"You don't have to do that." Brennan knew he needed and wanted help, but if he could convince Elly to go away, he would.

"But I have to! And I can't just leave without you! We're traveling together!"

"But..."

No buts! We'll do as I say!"

Brennan sighed and bowed his head in defeat. Never before had he let someone's assertive attitude beat him, so this feeling was completely new.

"Fine," he said. "Just be sure that you want to do this."

"Why are you so insistent that I leave?" Elly leaned forward into his face and stared him down.

"When I was Olivia, I asked a friend to help me travel the country, and it didn't end well." Even though she was practically in his face, Brennan still found a way to avoid eye contact. "Yes, a friend. Her name was Jessica. She was the one who bullied Olivia until she killed herself and I somehow fell in..." He began stuttering over his own words, but he decided telling the truth would be best. "I somehow fell in love with her, and I got her to drive me away from Olivia's hometown. I created such a mess that day. It was a mess I brought her into. The pressure was too much, and she ended herself."

Elly pulled herself back and picked at the ground with her toes. "When did this happen?"

"I met her the moment I switched bodies with Olivia. I woke up as her. And Jessica was waiting for her, but she got me instead."

"Was she waiting in the hospital for Olivia to wake up?"

"Yes."

Brennan started to visibly shake, and so Elly reached her hand out. She pushed herself up using her toes and laid a hand on Brennan's cheek.

"I treated her like shit when we first met, but I soon realized she just wanted to apologize to Olivia. She thought she was, but it was me she was talking to. She never got the chance to tell Olivia how she felt. All she did was tell me her true feelings."

"Brennan, I'm sor–"

"We can talk about this later." Brennan gently grabbed her hand and put it down. From there, Elly stood on her feet rather than her toes. They took a peek out the alley, but decided not to leave yet. There were still too many people wandering the streets.

"Let's wait," Elly said, blocking him with her arm. She stood like a sentry, but suddenly changed the mood when she declared, "Oh, I forgot to tell you. I have some skills that might be useful."

"Like what?" Brennan raised an eyebrow.

"Well, I helped Olivia find your ex-girlfriend by tracking down the places she took her photos. If you want to do something similar, I can help."

Brennan thought for a moment. He knew he wanted Olivia to look forward to coming back to life, but what could he change? He started counting off her hardships on his hand, raising one finger for each problem that needed fixing. By the time he lifted his thumb, he remembered that her stepfather was the worst part of her life.

"I just want to make her life bearable," Brennan said. "Trust me. I've seen first-hand the things she's gone through, and they're much worse than my hardships."

"Okay then, what do you want me to do?"

"Her stepfather is the reason her life is a living hell. We need to stop him. You said that you tracked down my girlfriend by using her photos. If I can find a picture of Mr. Benning, we can figure out where he is." Brennan didn't know what to do next. In fact, he already knew where Mr. Benning lived, but he didn't know what to do with that information. "Elly, what can you do when you track someone down?" Brennan walked closer to her as he hoped for an answer.

"Well, I know where they live according to the photos, because it shows their IP address. With that info, I can get into their electronics."

Brennan had no idea what she was talking about. All of it just seemed like a jumbled mess of words, but she spoke with so much confidence that he took her word for it. And if she could get into their electronic devices, maybe they could dig up something useful.

"Okay then, what do you need to get started?" Brennan asked.

"Get me a laptop with internet access, and some photos of Olivia's family online. Check social media accounts or news outlets or anything that showcases them. I'll worry about downloading the necessary operating systems and programs."

Brennan nodded. They popped their heads out of the alley to make sure no cops were waiting for them, and once everything was clear, they left without a trace.

Brennan and Elly had to wander the town on foot since Olivia popped her tire, but, amazingly enough, she didn't seem angry when telling Brennan how she found out. In fact, she seemed elated just to be around him, and he couldn't help but feel that she took this as some sort of date. Still, his concern never left him. Now wasn't the time to think of dates and love. His number one priority was to change Olivia's life while protecting Elly's sanity.

After minutes of her speaking at a pace that made Brennan wonder if she breathed in between, they finally found an electronics store. A giant sign hung from the roof that said, "Gizmo's Gadgets." The outside appeared to be horribly dirty, but the interior showed a completely different story. Every shelf was spotless, and the most recent pieces of technology were stacked in boxes on display cases.

While Brennan stood in awe, Elly walked straight to an aisle without hesitation, like she already knew the store. Seeing as there was nowhere else to go, Brennan followed her, but his eye caught one of the employees staring at them. The man eyed them with suspicion while hovering his hand over the phone. A bad feeling swelled in the pit of Brennan's stomach. He knew that they had to get what they needed as soon as possible.

"Let's be quick about this," he muttered.

"This might take some time. I don't have the money to buy any laptop. I need to find one that's powerful enough to do the job, but cheap enough for me to afford."

Brennan glanced over his shoulder and the employee frantically stabbed his fingers on the landline. "Well, you better start looking fast. I think that guy working the front counter recognizes us."

"Okay, then." Elly put on her strong face again and nodded. After that, she scoured the shelves while taking a careful look at each laptop. She put her face up to the glass like a detective searching for clues. Meanwhile, Brennan took advantage of his height by looking over the aisles to watch out for anyone who might be looking for them. He heard Elly muttering to herself as she checked each piece of hardware. "No, too expensive," she muttered after checking out a 2,000-dollar laptop. "This one is too weak," she complained at another. It hadn't been five minutes and she was already wasting their time with needless chatter.

An unmarked vehicle stopped in front of the store, turning Brennan's frustration into adrenaline. Two men in suits exited the car and headed toward the employee who used the phone. He looked horrified while the men stayed calm. They each opened the side of their suit, and Brennan noticed a gold flash just barely visible from his position. He stared more intently until he realized they were law enforcement. *Detectives?* Brennan ducked behind the shelf and whispered in Elly's ear.

"You have to hurry, now! There's some detectives in the store looking for us."

Elly's eyes popped out. She made a move to peek her head around the corner, but Brennan motioned her to keep searching through the shelves.

"I'll keep an eye out. Just get what we need." Brennan craned his neck to look around the corner. The detectives searched through the other side of the store. They thoroughly checked every corner, wall, and shelf. Brennan felt his sweat starting to drip from his forehead. "Hurry up!" he demanded.

"What am I supposed to do?" Elly asked, frustrated. "I found the perfect laptop for us, but it's stuck in the glass case. I can't open this shit!" One of the detectives shot his eyes in their direction and made eye contact with Brennan.

"Hey!" the man yelled.

"Fuck this," Brennan said, gritting his teeth. He pushed Elly aside and raised his hand high into the air. He closed it into a fist and punched through the glass case. A few drops of blood hit some of the devices.

"What the hell are you doing?" Elly yelled.

"That's the laptop you need?" Brennan pointed to the one directly below his hand.

"What?" Elly was still shaken by the situation, but Brennan remained decisive.

"Answer me! That's the laptop you need, correct?"

"Yes!" She nodded, and Brennan reached his bloody hand further into the display case. He lifted the laptop with the logo of a red spider printed on the top. He took the laptop and the charger from the case and tossed them to Elly.

"Let's go!" he yelled. She clutched everything to her chest while running alongside Brennan. In a panic, they ran to the back of the store, where they burst through the emergency exit. The alarm sounded, frightening everyone in the building, but they didn't pay any attention to them. And once they were outside, Brennan realized they couldn't outrun the cops. He knew they had to hide. He bit into his left sleeve and tore off a piece of his shirt before wrapping it around his injured hand.

"What are you doing?" Elly asked, still panicking.

"I'm making sure I don't leave a trail behind. We can't outrun them. We'll have to hide." His eyes darted around the parking lot as he finished tying the cloth around his skin. Eventually, his eyes settled on the dumpster a few feet from the door. "I hope you don't mind getting a bit dirty," he said.

"What?"

Brennan pointed to the dumpster and ran with Elly trailing him. He opened the lid with one arm and picked her up with the other. He lifted her like she was a child, then tossed her in like a rag doll. When her body plopped to the bottom, Brennan hoisted himself inside and shut the lid. They crouched in the dark atop the wet garbage bags. Silence enveloped them while the horrid smell assaulted their noses. Brennan listened intently for the detectives and heard them bursting through the door.

"Where the hell did they go?" one of them asked his partner. Brennan heard a sigh before the other man spoke.

"I don't know, but get on that radio. Alert everyone to keep an eye out for those kids."

"Got it." The static of the radio found its way into Brennan's ears. He shut his eyes and silently prayed that they'd get away.

After their scary but brief encounter with the men, their next battle became a hefty war of patience. Brennan and Elly sat in the darkness, with the unspoken agreement to stay quiet. Patrol cars boomed their sirens in the distance while they drove by. Cops stood outside the building talking to each other. Eventually, the noises ceased and, when Brennan was sure no one else waited for them, he opened the lid of the bin. Elly peeked out first, grasping at the chance to breathe in fresh air.

"That smell was awful," she whined.

"Let's go. It's already night, and we can't waste any more time." Brennan kept his voice stern, making it very clear that he wanted them to finish their task as soon as possible. The moonlight showed Elly's disgusted face stemming from the bin, and Brennan knew she wanted to rest, but at the same time, he single-mindedly sought to finish the mess he and Olivia had gotten into. He took a glance at Elly, but felt a tinge of compassion when his head replaced her face with Jessica's.

Brennan decided the next step was for them to hop out and find a place where she could rest. Dirty food, along with some unrecognizable liquid, covered his whole body. Elly wafted her nose and turned her back when he got closer.

"God damn, you smell bad," she said.

"Doesn't matter. Let's find a place where you can sleep."

A smile of relief spread across her face after hearing his suggestion. "Well, then let's find a motel to stay for the night." She trudged forward, clearly happy to take some time to relax.

"Hold on a minute." Brennan sprinted toward her and placed a hand on her shoulder. When she turned her head, he spoke. "I don't think anyone will let us rent a room. The whole country is searching for us."

Elly smirked. "I never said anything about renting a room. I got other skills that don't involve electronics. I'll get us a place."

THE DIRT
BENEATH THE
SURFACE

After following numerous street signs on their two-hour walk, they finally reached a motel. Brennan went straight for the stairs outside of the building, while Elly hid in a bush just like a thief from a fantasy novel stalking her enemy.

"What are you doing?" Brennan asked.

"I'm making sure no one's watching," she hissed under her breath.

"I'm pretty sure we'll be fine." He marched up the stairs and Elly ran out of the bush in a panic.

"Just wait!" she said.

"We're not living in a movie. Let's get in a room." Brennan sighed. He looked through the windows hoping to find an empty space.

"I found somewhere we can stay." He stopped in front of a door with the number ninety-six. From there, Elly got on her knees in front of the knob and took the two bobby pins holding her hair together. They fell to her shoulders, but she didn't let that distract her from messing with the pins. Brennan watched intently like she was performing a magic trick. She turned them into an odd shape and carefully inserted them into the lock.

"What are you doing?" Brennan asked.

"Computers aren't the only things I can work with. While Olivia was knocked out in that coma, I started to teach myself some new tricks."

"So, you taught yourself how to pick a lock?" Brennan meant to give out a short chuckle, but it came as more of a grunt. Everything she did came as a pleasant surprise to him, so he couldn't help but let his excitement show. Whether it was a smile or a short laugh, he just needed an outlet to express his gratitude.

"I got bored without her," Elly said, keeping her focus in check.

"Well, I'm not going to complain."

When the door finally opened, they stepped inside. Elly immediately ran to the bed and plugged the laptop into the socket next to the mattress. Her hands quickly began working.

"I'll get started with the Wi-Fi to download the software. In the meantime, you should shower. It'll be hard to focus with that stench lingering around." Elly stared intently at the screen while her fingers flew across the keyboard. Brennan desperately wanted to see her do her work, but decided instead, to heed her request.

"Okay, but you have to do the same after I'm done," he told her.

"Yeah, yeah." Elly dismissed him with a wave of her hand.

Brennan entered the bathroom with a new mindset. No longer would he run away from his problems. Defeating Lilith solidified that belief in him, and now was the time to practice it. As he stepped in the shower, letting the water caress his skin, he imagined what his life would be like after their adventure ended. *What will happen to Olivia? Will we stay in contact?* His mind went blank as he showered.

Once he refreshed his entire body with a river of water, he wrapped a towel around himself under his clothes, hoping that it would prevent the dirt on his clothes from sticking to him. Upon entering the bedroom, he found Elly still glued to the computer screen.

"You can use the bed. I'll sleep on the floor tonight," Brennan said. "Just promise me you'll shower at some point." She nodded without looking away from the laptop, and a smile quickly spread across her face. "What are you so happy about?"

"Oh, it's just that this laptop you stole is amazing. It works so fast. I can probably open multiple programs all at once."

"That's nice, but I don't know much about computers. Just don't get distracted."

"Don't worry, I won't." When Brennan lay on the floor, he swore he could've seen a reflection of the screen in her eyes. He was glad to be lucky enough to have her as an ally. In fact, her presence helped him heal from Jessica's death. It was like she offered a second chance. The feeling of having another friend, someone to protect, reminded him of Jessica. He just felt a little disappointed in himself for only seeing her as a replacement for his dead companion.

By the time his eyes felt heavy, she got up and walked into the shower. Brennan fell asleep at the sound of water running.

Brennan woke up the next morning to the sun shining through the window. He sat up and turned his head, expecting to see Elly. She was lying asleep in an awkward position that took up the entire bed. A towel lay next to her, and Brennan saw the imprint of her body left on it. He wanted to tap her shoulder and tell her to start working again, but decided against it. After all, his grogginess was in full effect, and he already worked her like a slave. She even passed out clutching the laptop to her chest.

Brennan assumed she stayed up all night, so he carefully pulled the device out of her hands, hoping she wouldn't wake up. Once he successfully retrieved it, he placed it on his lap and turned it on. He became satisfied to see all the things Elly had done. He may not have known much about technology, but the amount of code typed, accompanied by the numerous programs, told him that Elly kept herself busy.

After looking at them, he simply minimized their screens and proceeded to go to the internet browser. He knew that pretty much every adult used Facebook as their only social media. That was where he began looking for Olivia's stepfather, Mr. Benning. He went on the website and typed the man's last name into the search bar. After remembering that Elly needed to know where they lived to get into their electronic devices, he felt relief. That was a piece of knowledge he already had and could use, so he went out of his way to open a notepad file and entered all the information about Mr. Benning which was his name and street address. From there, he decided to peruse the Internet for the next couple of hours to get an impression of what happened while he was stuck in the afterlife.

He went from one news outlet to another, only to realize that Elly's journey was more chaotic than he thought. Brennan took another glance at her sleeping body, feeling sorry for her. But at the same time, he was appreciative. She had been through so much and all for the sake of finding him. That pleasant feeling of gratitude would stick forever.

Elly opened her eyes after hitting the two-hour mark. Her hair stuck up like a Christmas tree, and her face had the driest skin Brennan ever saw, but he didn't find it ugly at all. It was rather charming, even. After turning her head all around the room, she went to lie down again, but Brennan spoke.

"I didn't find any photos of Olivia's stepfather, but I left his street address."

Elly sat straight up after hearing his voice. "R-right." She nodded, and Brennan handed the laptop over. She shuffled closer to Brennan and brought the laptop to her face. He left it on the Notepad file, giving Elly easy access to her work.

She immediately downloaded typed the address into one of the programs and began clicking and dragging different tabs, typing away at the keyboard. "This will take a while, but I'll go as fast as I can."

"Take as much time as you need. I want to be fast, but also need to do this job thoroughly." Brennan stood and made his way to the front door, but stopped when Elly yelled at him.

"Hey! Are you crazy? After everything we've just been through, don't you think it'd be best to stick together?"

Brennan sighed, since he knew she was right. After the chaos of last night, he just wanted to take some time to walk in the sun, hoping that it'd calm his mind. But he agreed with her and stayed by her side and watched her work.

Once she finished, Brennan's eyes already began drifting shut from boredom. She playfully slapped his shoulder, making his eyes pop open. He turned his head just to see her smile.

"Look!" she said, rotating the laptop. It showcased three numbers that she copied and pasted into the note app.

"What's that supposed to be?" Brennan asked.

"Well, these numbers are coordinates. Knowing them can give me the exact location of their computer within their house. It's more accurate than going off an address."

Elly typed the numbers into a map and clicked on the option for a street view. Brennan saw Olivia's house pop onto the screen and flinched when he saw the window. He remembered jumping out of that when he was stuck in Olivia's body. Mr. Benning was doing the usual abuse he'd give Olivia, and Brennan decided to make a rough getaway.

"That's definitely their house. So, you know their IP address, now?"

"Not yet, but I will." Brennan gave her a pat on the back to show his appreciation.

"Good," he said. "Soon we'll be able to go through his stuff. Hopefully, we'll find something there we can use against him. No one believed Olivia or me when she was being abused, so we'll need to dig up some dirt on him." Brennan rubbed his chin. He knew he'd get this far, but didn't expect it to happen so quickly. He didn't know what to do next. "Hacking isn't something I have experience in," he said. "So, I have to ask, how much personal info can you get?"

"Given enough time, I can get anything."

Brennan nodded happily. "That's exactly what I wanted to hear. Look through everything on his computer. Leave nothing untouched."

"Yes!" Elly smiled and got back to working. Meanwhile, Brennan paced the room back and forth until he could come up with another plan of action.

After a couple more hours of watching her work, Brennan showed signs of admiration. She clearly proved herself to be a hard worker and, even though he felt uncomfortable at how clingy she was, he still appreciated her willingness to help. For a moment, while she typed away at the keyboard, she put a hand to her stomach as it growled. The onset of hunger must've been setting in, and Brennan sat next to her tired face.

"We can get something to eat. I'm sure we'll be able to go unnoticed," he said.

Elly shook her head. "No, I'm not willing to take the risk. Plus, I know this job is important to you."

Brennan breathed heavily. In his past he saw people as tools, but not anymore. He wanted to show more compassion, especially to the ones who were willing to aid him.

"You're right," he said. "It is important, but I'm not going to overwork you. You can relax for a moment."

Elly shook her head again. "I'm not going anywhere. I'm finishing this."

Brennan sighed and said, "Okay then, but tell me when you need something. I don't want you to pass out from exhaustion."

She gave him a thumbs-up before twiddling at the keys. He looked at her once again and knew that he wanted to protect her. He wouldn't make the same mistake he did with Jessica.

As Brennan got lost in wondering what Olivia was doing, his thoughts were cut short when Elly happily yelled, "I found something!"

Brennan was startled at her sudden yelp, but he returned to earth when she beckoned him to take a look. She pointed at a new set of numbers on the screen.

"I still don't know what I'm looking at," Brennan said.

"This is their IP address, and I already got into his computer. I'm seeing a lot of traffic coming from websites that specialize in pirating games, music, and movies."

Brennan just sighed in disappointment. "Piracy isn't enough to take him down. The cops don't care about it. In fact, everyone does it and no one gets caught. We need something else. Something more severe."

Elly squinted her eyes at the screen like she was legally blind. She meticulously searched each file, but a lot of them still came from common websites everyone knew; however, eventually, she found a ginormous number of files being trafficked from a site she'd never heard of.

"Well, this looks odd," she muttered.

"What looks odd?" Brennan scooted closer to her and grabbed the bottom of the laptop to make it easier for them to share the screen.

"This file. There are tons of stuff in it, but everything is encrypted." Elly opened a tab to one of her programs and began working again.

"Can you explain what that means?" Brennan asked.

"Well, to put it simply, this file is encrypted, meaning it's locked. Right now, I'm doing something that's the equivalent of picking a lock."

"How long does it take to do that?"

"A while."

Brennan let out a deep breath. This was going to take longer than he thought. His mind raced with anticipation. He just wanted to find some dirt on Olivia's stepfather, but it seemed like Brennan's optimism got the better of him. He turned his attention back to Elly and noticed that her eyes were glued to the screen, and the reflection of the mysterious programs shone in them.

"By the way, I forgot to say that there's no guarantee I won't leave a trace," she said.

"Leave a trace?"

"Yeah, there's a good chance what I do can be tracked back to this laptop."

"Why didn't you tell me earlier?" Brennan yelled.

"Relax, we'll just leave this thing behind and get as far away from here as we can." Elly didn't take her attention off the device until she gave an excited giggle. "Turns out he didn't put much thought into hiding the file," she said, looking at Brennan. He eagerly leaned even closer, and they both examined the file. When Elly clicked the folder, they were directed to a bunch of short videos. She hovered the mouse cursor over one of them. "I have a bad feeling about this. Usually, anything that's been encrypted contains something important."

"Let's just find out what it is. Stop being scared and click on it."

Elly started the video and gagged on bile when it popped up. Meanwhile, Brennan looked horrified. Brennan's mind brought him back to the moment he woke up in Olivia's house while he was stuck in her body. He could feel the bruises and pain in his lower regions again. Every video in the folder depicted the sexual acts Mr. Benning did to Olivia while she was unconscious.

"He must've uploaded this to a website and redownloaded them to keep for himself," Elly managed to say. Brennan's hatred toward Olivia's stepfather grew and fueled his desire to take him down.

"Now, we got something we needed. Leave an anonymous tip on the Island Bay Washington Police Department's website. They'll take it from there, and we can go." Elly quickly closed the video player and took a moment to breathe.

"I'm on it." She shook her body, as though it would wipe away the disgusting sight, and once she was done, she looked at Brennan. "Get up, we're leaving." She tossed the laptop onto the bed, and they headed out the door.

THE BOY SHE
NEVER KNEW

O livia followed Thorin everywhere. From his house, the time he
slept, and now at the end of his school day. The memories of this
exact year came back to her. She remembered the loneliness ending when
Jessica's torment started. But after seeing what Thorin's day consisted of,
she realized that he was just as isolated as she. They were both hermits
sitting in silence, wrapped in their cocoon of loneliness. The only form of
interaction Olivia had that day was spending time in the club room, de-
signing posters for new students. Earlier, when she watched herself talking
to a girl she had no recollection of, she wondered where everything went
wrong. Why did she leave the club and isolate herself?

Other than talking, she and that girl mass-produced letters of encour-
agement on the teacher's printer. Olivia had been given the opportunity to
act as the club's postman, but she declined. Whether it was out of anxiety
or not, she didn't remember. Instead, she chose to stay behind to clean the
room. All these memories came rushing in her head as her formless being
followed Thorin around the campus. Eventually, a female student with

blonde hair came up to him out of nowhere. She held out a letter which Olivia assumed was one they copied and pasted onto the computer.

"What's this?" Thorin asked the girl.

"Oh, our club wanted to give you newbies something to get you through the school year. One of our members wrote letters to everyone."

"Thanks," he stuttered. Despite his approval, he didn't seem happy at all. The door leading to the courtyard opened slightly and a breeze flowed in. It seeped into everyone's skin, making them shudder. Even though the climate in Washington was always freezing, this numbing air became too much for most to handle. Thorin zipped his jacket and shoved his hands into his pockets. From there, the walk back to his house remained as devoid of life as Olivia's walks. He was alone, too, both literally and emotionally. When he came to a turn that led to his neighborhood, Olivia was surprised he ignored it.

He marched up a large hill that paved the way to an abundance of luxurious houses. This area of town was always referred to as "Small Hollywood" because of the wealthy residents who lived there. A beach lined the shore at the bottom of the hill, and by the time Thorin reached the top, he had the same look of anger, resentment, and determination Brennan had when she met him. She followed him as he climbed the fence into someone's back yard. Confusion washing over her as she pondered why he would be trespassing. After all, he didn't look like the type of guy to wreak havoc on the town. But she finally realized what he planned to do.

With an intense feeling of terror, she witnessed him hop to the other end of the fence that stood right next to a cliff. He stood tall with a stoic face. The wind blew hard against him, making his clothes ruffle, and Olivia felt shocked to see him resist the breeze. It could've easily pushed his body over the edge and into the rocky ground below. Olivia floated next to him, hoping she'd see him turn around. That he'd go back into the yard, away from the jagged rocks that lined the shore, but she knew he wouldn't do that, because her personal experience told her that when someone intended to take their life, it became a mission they'd see through to the end.

Only physical intervention would stop him at this point. He heaved a big sigh and stepped forward. His toes hung over the edge, while his face told Olivia that a million thoughts raced through him. As a tear rolled down the side of his expressionless face, he reached into his pocket to pull out the letter he was given. His hands traced over Olivia's signature and unfolded it. Olivia floated by his side to read the letter.

Hey Thorin,

To be honest, we're supposed to send out generic letters to everyone, but I decided to write this one just for you! But don't tell anyone 'cause that'll show favoritism! Anyway, I just wanted to wish you luck. It's too bad I caught you by yourself the day we met. I felt sorry for you, but to be honest, I also thought it was a little cute. Sounds messed up to say, but you were like a lost puppy looking for his owner. Hopefully, you're not as lost now, and you've found a few friends. Other than that, I wish you the best of luck. If you need anything, feel free to ask me. I'm always hanging out in the club's homeroom after school. It's room 21-C. In fact, you can even come over just to talk!

Best regards,

Olivia Benning

Olivia floated behind Thorin as he read the letter, and as his hands shook, she wondered if telling him he could talk to her was her way of asking for attention. Olivia couldn't see herself writing this. She seemed so outgoing, but it amazed her that she didn't remember reaching out to him. Was life at school really destroying her that much? Maybe all her internal struggles kept her from making friends and retaining them. Thorin folded the letter, wiped a tear from his eye and looked down.

Olivia knew he was hesitant to jump, but it didn't take long for him to decide. Within a few seconds, his face looked as strong as stone and he placed on foot over the cliff. Olivia held her breath, but was surprised when a man pulled him back. She'd spent too much time watching Thorin that the elderly man sneaking behind them was completely invisible. They fought each other until he pinned Thorin into the grass, his face being smothered by the foliage.

"What were you thinking, kid?" the man yelled. "You were going to jump, weren't you?" But rather than answering, Thorin stayed silent. Olivia didn't know if it was because he was afraid to admit it, or he was too stunned to speak.

"I told you there was a boy out here," the man said to a woman walking out of the house. "Call 911. Let's get him to a hospital." Olivia watched over them, feeling sorry for the boy she ran into at school. She never would've guessed that his life would end up this way. A mixture of guilt and shock filled her, but before she saw more, the world turned black, as if the sun was a lightbulb that had suddenly been switched off. When she was able to see again, she found herself in the black void, facing Death.

"Do you see how your kindness helped someone?" he asked.

Olivia shook her head. "I didn't help him at all!"

"Are you sure about that?"

"Yes, of course, I'm sure! I just saw him to try to kill himself! He was about to jump and—" Olivia stopped for a moment to let the panic sink in. She quickly fell to her knees and started crying.

"Your letter caused a moment of hesitation. I don't know if you saw it, but he felt genuinely happy to have someone express affection. For a moment, your writing made him not want to die. Even if it was just for a moment, that short time frame was enough for someone to reach him."

"I still don't get it. I just don't get it! You're showing me all these terrible things! Why?"

"Because you truly had an effect on others. If you were never born, your friend, Hina would've always been abused behind closed doors, and Brennan's life would've been much different. By your doing, he now has a relationship with his sister and he and Elly have a chance of being happy together. You may not have done it alone, but you were the catalyst to ending her misery. And Thorin felt a tinge of hope that he could live happily because of your smile and small gestures of kindness. You should never underestimate the power of words, not matter if they're said or written."

Olivia slouched. "You might be right about that, but I still failed those people. Thorin still tried to jump off a cliff!"

"It's not your fault. I'm sure you already know that, when someone makes the decision to die, that's their choice, not yours." Death wasn't expressionless anymore. He had a fiery determination to make Olivia feel better. He raised his voice as if to hype her up, but it didn't work.

"It doesn't matter. None of it matters," she muttered. Olivia brought her knees closer to her chest and hugged herself. Death knelt down and placed a hand on her shoulder.

"You're different. You leave an impression on everyone you meet."

"Oh yeah? What about Thorin? Is he even alive?"

Death took in a deep breath before speaking. "Any living thing that ceases to live meets me, and I have yet to see him. I think it's safe to say he's alive, and if he is, it's because your words made him hesitate."

Olivia jumped after hearing him speak, and Death got onto his feet too. "Is that true?" she asked.

"I've never met him, so I'd say 'yes'. Think about how you could affect his life. In fact, you already have."

For a moment, Olivia felt excited, but that excitement ended quickly. "Wait, so if I come back, it's just so I can help him? I understand that he's hurt, but can't I live for myself? I'd be living for him instead!"

"That's not what I'm saying," Death stated clearly. "You don't have to live for him. I'm trying to show you the positive impact you have on others. Because even when you feel worthless, there's still someone out there who loves you for who you are and what you've done."

"I'm still not living my life for other people," Olivia muttered.

"Yes, I know. But from what I understand, you've been living for other people since you could remember. Is that true?"

Olivia picked at the ground with her feet, trying to buy some time for an answer. "Unfortunately, yes."

"Well, then taking the initiative to live your own life is new. Do you feel like a new person?"

"I feel like it, but at the same time I don't know if that makes me worse. Change isn't always good."

Death rubbed his chin. "Perhaps, but you're doing something that makes yourself stronger. Isn't that good?"

"I guess so." Despite her uncertain word usage, Olivia spoke as though she were sure of herself. "But changing like this is like killing a part of myself." She heard a crack form in the mirror and turned around to face it. The glass showed a terrified version of herself, on the verge of tears. Olivia looked into the mirror and sighed. She walked closer to her reflection and spoke to it. "I'm different now, but..." she turned her head for a moment to glance at Death, not feeling the confidence to take one final push to her new life.

"Will you leave the person who you were?" he asked.

"No." Olivia turned her attention back to the glass. "I'm not leaving you behind. You're a part of me, and I accept that." She bowed her head as though she were paying her respects to a dead friend. A ripple sent waves throughout the mirror, and her reflection emerged as a tangible being. She was identical to Olivia, with the exception of her skin. Her body looked like it had a shade of gray enveloping it. She bowed her head, making it so Olivia felt her touch when their forehead's connected.

"Do I infuriate you?" her reflection asked.

"You used to, but not anymore."

"Do I disgust you?"

"No. Even though I'm moving on from the person I once was, you'll never leave. I'll keep you in my heart." They raised their faces and looked at each other. Olivia smiled and put a hand on her reflection's cheek. The other half of her cried a few tears. "The past is the past. No matter the life I've lived. I'll make sure my presence is known. I've been dealt a bad hand, and there's many things out of my control, but I'll do what I can. I'll help the people who need it, so they don't end up like me."

"Will you keep me in mind?" her reflection asked.

"Always. You're the old me, and it's a version of myself that's the foundation of my change." After saying those words, her other self transformed into a statue that quickly crumbled.

"I've made my choice, she said, turning to Death. "I'll go home."

He nodded. "I can take you back to the station, but just like Brennan, you must give up something valuable to get the ticket you desire." Olivia picked up one of the stone pieces and held it out in front of her.

"This will do. I'll give up a small piece of myself."

"Are you sure about that?"

"Yes, I'm very sure. I'm giving up my attachment, not the promise I made."

"Very well then. On to the train station we go." Death extended his right arm and opened his palm. He then closed his eyes to concentrate. A black sphere spawned underneath his hand. It spun at a great speed, throwing bits of itself into the air around him until it gradually slowed down and turned into a scythe.

"Would you please move?" he asked. Olivia stepped out of the way, and Death raised the blade into the air. In one swift motion, he cut a line through the void and a portal appeared. At first, it filled her with dread as an even darker cloud seeped through it, but Death's calm look reassured Olivia. She nodded and stepped through.

The world went dark, and for a moment she couldn't see anything. All she felt was her breath touching her chin. But within a minute, she suddenly found herself at the far end of the train station. A small machine stationed in front of her held out a tray.

"Go ahead and put your stone piece on the metal," Death instructed. Olivia did as he said, and the tray immediately retreated inside its slot. After a few seconds, a golden ticket with her name on it slid out of the other end.

"I guess, it's time to go," she said. "Will I see you again?"

Death shook his head. "In due time, you, Brennan, Elly, and everyone who's seen the supernatural will forget about all of this. To you, this will just be one wild adventure. Your mind will fill in the blanks with fake but believable stories.."

"But why?" Olivia made sure to show her disappointment.

"Because, the afterlife is based on faith, not definitive proof. I hope that the day we meet again will be the day you have no regrets. Farewell."

Death walked away into a shadowy corner and disappeared. Olivia sighed in both relief and sadness. She felt happy to go home, but at the same time, these events were something she'd rather not forget. After reflecting on everything that transpired, she walked to the tracks and waited for a train to pick her up.

BACK TO THE BEGINNING

After Brennan and Elly finished digging up Mr. Benning's criminal activity, they made haste to leave. However, the first step was making sure everything looked untouched. They didn't want the staff or other guests to realize that the room had been invaded. They made the bed, straightened the pillows, and closed the blinds. By the time their trespassing crime seemed to be covered up, they made the decision to flee. With the quiet opening of the door, their feet brought themselves out of the room, but the sight of police officers patrolling the parking lot caught their eye. Two more were going by each room, knocking on the doors.

"Shit," Elly whispered. "They must've followed my digital footprint faster than I thought. We need to leave before they catch us." She and Brennan began speed walking in the opposite direction. If he could burst into a sprint, he would take Elly on the fastest run of her life, but they had to remain discreet. They kept their heads down as they walked by, but when one of the officers yelled, "Hey stop!", stealth was completely thrown out the window. A chase began in the blink of an eye.

Brennan and Elly ran as fast as they could, while the officers pursued them. In their rush to get away, Elly accidentally dropped the laptop, making pieces of it shatter on the stone flooring. And when Brennan looked at her, he watched the most fearful look he'd ever seen dawn on her face.

"Don't look back. Just keep going," he told her. Much to his surprise, her short legs sprinted faster than him, but none of that mattered. All that waited for them was a wall blocking their path.

"God dammit!" Brennan yelled once they got to the wall. Their faces turned toward the cops trailing them. His eyes rested on their badges, and he felt a strong sense of dread. Brennan knew that the events leading up to this moment could never be undone. Elly hid behind him, and he stood in front like a knight holding out his shield.

"What do you want?" Brennan tightly gritted his teeth while giving an angry glare.

"You're not in trouble," one of them said. "We just want to take you in to ask some questions."

"You're not taking us anywhere," Brennan talked back.

"Listen, I understand that life's been tough on you kids, but we've dealt with runaways before. We can help."

"Bullshit." Brennan genuinely believed that they were pulling his leg. To him, nothing ever came without consequences, good or bad. He wasn't willing to take a chance at this moment.

"You kids aren't in trouble." The officers changed their tone to a more neutral one, as if to lower Brennan's guard, but he continued to stare them down. Despite Brennan's tough look and the officer's somber expression, it felt like they understood each other. When Elly stepped out of Brennan's shadow, he turned to look at her.

In his moment of distraction, he felt his body hit the floor. One of the cops tackled him, and it wasn't long until the cold sensation of steel handcuffs was on his skin, but that wasn't the worst feeling. The pain of being separated from Elly hit him harder than expected.

As they were put in different patrol cars, he couldn't help but feel shame and regret. She might've been willing to help him, but he believed he was the reason she got in trouble. During the ride to the station, Brennan remained silent. However, the inner mechanisms of his mind were working overtime. *What's next? I've committed some crimes.* Trespassing, breaking and entering, theft, and so much more. He didn't know much about the law; he just knew that he was eighteen, which meant he was an adult, so his age wouldn't do much in convincing the law to go easier on him. Fear swelled inside, but he feared for Elly's well-being more than his own, and that feeling persisted for the rest of the day.

Olivia woke up under a bridge. Her clothes were messy, and she smelled the horrible stench of the ocean nearby. Lying in the dirt at the edge of the water, her shoes became soaked, forcing her to wander around in wet socks. The condition of walking on wet fabric always annoyed her, and this time was no different.

How far am I from home? She made it her mission to find a telephone, or at least a place where she could get help. Even though she returned to her world, being back in her body wasn't something she could easily readjust to. It took time for her to set goals for the day, which she opted to do rather than rejoicing in her return.

In the end, she decided it was time to leave her stepfather and tell her mom how disappointed she was in her. *I have an impact on others. A huge impact.* Her last encounter with Death taught her that. Maybe taking the initiative to express her wants would force people into a position to make the choice to respect her more. She knew the same couldn't be said for her stepfather, but she knew she could beat him. She had the strength to do things on her own, even if that meant leaving her home. But first, she had to talk to her mom.

Olivia walked away from the beach and into the forest that lined the sand. When she stepped into the trees, it was like a different world had swallowed her up. Their brown trunks along with the rocks littered the place, but a clear hiking path showed her the way out. It led up the hill to a bridge that she quickly crossed. On the side, she ran into a woman.

"Excuse, me, young lady," she said.

Olivia turned her attention toward her. "Yes?"

"Are you okay? You seem a little lost." She had an odd tone to her voice, like she was worried and feeling sorry at the same time. Olivia knew by her body language that she planned to do more than just talk. The woman's eyes were on her, but her hands fumbled in her purse. That's when Olivia made her hypothesis that this woman recognized her from the news. Olivia reminded herself that she had disappeared for weeks, and her face was on every television station in the country. Assuming that the woman recognized her and planned to alert the authorities came as an easy conclusion. She couldn't think of a nice way to leave her behind, so she hastily marched up the hill, leaving the woman behind. And when Olivia reached the top, she felt accomplished, her pride at its highest.

Even though fear still lingered in the back of her mind, she knew she was about to take a step in living the life she wanted, and the griminess of her appearance just made her look like a warrior who had gone through hell. Her shoes were covered in dirt, and sweat made her clothes stick to her skin. Getting home to face the people who made her life hell was the next step. It was just too bad she didn't recognize where she stood. *I must be miles away from home.* However, she now believed that if there was a will, there was a way. This may not have been the small town she came from, but she'd do everything it took to return to the place she once called home.

It took a few hours until Olivia finally saw another human being. She noticed a woman from a distance when the sound of her car came cutting through the air. Olivia waved at her, and she came to a halt. The tires screeched at the sudden stop, but when she walked up to the vehicle, the driver rolled down the window.

"I need a ride," Olivia said.

"No way. I don't trust hitchhikers. For all I know, you could be some serial killer."

Olivia swallowed hard and put on her best 'sad face'. "I just want to see my parents. I got lost."

The woman eyed her before caving in. "How old are you?"

"Seventeen."

The woman stared at her a little longer. "Fine then," she said with a sigh. "You're lucky I have a soft spot for kids." With one small click, the door unlocked, and Olivia hopped in. She sunk into the leather chair. "Where are you headed?" the woman asked.

'Take me to a small town called Island Bay."

"That's pretty far. How the hell did you get over here?"

"I rode in with a couple of friends, then they ditched me." Olivia shrugged her shoulders and added a short pause to really sell her fake story. The woman nodded and sped down the road while Olivia closed her eyes to rest. This time, she stayed asleep, rather than entering the void.

Brennan did his best not to black out at the police station. He was scared and wasn't afraid to acknowledge it. However, he wasn't living in momentary fear of the police. Rather, he was horrified of what may happen when he forgot the entire events leading up to this moment. He'd learned so many things about himself and the people around him. If these things slipped from his memory, would he repeat his past mistakes? He contemplated this as he waited in the interrogation room. The camera above him rotated silently while his leg shook. His heel tapped against the stone floor until a detective walked in to have a chat. The man pulled out a chair and got ready to talk.

"Okay, now that all the paperwork is done, we can talk." The detective smiled. "I guess I'll start with asking you why you ran away." As their conversation began, Brennan made a mental note to speak as little as possible. "Why'd you leave the city?" The detective leaned forward with his fingers intertwined.

"A friend of mine was in trouble, so I left," Brennan said.

"And you're telling me the truth?" the man asked, raising an eyebrow.

"Yes." Although it was a lie, it came out naturally. "She was in a rough situation."

"So, tell me about your friend, then."

For a moment panic filled Brennan's heart. He knew he messed up. He couldn't outright say that he switched bodies with Olivia and neglected to find her after taking a detour in the afterlife, since that would truly be unbelievable, and at the same time mentioning their names would connect them to even more trouble.

"I had a suicidal friend," Brennan muttered.

"Go on."

"His name was Duncan." Brennan knew he had to be careful with his lies. He didn't want to dig himself deeper into a hole, and since he'd inevitably forget everything, he'd be stuck with a story he didn't know he made up.

"Is he okay?" the detective asked.

"Yeah, but after a while, I lost touch with him. We had a falling out."

"Have you tried following up with him?"

"I don't want to talk about this anymore."

"Now, we can only help you if you're being honest and open with us." Brennan wanted to snarl. He knew the detective had ulterior motives. He must've been trying to pry into his brain to get down to the truth of the matter.

"I'm not talking about Duncan anymore." Brennan stayed firm, and the man stared at him.

"Okay, I see." He reached into his bag and pulled out a water bottle. "We'll talk more when you're ready. In the meantime, you should have a drink. You kids must be thirsty."

"Thanks." Brennan took the bottle but didn't open it.

"Is there anything else you'd like? Some food? Clothes maybe?"

"No." Brennan kept his response short and made sure he wouldn't allow himself to lower his guard. The man stepped out of the room while Brennan remained silent. He stared at the wall in front of him, but he didn't feel alone. He swore he felt the presence of people watching him through the camera. Deceit lingered in the air, and he wondered what the detective was planning. *Will he have more questions? Will he be more aggressive?* Brennan folded his arms and leaned back in his chair. *What to do? What to do?* His thoughts were cut short when a woman came in.

"Hi, I'm Detective Marsh, but you can call me Violet."

They clearly made sure to bring another detective into the room. Not only that, but someone who seemed friendlier and much to Brennan's dismay, he almost let his guard slip. He regretted waiving his right to remain silent, but the cops were just so damn good at convincing him to do what they wanted. Sometimes questions weren't even spoken; he could just look at their body language and tell they wanted to learn more. "So, I hear that one of your schoolmates brutally assaulted you. I'm sorry to hear that."

Brennan didn't say anything. He didn't even glance at her.

"Is that why you were in a coma a few weeks ago?"

Again, Brennan remained silent. Even though he made sure to be aware of their tricks, he knew that at some point he'd fail. He just hoped that if he accidentally told them something about the afterlife, they'd forget about it, just like he, Olivia and Elly would.

"We need you to open up to us," Detective Marsh said softly.

"My friend's name isn't Duncan. Her name is Olivia, and her stepdad has been raping her. He even films it." Seeing as there was no way he could get past the trap of being questioned, he decided to just drop a massive claim on their heads.

"Hold on." The detective left the room for a few minutes only to return and resume their conversation like nothing happened. "Tell me more about this friend."

"Her stepdad's last name is Benning, and he lives in Island Bay, Washington. He films his sexual crimes and stores the files on his computer."

"And you're sure about this?" she asked.

"Yes. In fact, I know your deputies remember Elly and me stealing a laptop. We used that to track down Mr. Benning's computer. You can ask Elly to explain the rest. I don't know much about technology, but she does." The detective wrote down a few more notes while the recorder continued keeping track of their conversation.

"Thank you. This information is important."

After she left the room, Brennan wondered what would happen next. Surely, he'd accomplished his goal of helping Olivia, but since their memories of each other were only for a limited time, he didn't know how these events would replay in their head. He just hoped she and Elly would find solace after this.

The woman woke Olivia when they reached a bus stop.

"We're in town now. You can take the bus from here."

Olivia groggily nodded before stretching her arms and getting out of the car. After the woman drove away, it was a thirty-minute wait for the bus to arrive. When the driver finally pulled up, she told him her address so he could drop her off at the closest stop. As she walked past every seat, she held her breath, hoping that no one would recognize her. This was a small town, and she was born and raised here, but it seemed that the time she spent separating herself from everyone did her wonders. Just like no one noticed her when she went to school. Normally, she'd hate feeling invisible, like no one cared about her, but right now she was thankful for that. She passed by a boy sleeping in his seat, but when she caught a glimpse of his face, she turned around. He might've looked a bit different, but she knew him. He was Thorin. The memories of what she saw came flooding back, so she sat next to him, and as the bus started its engines, she sat still, imagining herself talking to him.

I'm sorry for leaving you.

It's okay. She imagined his voice saying.

No, it's not.

You didn't know about me. And I didn't know about you. It's an even trade. Don't worry.

Olivia stared at his sleeping face. He seemed thinner, almost as though he were starving himself, and as she looked at him, the bus went over a speed bump that shook him awake. When he opened his eyes, he rubbed them, but when he noticed Olivia, he looked astonished.

"Do I know you from somewhere?" he asked.

"Yes," Olivia said with a faint smile. "Thorin is your name, correct?"

"Um, yeah."

"I don't know if you remember me, but I'm Olivia. I found you wandering the high school when you got lost on your tour." He paused for a moment, but then his eyes grew wide. "So, you do remember me," Olivia said.

"Yeah, it's just been so long. What have you been doing so far?" Olivia realized his hands were shaking, and his breath losing its steadiness.

"I know your life was tough."

"Oh." Thorin put his head down, but Olivia never broke eye contact.

"Can we be friends? I mean, actual friends. We just knew each other back then, but we were only acquaintances."

Thorin brought his head up to her and with a smile spreading across his face. "Yeah, that's fine." He seemed weak, but Olivia made sure to beam with joy.

The bus came closer to its next stop, and since their life story would take hours to tell, Olivia frantically sought out ways to keep in contact with him. She noticed a marker sticking out of his bag. Her hand quickly shot over his lap to pull it out and grabbed his arm.

"What are you doing?" he asked.

"I'm getting off at the next stop. Use this number so we can talk later." After they came to a halt, she tossed the marker back into his bag, and walked away after giving him an unexpected hug.

She started down the sidewalk, with her mind conjuring scenarios of what may happen next. She could face her parents, but what if they retaliated? What dangers lay ahead? She knew she'd be putting her safety at risk, but that didn't stop her from getting what she wanted. She couldn't let her stepdad have control over her. Eventually, she decided to just stomp into the house and proudly proclaim her decision to leave. It would've looked petty to most people, but to her, it was like declaring freedom. By the time she finalized her plan, she stood in front of her house. She punched the passcode into the keypad next to the garage door, and, when it slid open, she stepped inside.

The dusty air felt like a pillow smothering her. Olivia carefully stepped over the piles of junk that littered the floor and walked up the short steps that led into the living room. Once she reached the top, she gave out a short cough, and someone from the other side of the door seemed to hear her. Her stepdad swung it open and pulled her in.

"You bitch!" He threw her to the floor, and Olivia's back smacked the wood, making her go into a violent coughing fit. "You think you can just run away?" He got on top of her in a mounting position while slapping her face. She flailed her arms in front of her, hoping to land a lucky hit.

"Get off me!" Her nails cut his cheek, and he let out a yelp. But rather than backing off, he gripped her wrist and spat in her eye. She flinched at the saliva as it gave a stinging sensation. She rolled onto her side as if it were possible to shrink into the floor.

"You need to learn your lesson," he said, gritting his teeth. Her stepfather stood and headed into the kitchen. In the meantime, Olivia wiped her eye before getting on her feet.

"I'm leaving for good," she declared.

"What?" She heard his footsteps stomping around the corner, but instead of running away, she stood her ground.

"I said, I'm leaving! I don't want to have anything to do with you or mom!"

As she stood by the door, her stepfather towered over her. "Now, that just won't do."

"No, I'm making my own decisions now."

He grabbed her throat and used all his might to slam her skinny body against the wall. By now, he added his other hand into the mix by choking her. Olivia's face turned red as she tried to fight back, but it didn't take long until her vision became blurry.

"I'll kill you!" she managed to say in a hoarse voice. "I'll fucking kill you!" By now, she almost had no more strength to fight, but the sound of a doorbell saved her life. Her stepfather let go of her, causing her to drop to the floor like a rag doll.

For a moment, she could only cough, but when she heard the voices of police officers conversing with him, she tried to muster the strength to scream. Unfortunately for her, her voice was only a faint whisper. She couldn't speak at all. Her throat burned with so much pain, so she looked for the nearest breakable object and limped toward a potted plant displayed on the bookshelf. She slammed the flowers onto the floor. The men stopped speaking, notifying Olivia that her plan was working. She flipped tables, threw remotes, and smashed the television with the leg of a coffee table. And after all that damage was done, the police came to investigate. Her red eyes and bruised neck immediately told them the story of what just happened.

"I guess that report from the detective in Alabama was right," one of them said. The cop immediately pulled out his radio while his partner detained Mr. Benning. "Don't worry, kid, we've got you." Olivia's eyes fluttered shut before she fell over.

The next thing she knew, she was in the black void with Death. He stood tall, taking down all the clocks.

"Did my stepdad kill me?" Olivia asked.

"No," Death answered without looking at her.

"I see, so I guess I didn't die, but I almost did. Just like when I was beaten into a coma, right?"

"Yes." He nodded and continued to take down the clocks.

Olivia was already familiar with the void, so she knew that predicting the time she'd spend here was impossible. "So, why are you taking those down?" She pointed at the wall, hoping to pass the time.

"It's because your time with me is over. Your journey has ended."

"So that's it then," she said relieved. "I'm free of them?"

"No, you're free of yourself."

"I don't get it." Olivia walked next to him. She believed she spent her whole life living with only the abuse of her father, but now she understood that even though her brutal home life wasn't her fault, she still had the power to change who she turned into.

"Yes, you're free of yourself. Your inner turmoil is over. You've recovered mentally, and soon, you'll recover physically."

Olivia silently accepted his words and reached for one of the clocks to help him take the rest down.

He gave her a sideways glance before speaking again. "If you're curious about Brennan, you should know that his journey with the afterlife is also over, and within time, anything that reveals the existence of my world will be erased from his memory, just as it will happen to you."

Olivia couldn't help but feel saddened by the news. Even though this had been one crazy adventure, she didn't like the thought of losing some core memories.

"But what if I return to my old self? What if I don't retain all the lessons I've learned?"

"Oh, you don't need to worry about that. Your mind and everyone else who was involved will be filled with a 'realistic' story that will substitute for the afterlife. You'll still retain the lessons you learned. It'll just be in a different way."

"I guess that settles it, then." She held the last clock in front of her.

"Would you kindly hand that over, so I can put it away?" Death asked.

Olivia obliged and handed it over with a smile.

EPILOGUE

B rennan sat on the beach with Elly by his side. His hand laid beside him as she held hers over his. Today marked the fifth year since their crazy adventure into Alabama. He still couldn't believe that he ran away for a few weeks with a girl he barely knew. He didn't know what he was thinking at the time, but then again, everything from his last year of high school was a blurry mess. However, he could truly say he was happy for now. Five years ago, he ran away with Elly and immediately entered one of the best relationships of his life. It was a relationship he planned on staying in forever.

They looked out into the ocean lit up by the moon. A boy walked across the sand and handed his mom a white flower. The sight brought on a calming feeling within Brennan, and he wished he could live in that moment forever.

"Thanks for taking me out," Elly whispered.

"No problem. Maybe more nights can be like this?"

"Of course," she said with a giggle.

Their conversation was cut short by his phone buzzing. Feeling annoyed, he pulled it out of his shorts and answered.

"Brennan!" Nora yelled into his ear.

"Jesus, stop yelling. What is it?" he asked.

"I just wanted to remind you to be on your best behavior. Elly is a great girl, and I don't want you to mess anything up!"

Brennan sighed. "I get it, calm down." Even though his sister annoyed him sometimes, he couldn't help but give a chuckle. Nora still had a certain charm that made him elated whenever they talked, no matter how much she got on his nerves.

After he hung up, Elly asked, "Was it Nora again?"

"Yeah, I'm sorry about that."

"No, it's fine. Just be happy you have her." She smiled and rested her head on his shoulder.

"Oh, trust me, I am happy." Brennan looked to the moon in the sky and enjoyed the time he had with her.

Olivia and Thorin's family had finally saved up enough money to take a vacation in Florida. Even though she still felt uneasy being alone with thoughts of her stepfather, having friends like Thorin brushed them away momentarily. They walked along the shore, talking about their lives, what they planned to do in the future.

"So you're planning on being an editor?" Thorin asked her.

"Yes!"

"Why not just become a writer instead?"

Olivia stopped and put a finger to her chin. "I do enjoy writing, but I find it more enjoyable to read other people's stories and help them grow it. It's a lot like seeing a person mature and turn into a different version of themselves. Not only that, but you don't exactly rewrite their story. You just make simple suggestions to create something wonderful. It's like nudging someone in the right direction to become someone better. Someone great."

She stopped speaking when she became distracted by a tall man with dark hair. He sat on the beach, talking to a short girl whom she assumed to be his girlfriend.

"Is something wrong?" Thorin asked.

"No, nothing." Olivia gestured for them to continue their walk. She genuinely felt happy around him, but she couldn't understand why she felt such a familiar feeling around the dark-haired man. It was like she understood him on a different level. Like she'd once crawled into his skin and lived his life. Seeing him really made her wonder what it would be like to live as someone else. But she thought it was strange of her to think that. Yet, for some reason, this man gave her the impression that she knew his life and everything he'd gone through.